I0589872

# A SEASON TO LOVE

## BOOK 2

### REBECCA HEFLIN

A SEASON TO LOVE

Copyright©2020. All rights reserved.

REBECCA HEFLIN

Cover Design by The Killion Group, Inc.

This book is a work of fiction. The names, characters, places, and incidents are the products of the author's imagination or are used fictitiously. Any resemblance to actual events, business establishments, locales, or persons, living or dead, is entirely coincidental.

All rights reserved. No part of this publication may be reproduced, stored in a retrieval system, or transmitted in any form or by any means (electronic, mechanical, photocopying, recording, or otherwise) without the prior written permission of both the copyright owner and the publisher. The only exception is brief quotations in printed reviews.

The scanning, uploading, and distribution of this book via the Internet or via any other means without the permission of the publisher is illegal and punishable by law. Please purchase only authorized electronic editions, and do not participate in or encourage electronic piracy of copyrighted materials.

Your support of the author's rights is appreciated.

Published in the United States of America by:

Rebecca Heflin Books, LLC

Gainesville, Florida


ISBN: 9780997181289

www.RebeccaHeflin.com

❀ Created with Vellum

# ACKNOWLEDGMENTS

For my readers.

2019 was quite the year, so much so that I did not finish this book on time, so I appreciate your patience and understanding.

I would be remiss if I did not express my gratitude to my husband and beta-reader—the man who also must sacrifice time spent together, so that I can write my books. And to my other beta-reader, Yvonne, you keep me on the straight and narrow when it comes to my characters and their behavior.

As always, I'd like to thank those who listen to my tales of woe as I labor over my books. It's not always an easy or pretty process, and venting to you (you know who you are) keeps me sane. I especially want to thank my GARA ladies for supporting me through my struggles. I know you know exactly where I'm coming from.

I appreciate Luke for spending so much time with me,

answering my multitude of questions, as I learned about the brewing process, and for taking me on a tour of his incredible brewery. Oh! And for the tasting!

I spent a great deal of time speaking with Joanne, a local oncologist, regarding Hodgkin's lymphoma—its symptoms, its treatment and the side effects and long-term consequences of that treatment, and survival rate.

Any mistakes in my portrayal of the brewing process and the craft beer business, or the specifics of Hodgkin's lymphoma are purely my own.

I researched carefully the film location approval process in Georgia, but where the actual process did not fit my plot, I took some liberties. It is fiction, after all.

Finally, to my editor, Paul. Thank you for being my eagle-eyed friend and my grammar guru.

Forgiveness is the final form of love.
~ Reinhold Niebuhr

# CHAPTER ONE

IF LOOKS COULD KILL, Kristen McKay's glare would be a lethal weapon.

Tyler Kincaide entered the conference room searching for an open seat at the conference table and grimaced when the first open seat his gaze landed on happened to be next to Kristen.

Not that he had anything against her. He liked her. A lot. But for some reason, she felt about him the way he felt about Brussels sprouts and kale—intense loathing.

Just as he'd made up his mind to take the seat anyway, she lifted her startled gaze to his, then turned the glare up a notch to death ray.

*Well, okay then.*

Another seat across the table next to Tabitha Gillespie, owner of Pints and Paints, appeared to be available. Turning his footsteps in that direction, he felt the heat of Kristen's glare burning holes in the spot between his shoulder blades, like a laser blast from Cyclops.

Resisting the urge to twitch his shoulders, he set his iPad on the table, pulled out the chair, and nodded to

Tabitha, just as Carter Watson, the council chair, called the meeting to order.

The Town Hall conference room served as the monthly meeting venue for the Northridge Economic Development Council, or EDC for short.

The little town of Northridge, population six thousand twenty-three, had an active Economic Development Council that advised the Town Council on things like business retention and expansion, new development (within strict zoning ordinances to maintain Northridge's historic charm), marketing opportunities, and tourism.

As the owner of Firehouse Brews, a local craft brewery, and its sister business the Firehouse Taproom, Tyler had a vested interest in Northridge's economic success. So, despite the unwelcome chill from Kristen's side of the table, here he sat, making a concerted effort not to fidget in his seat.

He noticed today she had her long red hair plaited down her back, stray bits coming loose to curl around her face. The olive green sweater she wore deepened the color of her bottle green eyes and played up the peach of her cheeks. The chill of fall had yet to show its face, but Kristen was bundled up as if a blizzard was imminent.

She had this rolled-out-of-bed quality that intrigued him. Hair just this side of messy, clothes that seemed an afterthought but that hugged her curves, little to no accessories. It suited her devil-take-it attitude. For a petite woman, she packed a powerful punch.

After working with women in his former profession on Wall Street, buttoned up and suited in dark colors, sleek skirts, and red-soled, sky-high shoes, Kristen's fuck-it appearance was refreshing. And sexy as hell.

*Ooh boy.* He needed to get a grip before he did something stupid, like compliment her appearance. Such a move could start World War III.

Sliding his iPad open, he tapped on the Notes app, ready to jot down his thoughts during his second meeting since joining the council in August.

After approving the minutes of that meeting, Carter brought up the first item of business. As he spoke, Tyler scanned the agenda, stopping halfway down the page where he saw the bullet for "Film Location."

Interested, he drummed his fingers on his lap, wondering what that could be about.

Kristen McKay tapped her pen on the table as Mason Porter, owner of Forget-Me-Not's Florist, droned on about the latest sales tax increase, and averted her eyes from the man directly across the table from her.

Why, she asked herself for the thousandth time, did he have to join the EDC?

Whenever she was in his presence, she felt the familiar push-pull. The shame of that night so many years ago, coupled with the confounding and unwelcome desire to be with him despite it. The desire to keep her secret, and the guilt over doing just that.

Damn him and his dark blond hair and crazy chameleon eyes in that mixture of blue, green, and brown. Seemed like every time she saw his eyes, the color changed. What color would they be now? she wondered.

*Don't look, don't look, don't look,* she repeated to herself.

Okay. She looked. And beneath the jarring fluorescent lights, they were a deep olive green with flecks of blue and gold. He gave her a flicker of a smile, and she rolled her eyes, more at her own weakness than at his impertinence.

*Enough.* Stifling a groan, she studied September's agenda for topics of direct interest to her.

She'd only recently become a business owner in her hometown of Northridge, having purchased what had been the bookstore two years ago when Patti Cotton decided to retire and move to Florida.

Kristen had put every dime she could spare into the business, converting a section of the bookstore into a café where she served fresh-baked goods and coffee, renaming it Beans 'n Books. She'd also taken out a small-business loan and applied for small-business grants from the Georgia Chamber of Commerce.

As one of the junior members of the EDC, she'd joined determined to make herself heard and have a hand in Northridge's economic success. She also wanted to prove to everyone that she wasn't her mother's daughter (or, even worse, her father's). That she could be a success, be independent, and unlike her mother, not fall back on a string of questionable relationships and the occasional hook to make ends meet. And, unlike her father, stay out of prison.

She knew she had a good business model, but in addition to regular patronage from Northridge's local citizens, her business' success depended on the tourists from neighboring Atlanta who craved a day away from the big city where they could stroll the quaint historic downtown area, visit trendy shops, and sample excellent food and beverages that Northridge's businesses were proud to offer.

Gliding a finger down the agenda, she passed an item, then backed up. "Film Location." She sat up, intrigued.

The State of Georgia had invested a great deal to become the "Hollywood of the South," and they'd succeeded. Some of her favorite binge-worthy TV shows were filmed in Georgia, including *The Walking Dead* and *Stranger Things*. And those productions had boosted the economy in both filming locations.

Was a production company looking at Northridge for a TV show or feature film?

Salivating at the possibility of a regular catering gig for a production crew, she anxiously waited for the meeting to move along. This could help her little business turn the corner.

Finally, Carter cleared his throat. "The next item on the agenda involves the proposal submitted to the Film, Music & Digital Entertainment Division of the Georgia Economic Development Council for Northridge to serve as the location for the feature film adaptation of the best-selling novel *Battle of the Heart*, by Jordan Raven."

Kristen sucked in a breath. She tried her best to squeeze in time for reading—a crucial activity for a bookstore owner —and had actually read that book. And she'd loved it! Who *hadn't* read that book? she wondered. It'd been promoted on news programs, talk shows, and magazines all over the country. She'd even featured it in her Georgia authors section at the bookstore.

Set in the Post-Civil-War-South in the late 1870's, the story focused on Samuel and Eleanor Wesley, a couple trying to put their lives back together after the Civil War. The hero's haunted past threatens to destroy everything the couple has worked so hard to accomplish.

Northridge was the perfect location with its railroad history, original post-antebellum buildings and nineteenth-century charm. Excitement surged through her but waned as she returned her attention to the meeting discussion.

"I don't think we want to subject our town to this invasion," Mason said, brow furrowed.

"Yeah," Tabitha seconded, tucking a strand of her weave behind her ear. "It will disrupt our lives and the tranquility of our little town."

"It will also be a shot of adrenaline for Northridge's economy," Kristen interjected, surprised by her own temerity, especially when all eyes turned to her, including Tyler's.

Screwing up her courage she continued, raising her voice to be heard over the base drum of her heart. "Tony," she pointed at Dominick Bertolli's son, who now ran Dominick's Pizza, "what about catering for the film crew? Or Meghan?" She jutted her chin toward Meghan Redmond, owner and chef of The Whistle Stop Pub.

She then turned her gaze to Mason. "You might be called on to provide flowers for scenes. And, Tabitha, the crew will be looking for things to do during their time off—they could go to Pints and Paints."

She leaned on the table to make her point. "Carter, you and Anita did such a beautiful job renovating the 1885 Bed & Breakfast, you could make a mint serving as the setting for the boarding house in the book. After filming, fans of the book will want to stay at the 'Magnolia Boarding House.'"

Her heart expanded in her chest with both nerves and excitement—and being the center of attention for all the *right* reasons—rather than for pity or disdain.

She lifted her hand then let it drop to the table. "For me, it's a no-brainer."

TYLER'S HEAD had swiveled in Kristen's direction at her first words.

*Huh.*

He didn't know why, but he never expected to be on the same side of an issue as her. Maybe because whenever he was around her, she was so . . . contrary, almost for the sake of contrariness. If he said the grass was green and the sky was blue, she'd say the opposite, despite the evidence to the contrary.

"Kristen's right. The economic boost to Northridge is incalculable. Everything from job creation to attracting tourists, this opportunity will bring nothing but good to our businesses."

This set off another round of arguments from the naysayers. Feeling Kristen's green eyes on him, he tilted his head and returned her stare. The angry voices receded, and in his mind anyway, it was just the two of them—alone.

She lifted a brow in challenge, but her eyes remained calm.

This was the first time since he'd returned to Northridge a year earlier that she'd looked at him without hostility. Maybe they were making progress. He liked it.

"Well, Tyler and Kristen, since you two are currently the only ones in favor of this, the council requests a full report from you on the economic impact—good and bad—this could have on Northridge."

He slid the proposal down the table where it came to a halt in front of Tyler.

"We'll expect the report at the November meeting."

*W*AIT. *What?* Kristen's gaze bounced between Carter, at the head of the table, and Tyler, seated across from her.

Surely Tyler wouldn't agree. She'd certainly given him

enough reason to steer clear of her. Clenching her fists under the table, she held her breath awaiting his refusal. As one of the newbies on the council, she didn't want to be the one to turn down an opportunity to show the council how vested she was in the community and that she deserved their respect. But this? No way.

She couldn't spend time with Tyler working on a report, meeting to discuss the pros and cons of the proposal, possibly over lunch, or worse . . . dinner. For one, she couldn't afford it, and for two, she couldn't handle it. Since his return, keeping her distance—and her secret—had been difficult enough. Spending time with him would make it just about impossible.

But as she opened her mouth to protest, Tyler said with a nod in her direction, "We'd be happy to."

# CHAPTER TWO

As Kristen pulled the trash bag from the twenty-gallon trashcan behind the coffee bar, the bell over the door tinkled and she stifled a groan. Sure, it wasn't quite closing time yet, but she was dog-tired and wanted nothing more than to get off her feet.

"Tough day?"

Kristen sighed in relief at the sound of a familiar voice. At least her friend's visit would serve as a welcome distraction from her angst over working with Tyler.

High school rival-turned-friend, Olivia James—soon-to-be Ryder—often came by on her way home from the dance studio she'd taken over following her mother's death. Once an internationally famous ballet dancer with The Joffrey Ballet, Olivia's career had ended abruptly with a ruptured Achilles tendon.

Olivia had returned home from Chicago to handle the estate after her mother died, and she never left. Now she and Zach Ryder, her high school sweetheart and police chief of Northridge, were planning their nuptials.

"You've no idea," Kristen muttered with a sigh. "French press?"

"Sure," Olivia said with a shrug. "And some of those pecan chocolate chip cookies."

Kristen swung around behind the counter, hands on the French press, then paused and lifted a brow in amusement. "I thought you didn't indulge in sweets."

"They're not for me." She bit her lip. "I need to butter up Zach before I tell him I have to fly to New York for a guest appearance on *The Today Show* in two weeks."

"Ah. For the new book?"

"Yep." She tilted her head. "Well, to put my story out there to catch the interest of potential readers."

A few months ago, Olivia's agent had approached her regarding a book deal about her rise to fame and her adjustment to life away from the spotlight. Olivia had been interviewing with Kari Rosenberg, the biographer, via phone or FaceTime for weeks. Later in the fall, the biographer was flying down from Delaware for a week for in-person discussions, visits to the dance studio, and interviews with family and friends.

The book wasn't due to be released for another year, but the publisher was already pushing the promo. Kristen relished the idea of featuring the book in her shop, maybe having a reading and a book signing with both Kari and Olivia.

"Well, those cookies should do the trick. And the wedding?"

Olivia groaned and rolled her eyes.

"Problem?" As the coffee steeped, Kristen boxed up the cookies, adding a rare leftover chocolate croissant for good measure, and tied it up with twine. Finances might be tight, but she loved the old-fashioned white baker's boxes tied with white twine, and if something was worth doing, it was worth doing well. For in-house orders, she preferred the heavy white glazed cups, mugs, saucers, and plates, only using the thermal paper cups and plastic lids for to-go orders.

She often perused Pinterest for those small touches that would take her business to the next level, like the stickers with her logo—a stylized steaming cup of coffee sitting atop a stack of books. Although not necessary in this case, she peeled a sticker off the roll and pressed it to the top of the box.

"Other than lack of time, no. We selected the date, June twentieth, after the recital. We booked the venue—The Barn at Magnolia Farms—"

"Ooh! Great location!" Kristen interrupted. Magnolia Farms featured an enormous renovated barn, complete with open rafters, polished hardwood floors, and glittering chandeliers. In short, it was gorgeous. She couldn't imagine how much *that* rental cost.

"Yeah, but we've done nothing else. No dress, no invitations, no flowers. No caterer, no photographer . . . well, you get the idea."

"Still, a venue is a start, right?"

"Yeah. So, speaking of the wedding . . ." Olivia worried her lower lip with her teeth.

*Uh-oh.*

"I know this isn't really your thing, but would you be my maid of honor?"

"Maid—" Stunned, Kristen drew back. She thought Olivia might ask her to be a bridesmaid, but maid of honor? Her first inclination was to decline. What did she know about being a maid of honor? Especially for a wedding that would likely draw media attention? Then there was the cost of a dress and shoes . . . . "*Me?* What about your sisters?"

The fingers of Olivia's right hand twisted the enormous diamond ring on her left hand.

Earlier that year, Olivia had discovered a family she never knew she'd had, complete with two sisters, Satira and Alexandra, their husbands Zander and Neil, twin nieces Gabriella and Isabella, and nephew Aaron.

"I spoke with them about it. I couldn't choose between them for matron of honor, and they were totally onboard with being bridesmaids. And Gabby and Bella will be my flower girls, and Aaron the ring bearer."

"I—are you sure?" She touched Olivia's hand. Until six months ago when Olivia had returned to Northridge and generously set aside their contentious past relationship, Kristen had had no other woman she could call friend.

"Of course."

Olivia turned her hand up and clasped Kristen's, and Kristen felt tears gathering. WTF? She blinked as if she had an eyelash in her eye, then looked at Olivia. "I'd be honored." Olivia squeezed her hand and squealed. "But," Kristen held up a finger, "don't expect me to hold up your wedding dress while you pee."

Chuckling, Olivia brushed away a tear that was tracing a path down her cheek. "Wouldn't dream of it."

"And don't become a Bridezilla."

Olivia shook her head with a smile, and another tear spilled down her cheek. "It will be a small wedding party, since I just moved back and don't really know that many people." She lifted her shoulder in a shrug that said anything but what a shrug usually says. "Jennie is giving me away, since," she sniffed, "well, since mom won't be here."

Kristen squeezed her hand in understanding. "It will be beautiful."

Olivia nodded.

Feeling awkward now that the moment was over, Kristen cleared her throat, handed Olivia a napkin for her eyes, and lifting the bakery box, placed it in front of her on the bar.

"So what's up with you?" Olivia asked before blotting a tear and blowing her nose on the napkin.

It was no secret Northridge had received an application to film here, so she leaned on the counter, her elbows bent, relieving some of the pressure on her lower back, and spilled the news.

"Really? That's so cool! I loved that book. Too bad there isn't a dance studio scene," she added with a cheeky grin.

At Olivia's words, Kristen stood upright. "You'd support it?"

"Of course! It'd be crazy not to. Anyone can see the economic benefits to the community. Why? You don't?"

"No, I definitely see the opportunity. But several people on the EDC only see the inconvenience."

"Well, yeah. I'm not saying it won't cause some aggravation, but it would be worth it in the end. Anyone else on the council support it?"

"Tyler." She couldn't hide the disdain in her voice.

Olivia eyed her. "Sure he does. He's a smart business owner, just like you. How's that a problem?" Before Kristen could answer, Olivia continued, "Oh, yeah, you don't like him."

Kristen turned her back under the excuse of pouring Olivia's coffee. "I never said I didn't like him."

"Didn't have to. It's written all over your face right now —and your body language speaks volumes whenever his name comes up. Not to mention the look on your face when you see him, like you've just swallowed bad coffee or something."

Kristen handed the cup to Olivia, avoiding her gaze.

Olivia lifted the cup to her mouth and blew gently, steam rising against her breath.

Kristen lifted a shoulder then brushed it off. "Whatever. We just don't get along, that's all."

"Uh-huh. That's like saying the Ice Queen and I don't get along."

Kristen snorted at that. "Now, if there's anyone in this town I don't like, it would be that . . . woman." She pointed her finger for emphasis.

Lily Larson, aka Ice Queen, was the town's First Lady and self-appointed social dictator. She and Olivia had had a little run-in earlier in the year when Olivia hadn't cast her daughter in the role of Cinderella for the recital. But it was her troubled son, Peter, who'd attempted to exact revenge against Olivia and had almost succeeded in unintentionally killing her.

Her husband's term as mayor was coming to an end next year, and while he was a good enough guy, the whole town would breathe a sigh of relief to have a kinder, gentler First Lady, or Gentleman, in the role.

"So, circling back to Tyler—"

"Do we have to?" She rolled her eyes.

"If you two support the opportunity, and the rest of the council doesn't, where do you go from here?"

Kristen told Olivia about the investigation and the report she and Tyler were assigned to prepare.

"But that's good, right?"

"Only if by 'good' you mean 'painful.'"

Olivia chuckled and shook her head. "If this is important enough to both of you, you'll figure it out."

"Yeah, if we don't kill each other first."

Olivia gathered her coffee cup and pastry box. "One of these days you're going to have to forgive him for whatever it was he did to piss you off."

"Yeah, well, forgiveness is not my strong suit."

THE NEXT MORNING, Tyler and his best friend Zach made their customary post-run stop at Beans 'n Books for a coffee, and if truth be told, to catch a glimpse of Kristen's mighty fine ass—at least on his part.

The café bustled with activity. The tables were occupied with patrons, some with laptops open and cups of coffee or tea at their elbows, others reading books or talking amongst their tablemates. In the back, customers perused the shelves for their next read. An old-fashioned sliding ladder sat at the ready for those browsing titles closer to the open-beamed ceiling. Two cozy seating areas invited shopgoers to select a book and sit a while.

The coffee bar ran along the exposed-brick wall to the left, and glass cases in front displayed a wide array of baked goods—everything from muffins and breakfast pastries to cupcakes and cookies. The scent of fresh-roasted coffee and those tantalizing sweets were difficult to resist.

Overall, it was a warm and welcoming atmosphere. He had to hand it Kristen, she'd turned the dusty old bookstore he'd remembered into a vibrant business.

Zach settled at the coffee bar next to him and, snatching a couple of napkins from the dispenser, wiped the sweat from his face.

Kristen chose that moment to come out of the kitchen. "Hey! Go to the bathroom to do that. This isn't your personal locker room."

Zach just grinned and handed her the two sweaty napkins. She gave him the evil eye, but took them from him just the same and tossed them in the garbage behind the bar. For all her animosity toward Tyler, she seemed to tolerate more from Zach.

As she turned to wash her hands, she asked, "The usual?"

"Yes," they chorused.

Tyler and Zach grew up together, hung out together, played sports, and otherwise got into the typical trouble boys in a small town could get into. It wasn't until Tyler went to college that they went their separate ways. But even so, they'd managed to keep up with one another via the ever-evolving social media options and, of course, email and text. And when Tyler had returned to Northridge, they'd fallen back into their friendship as if he'd never left.

Now, Zach was just months away from becoming a husband and, maybe someday, a father. Tyler had known his friend's fiancée, Olivia, growing up too, and like Tyler, she'd left Northridge to pursue a career. Also, like him, she'd returned to make a new life for herself.

But unlike Zach and Olivia, Tyler's prospects for marital bliss and family were poor at best. Not that he had a burning desire to get married any time soon. Or even engaged.

Tried it once. It didn't take.

Then there was the possible fertility thing. Or *infertility* thing, he should say.

"So," Zach cleared his throat. "The wedding plans are

under way, and we've selected June twentieth for the ceremony."

"That's great, man. I'm happy for you and Olivia." Tyler clapped him on the back.

"And, well," Zach continued, "I need a best man. I was hoping you might stand up with me when I bid goodbye to my bachelorhood."

"Seriously? Of course! I'd be honored to be your best man."

Kristen, who had just set their steaming cups of coffee on the counter, choked.

"You okay?" Zach asked. "You look like you swallowed a bug."

She grimaced and waved him away, then huffed out a sardonic laugh and shook her head as if exasperated.

"What?" Tyler asked.

Avoiding his question, she asked, "Anything else?" She lifted a brow at Tyler.

"Maybe one of those cinnamon rolls."

She snatched a sheet of wax paper from the box, as if the inanimate object had pissed her off, and reached inside the glass case to select a gooey, spicy roll and place it on a white plate. "Warmed?"

"Yes. Please." He tried one of his nerdy grins on her, the kind that generally melted even the coldest of female hearts. Apparently not hers.

With an eye roll, she walked over to the TurboChef oven and popped the roll in. He took advantage of this to admire her world-class ass, wrapped tight in black leggings, her feet stuffed into some fuzzy boots against the first chilly morning of fall.

Zach elbowed him. "You have a little drool," he said, pointing at the corner of his own mouth.

"Funny." But the heat of a blush worked its way into his face.

The timer dinged and the scents of sugary melted icing and spicy cinnamon mingled with the smell of roasted coffee beans, making Tyler's stomach rumble.

Zach leaned back and eyed him. "Damn, dude. When was the last time you ate?"

"Last night." Tyler took a hearty bite of the cinnamon roll and nearly fainted with pleasure, not to mention burning the tip of his tongue.

"Careful. It's hot," Kristen supplied, her voice flat, relaying the exact opposite of concern.

"Yeah." He wiped his mouth with a napkin. "Thanks for the warning."

"That smells good," Zach put in. "I'll take one too. So, I hear Northridge is a film location prospect."

"Yeah, though most of the EDC opposes it."

"It can be a hassle. When I was with the Atlanta PD, I served on a few security details when they were filming there—mostly commercials and what-not—and it can be a big inconvenience to local businesses impacted by road closures."

"But the city benefits in the form of fees, jobs, and good will."

"True. I'm not saying I'm opposed. I'm just saying I can understand folks' hesitancy over the disruption it will cause. Because it will cause disruption." Taking a bite of his own cinnamon roll Kristen had placed in front of him, Zach moaned as the icing melted in his mouth.

"Be that as it may, I believe the economic benefits will far outweigh the inconvenience."

After swallowing, Zach sipped his coffee then held up the cinnamon confection. "These are your best yet."

"Thanks." Kristen stood not far from them filling containers with various sweetener packets for the self-serve area.

"So, when do you want to get together?" Tyler pushed his empty plate away and picked up his coffee.

"What?" Kristen gawked at him, her brow furrowed.

"You know, to look over the proposal, decide on a game plan for the investigation, and start our report for the committee."

"Oh. Um. Well." Kristen's gaze slid away, then back. She drew in a deep breath as if she'd come to a decision. "I'm . . . busy today."

"Okay. How about tomorrow?" Tyler pushed. He could practically see the gears turning in her head as she tried one excuse after another, abandoning them before they were fully formed.

She sighed in resignation. "Tomorrow's fine." She held up a finger. "But not until after the morning rush."

"Eleven, then?"

"Sure." Her response wasn't what he'd call enthusiastic. He shook his head. What did he do to make her dislike him so much? he wondered for the hundredth time.

When she returned to take his empty plate, he addressed the elephant in the room. "Hey, you ever going to tell me why you hate me, so I can ask for your forgiveness?"

She stiffened, and her death-ray glare returned. "If you have to ask, you don't deserve my forgiveness." Spinning on her heel, she stalked into the kitchen, leaving him to stare after her.

"Ouch. That didn't go so well, did it?" Zach said around a mouthful of his breakfast.

*Damn.* No it didn't.

❄

"OF COURSE HE IS," Kristen muttered, as she scrubbed the kitchen counter with the force of a carpenter sanding wood.

"What?" Calypso Benoit, her assistant manager and barista asked in her pleasing Cajun lilt.

"Hmm? Oh, nothing." Nothing except one more reason she and Tyler would be forced to spend time together.

*Joy.*

But what did she expect? Tyler and Zach were best buds. Who else would Zach ask to be his best man?

Between the film location proposal investigation and report and the wedding, it looked like she and Tyler would be in close proximity, at least for the near future.

Despite the size of Northridge, she'd been able to avoid Tyler for the most part. Sure, he came to her café often, and she appreciated the business in any form she could get it, but those visits never lasted more than half an hour at most.

She also frequented his taproom on occasion. She was woman enough to admit he brewed a tasty beer. Most times he wasn't there, and even if he was, he wasn't behind the bar; he was in his office doing whatever it was he did there. And now there were the monthly Economic Development Council meetings. But, other than that, she'd managed to evade his company.

Until now.

And the gall of the man to ask what he'd done to make her hate him!

There was no way in Hell she'd ever admit to him, or anyone else, why she felt so strongly about him, especially if he had to ask. She'd never admit how she let her guard down. How she let him hurt her. Humiliate her. Never returning her phone calls. Then pretending like it never happened.

She, however, could not pretend like it never happened.

Most men were shitheads. Zach Ryder and Marshall MacKinnon were the rare exceptions. If she hadn't learned that from her father and her mother's boyfriends, she'd learned that hard lesson from Tyler Kincaide, a guy she once thought of as sweet and kind. Turned out he was a wolf in sheep's clothing.

She prided herself on being a quick study, and she carried that lesson close to heart. Didn't need to tell herself twice. Tyler Kincaide was out of her league. He'd more than made that clear seventeen years ago when he'd had his way with her then tossed her aside her like a pair of worn shoes.

But even if she could bring herself to forgive him, the truth was, she didn't trust herself around him. Despite his treatment of her, she still harbored a little of that school-girl crush she'd had so many years ago. It wouldn't take much for her to fall all over again. And that couldn't happen.

Nope. Never again.

# CHAPTER THREE

THE NEXT DAY, Tyler took in the charm that was Northridge, whistling as he walked. The red brick buildings, the tree-lined Main Street with its decorative lampposts, decked-out with hanging baskets of flowers in oranges, yellows, and deep reds.

Since he'd been away, some of the businesses had changed hands, but many remained the same, including Dominick's Pizza, Carmichael's Bike Shop, and Sweet Cream Ice Cream. It spoke to the Northridge community's support for local business.

Alongside some of the traditional businesses, trendier shops had opened. Tabitha's Pints and Paints had taken over where the local hardware store had once been. Tony Mosby's pet bakery stood next to the post office, and Matt and Sophia's chic wine bar and restaurant, dubbed The Old Bank, resided in the First Bank of Northridge building.

He thought the brass plaques on the historic buildings displaying the names of the original tenants was a nice nod to those who had come before. The Town Council had clearly done a good job attracting new businesses while maintaining the charm of the nineteenth-century railroad town.

The railroad tracks bisected the downtown area, separating the commercial side from the residential, and consequently, the affluent from the impoverished. Katrina Gold swept the steps of the old train station, now The Whistle Stop Pub. Trains still roared through town, some carrying goods and others carrying passengers, but they no longer stopped in Northridge on their journey.

The town's existence post-dated the Civil War by about five years, so it didn't boast any antebellum homes, but it had its share of notable historic homes dating back to its early days, most in the American Craftsman style like the one he'd bought and renovated when he returned.

Only about five square miles, the town proper was built on a ridge some twelve hundred feet above sea level and some two hundred feet above its neighbors, making Northridge's temperatures about ten degrees cooler than the surrounding area.

The beautiful blue-sky fall day reminded him that life was good and that he was grateful to be alive. He had reason to be.

Since his homecoming a little over a year ago, the one fly in the ointment had been Kristen. He'd returned home to find she'd opened her own business, which was thriving by all accounts. But any time he tried to strike up a conversation with her, she gave him the cold shoulder. It wasn't like they'd been best buds in high school, but they'd at least been friends. Now she treated him like he had the plague, which made the EDC meetings a tad uncomfortable.

And now they had found themselves on the same side of an issue, squaring off against many of the other members of the council and the community as a whole.

Not that he wanted a romantic relationship with her—or any other woman for that matter—his last relationship having ended at the worst possible time in his life, but he'd like to at least have a cordial relationship with her.

He arrived at the café at eleven-fifteen, his iPad under one arm, the proposal the film company had submitted to the Gwinnett County Film-Ready Liaison tucked into the device's cover.

The way he saw it, this would be a brainstorming session. He and Kristen would toss around ideas on next steps and then come up with a game plan. In preparation for their meeting, he'd compiled a list of issues based on his research of other county film liaison websites.

Grabbing a table in the corner where he and Kristen could talk, he set his things down, pulled out a chair, and took a seat. After her response to what he thought was a perfectly reasonable question, he didn't know what kind of reception he'd get from her today.

Kristen chatted with Marshall MacKinnon, attorney and lifetime resident of Northridge. His family had been in Northridge since its inception. His office was just a few doors down from the café, so stopping by the café for a cup of Kristen's delicious coffee was convenient. Tyler didn't know him that well, but Olivia adored him, so he must be a great guy.

"I'll see you later today?"

Kristen nodded.

They said their goodbyes and Marshall turned to leave then spotted Tyler and approached his table. "Tyler," he said with a nod of his gray head.

"Morning, sir," Tyler responded politely.

"I hear you're in support of filming in Northridge."

"I am," Tyler said, prepared to launch into his arguments in support of it.

"Good. Town needs shaking up a bit."

Taken aback, Tyler barked out a laugh.

Marshall turned back to Kristen. "And speaking of shaking things up a bit, did I tell you my granddaughter is moving back?"

"No. When?" Kristen paused in the middle of refilling a napkin dispenser.

"Next month. She's made an offer on Edgar Evans' real estate business. Expects the deal to go through in the next couple of weeks."

"That's great news, Marshall."

"It is. It is, indeed." He made his exit, cup of coffee in his hand and a spring in his step.

His granddaughter, Georgia, had been two years behind Tyler and Kristen in high school and clearly held a special place in Marshall's heart.

She'd been a whirlwind growing up. His mother had said Georgia couldn't wait to get the hell out of Dodge—taking off for California the day after high school graduation. If he remembered correctly, UC Berkeley for undergrad, then Stanford for law school. She'd reportedly become a hotshot real estate broker in L.A.

Tyler wondered what was bringing her back to little Northridge and Edgar's rinky-dink real estate office. Then he snorted. He'd come back, hadn't he? As had Olivia. Somehow Northridge never left you.

He looked up as Kristen sat down with a groan.

"Problem?"

She rubbed her low back. "Just been on my feet since four-thirty this morning."

Tyler grimaced. "Four-thirty?" he asked, incredulous. "Couldn't sleep?"

She snorted. "Those cinnamon rolls don't bake themselves, you know."

*Huh.* He'd never thought about what it took to have all those luscious baked goods ready to sell and eat by seven a.m. when she opened her doors.

"What time do you go to bed?"

She lifted a shoulder. "Usually between eleven and midnight."

"Midnight! Jesus. There isn't enough coffee in this café to keep me awake and functioning that long."

"You do what you have to do." She sighed and closed her eyes.

He studied her. For the first time, he saw the dark circles under her eyes, the fatigue around her mouth. He'd never noticed before. Or maybe it was just that he'd never had the opportunity to study her before she could cut short their encounter.

"You close at seven, what do you do until midnight?"

Her eyes flew open, as if she'd forgotten he was there. "I might close at seven, but then I have to clean up, resupply, run inventory. Then I go home and manage my social media, and do other . . . things."

"Like bookkeeping? You know there are these things called computers and they talk to one another. Your register could talk to your accounting software, and your inventory system could talk to your computer."

She shifted in her seat then waved her hand dismissing his comment. "I know, but I run reports, crunch numbers, that sort of thing." She lifted a defiant brow. Before he could push the matter, she spoke, "Aren't you here to talk about the film location application? Let's get to it."

He eyed her another moment then resigned pulled the report out of his iPad case.

She wagged her finger at the proposal he was holding. "When do they want to start filming?"

"Summer."

She nodded. "Makes sense, since that's when the story opens in the book."

"Film permits are issued at the municipal level. Gwinnett County has film guidelines, and an application, but Northridge is allowed to have an additional permit application and requirements, as well as our own fee schedule."

Kristen breathed a sigh of relief when their conversation finally turned to the reason for this meeting. She didn't need any further prying from Tyler. He didn't need to know how she spent her evenings after closing, and sometimes her afternoons when business was slow.

"We'll need a location agreement and a roads-use agreement," Tyler continued, and she redirected her attention to what he was saying. "They're pretty standard, but the county liaison can help with that."

Tyler's earlier interrogation wasn't the only thing distracting her. His cologne was doing a mighty fine job of that too. He smelled spicy and woodsy. And expensive.

She knew Tyler had been a huge success in New York. He'd come home with the Maserati to prove it. And now his two businesses appeared to be a tremendous success as well. Two of his craft brews had been written up in *DRAFT Magazine,* and his taproom had been featured in *Atlanta Magazine.* And he'd accomplished it all in the space of a year.

Wouldn't she just love to have her café featured in *Atlanta Magazine?* Northridge as the movie location could go a long way to making that a reality.

Despite Tyler's success, he'd come home thin and worn looking. At first she'd thought he'd been sucked into the world of cocaine and other designer drugs that those with more money than sense sometimes succumbed to. But no. He must have just been overworked. Upon returning to Northridge, he'd bought and renovated a house, put on a bit of weight, and became more like the fit, healthy man he'd been when he'd left.

And there was nothing wrong with his health now. He seemed the picture of fit and healthy in his worn jeans and his blue-green Henley that set his eyes off perfectly. And dammit if sitting this close to him didn't set off some weird vibe, like a low hum of electricity. She found herself staring at the pulse in his throat wondering what he would do if she pressed her lips to it.

"Kristen, are you listening to me?"

"Huh? Of course." She shook herself. *Get with the program, McKay.*

"You okay?"

She gave him a look that said, *Hello, been going since four-thirty.*

He studied her just long enough to make her twitch, then continued.

"We need a minimum of two off-duty officers on location the duration of the shoot. We'll need to check with Zach to see what the department's policy is for hiring and paying off-duty officers. I want to make sure we've covered all the bases, in case we get questions."

She felt his eyes on her again.

"You've read the book, right?" He accidentally nudged

her arm with his as he spoke, and she felt it all the way down to her toes. *Oh, hell no.* We'll have none of that, she told her traitorous body.

"Of course. Hello. Bookstore." She waved her hand toward the back of the café. Up to that point, Tyler had done all the talking. Not that she'd minded. Her brain had been elsewhere— in the gutter with her body.

"I just started it. So based on your read, what locations do you think they'll need?"

"It's just speculation, since I don't know anything about filming, or even how the whole screenplay and location selection process works. I assume not everything from the book will be in the movie, but they'll need something for the boarding house—it plays a major role in the story." She held up her hand, lifting her fingers as she listed the locations. "The B&B would be perfect if Carter and Anita are willing."

"The Whistle Stop Pub, since they'll need the train station. Not sure how they go about that. The exterior would likely be easy. It's how they handle the interior setting that will be interesting. Sound stage, maybe?" She shrugged.

"Main Street." She continued to tick off the scenes as they came to her. "The old bank will need to be, well, the bank."

"Well, I can promise you one thing: they aren't going to turn the Firehouse Taproom back into the livery stables," he said with a grin and a wink.

She rolled her eyes and continued, "They'll need a general store."

"That's what your café was back in the day." He gave her a playful elbow bump.

Biting back a smile at his enthusiasm, she continued,

"Yeah. I know. Assuming they intend to use the interior, that wouldn't be too difficult to pull off again." And the production company would pay to remodel it and then put it back to rights. Maybe she could even keep any changes that were beneficial to her business. *Bonus.*

She wondered how long before the economic impact to Northridge and its businesses would be felt. Before this opportunity came along, she wondered how she was going to keep her dream alive. This. This was her lifeline. If she could hang on, she knew this would be the boost her business needed.

This had to happen. That was all there was to it. She wasn't the only one relying on her success. And if it meant spending more time in close proximity to the hard-to-resist Tyler Kincaide, then so be it. Her business, her livelihood, and her reputation depended on it.

The bell over the door tinkled, and shadowed against the light pouring in through the open glass door stood a tall, rangy young man. She sucked in her breath and cut her eyes at Tyler.

The kid ambled in, a duffle bag over one shoulder, a violin case in his other hand. He set the case on the table, dropped the duffle at her feet, and said, "Hi, Mom."

# CHAPTER FOUR

So, this was Seth. Tyler had seen him here and there around town but had never met him. The kid was away at school, Zach had said. Juilliard. Damned impressive. Supposedly he was a violin prodigy.

When Tyler had first learned from his mom sixteen years ago that Kristen had had a son, you could have knocked him over with a feather.

Seth had had a growth spurt since Tyler had last seen him six months before. He had his mom's green eyes and hints of her red hair in the strawberry blond. Tyler couldn't help but wonder who the father was, and an unexpected shot of jealousy pierced him.

Clearly stunned by her son's appearance, Kristen stared up at him open-mouthed. Late-September—he assumed the kid was supposed to be in school. She finally stood and hugged him, her eyes closing as her arms wrapped around him. So Kristen had a soft side, Tyler thought. *Who knew?*

Whereas she was short, Seth was very tall. He already towered over his mother. Leaving his mother's embrace, he nodded at Tyler.

"Um, Seth, this is Tyler Kincaide. Tyler, this is my son, Seth." She wore a proud, yet defiant expression Tyler couldn't unravel. Did she expect him to rebuke her for having a son out of wedlock? At least he assumed it was out of wedlock, since there had been no mention of a husband, past or present.

Tyler rose and shook Seth's hand. "Nice to meet you, sir."

Tyler nearly choked. *Sir?* "If it's okay with your mom, please, call me Tyler."

"Tyler," Seth said with a nod.

"You hungry?" Kristen's face softened as she spoke to Seth. "There's fresh bread in the kitchen, along with some sliced sandwich meats and cheese I bought for lunch. Go fix yourself a sandwich."

They both watched the kid amble across the café and behind the bar before entering the kitchen. She shook her head and sighed in what sounded like exasperation.

"I take it he's not supposed to be home."

"Huh? Oh. No. He's supposed to be in school. In New York." She collapsed into her seat again as if she could no longer bear the weight of the world on her shoulders.

He bent to close the cover on his tablet, tucking the application back in. "Well, I'll let you speak with your son. I'm sure you, uh, have a few things to discuss."

"Yeah, you could say that," she said, rubbing a spot in the middle of her forehead.

"We'll finish up our plan in a day or two."

For once, he didn't feel Kristen's glare on his back as he exited the café.

❄

"WHAT ARE YOU DOING HOME? Your classes started two weeks ago."

Seth dropped into the seat recently vacated by his father and set the plate in front of him. "I'm taking a semester off."

Stunned, Kristen sat back in her seat. "You're—what the hell?"

"I need a break, Mom." Seth picked up half his sandwich and took a man-sized bite out of it.

"But you love Juilliard." She reached out for his hand. "What changed?"

Seth shrugged as only a sixteen-year-old who knows nothing about the consequences of his actions can, then let his gaze roam around the café before finally resting on her face. The color rose in his cheeks. "I missed you."

"Oh, honey." Her heart swelled. "I missed you too, but this is your future." She released his hand, in firm command of her mom-voice again. "What about your scholarship? And what about school?"

"I'll take classes at Northridge for the semester."

"Those classes started two weeks ago."

"I'll catch up," he said, his voice thick with exasperation.

And she had no doubt he would. He was wicked smart like his father.

"And your violin training?"

"Northridge has an orchestra."

"Pfft. Like that's going to get you to Carnegie Hall."

"Mom. Stop."

She leaned across the table. "If you lose that scholarship, I can't pay. You know that, right?"

"I know, I know. I won't lose it. I may have to audition again, but I'll get in."

"Says the kid who begged me to go to New York." She

paused, watching him devour the sandwich like he hadn't eaten in days. Maybe he hadn't. "How'd you get home?"

"Bus," he said around a mouthful of food.

"And what about the Woods'? Please tell me you didn't take off without letting them know."

Rolling his eyes, Seth sighed. "Of course they know. They tried to talk me out of it, but in the end, they let me go. I texted them to let them know I was home safe."

Of course, she should know better. If Seth had disappeared without a word to them, they would have been on the phone to her immediately. Gabe and Cordelia Wood were friends of Marshall MacKinnon's. They were attorneys in New York with no children of their own, and because they came with Marshall's stamp of approval, she knew she could trust them. They had welcomed Seth into their home and become surrogate parents to him. Attending concerts, chauffeuring him to activities, and providing a roof over his head and food to feed his growing body.

"I only have a one-bedroom apartment, remember? We agreed when you left for school that I would save money by moving."

"So I'll sleep on the couch."

She eyed her son, happy to see him, but worried about his future. She hadn't worked hard and sacrificed for him to attend Juilliard's High School program just so he could become like her. He'd go to school, make good grades, get into Berkeley or Juilliard's music programs, and become another Joshua Bell or Itzhak Perlman.

She would never have sent her son away just to conceal him from Tyler, but his desire to go to Juilliard just as Tyler came back had been a bonus. When Tyler returned to Northridge and saw Seth, he hadn't put two and two together. He hadn't connected their night together with

Seth. And she was happy to keep it that way. But unless she could talk Seth into going back to New York, Tyler might eventually figure it out.

Growing up, she lived in fear of being taken away by child protective services. She saw too many of the kids who lived in the trailer park taken away from their parents, some returned later, while and others remained in the foster care system. She often thought she'd be next. Especially after her father's arrest. Anytime a police car drove through the trailer park, she'd run away and hide, thinking they were coming for her.

While her mother didn't exactly provide a stable environment, Kristen could neither leave her mother to fend for herself nor imagine living without her. Many wild animals were better mothers to their young, but Kim McKay did the best she could with what she had.

When Kristen found herself single, pregnant, working two jobs, and living in that same trailer with her mother, she'd been young and scared. No. Not young. She hadn't been young since her father's arrest when she'd had to take on grown-up responsibilities. But she'd been plenty scared. How the hell was she supposed to take care of a baby when she could barely manage to take care of herself?

So she'd called Tyler to tell him—several times—but he'd never called her back. And with each message left with no return call, her anger and resentment grew. Maybe it was for the best, she'd told herself. If he and his family had known, they might have denied it. Or worse, believed it and tried to take her son from her.

And then, after her beautiful son was born, she'd convinced herself that Tyler didn't deserve to know. He had left for Princeton without a word, making her feel like the worthless slut everyone thought she was. No. He hadn't wanted her seventeen years ago, and he hadn't bothered to call her back when she discovered she was pregnant, so she had no inclination now to welcome Tyler into Seth's life. He'd lost that chance long ago.

KRISTEN WAITED in Marshall's waiting room for her appointment. As part of his mentorship through the Small Business Association, he provided pro bono legal services to Kristen, reviewing her purchase agreement when she bought the bookstore, advising on the lease agreement, loan agreements, and much, much more.

He was the reason Seth had been able to go to Juilliard. While Seth had received a scholarship for weekly instruction at the school, he needed a place to live with a responsible adult who could help him navigate the ins and outs of going to high school in New York, and support him so far from home.

And Marshall's kindness hadn't started with Seth. Thanks to his generosity, she'd been a cheerleader for Northridge High School her junior year when she was going through her short-lived trying-to-fit-in stage. Marshall had stepped up and bought the uniforms she and her mom could never afford to buy. He'd paid for her mother's funeral, and when the bookstore went up for sale, he gave her a low-interest loan for the required renovations.

And he did it all without making it feel like a handout. He always told her he was "investing in her future." He' believed in her more than she believed in herself. He listened while she bounced ideas off him and gave her the fatherly advice she grew up without.

"Kristen, Mr. MacKinnon is ready for you."

Kristen stood, smoothed the denim skirt over her brown tights, and tossed her ponytail over her shoulder.

Marshall MacKinnon looked every bit the lawyer, seated behind a massive mahogany desk, horn-rimmed glasses perched on his nose as he reviewed the document he was holding. His thick silver hair gave him a distinguished, but grandfatherly appearance.

He glanced up when she came in.

"Kristen. Come in, come in. Sit down." He indicated the chair across from his desk.

She set a cup of his favorite concoction on his desk.

"You are a lifesaver, Sugar. A lifesaver." His Southern charm and promotion of social justice had earned him the reputation of Northridge's response to Atticus Finch. He sipped from the cup then grinned. "Just the way I like it, sweet and creamy."

Marshall had a sweet tooth and liked a little coffee with his cream and sugar.

She cut right to the chase. "I know we were supposed to discuss the potential upgrade of my bread ovens, but I got a little surprise today and I could use your advice." Shifting in her seat, she said, "Seth's home."

"Well, tarnation."

Kristen bit back a smile at Marshall's polite oath.

"Did he say why?"

"He said he was taking the semester off because he missed me." Just saying it warmed her heart but made her feel guilty at the same time.

"Well, of course he does. But he needs to focus." He jabbed the desktop with his finger for emphasis. "Once he'd returned to his busy fall schedule, he'd be fine."

"I'm worried about the scholarship. Marshall, I can't pay for Juilliard if he loses this scholarship."

Marshall rose from his chair and came to perch on the front of his desk. He nodded in thought. "Is he set on staying in Northridge?"

"I think for now. I hope to convince him to go back in January."

"I'll write a letter to the dean at Juilliard. Tell her there are some family issues and Seth needs a leave of absence and see where that gets us."

"Thank you, Marshall."

He nodded and slapped his hands on his thighs. "Now, let's talk about that upgrade."

"So, what's the word?" Zach sat at the bar, shoulders hunched, eyeing Tyler.

Tyler resisted the urge to sigh. He knew Zach only asked because he cared, but sometimes Tyler just wanted to put it behind him once and for all.

As if that were even possible. Especially with the news he'd received today.

"Tumor markers are clear, and so are the scans."

Zach's shoulders visibly relaxed. "Great news, man!" He reached out a fist and Tyler bumped it with this own.

Yeah, it was great news. If only it had been *all* great news.

Growing up, he'd had no real drama in his life, other than that of any other adolescent boy. His parents didn't drink to excess, they had steady middle class jobs, and they were still happily married after forty-three years. He'd never been abused, always had a roof over his head, and knew where his next meal was coming from.

Sure, he got into his share of trouble from time to time,

suffered through groundings and other such punishments, but everything considered, a charmed life by most standards.

His charmed life continued through college and early into his career. The long hours as an investment broker hadn't bothered him too much—the money had been good. Very good. His client focus had been sports superstars with massive portfolios. He'd been able to pay off his parents' debt, including their mortgage, and sock away a substantial savings for himself.

While his colleagues were busy buying million-dollar apartments in Manhattan and fancy cars, he lived in a one-bedroom apartment in Queens and took the subway. And other than wining and dining his clients on occasion, partying had never been his thing. He grimaced. The night before he left for Princeton had taught him that.

His charmed life had all come crashing down when, a month past his thirtieth birthday, he'd been diagnosed with Hodgkin lymphoma. Determined not to let the cancer win, he'd delved into all the latest research, chosen the best oncologists, and pursued remission with the same single-minded focus with which he'd pursued his degree and his career. It had been the most difficult period of his life for more reasons than the cancer.

He came out the other side physically and mentally burned out and ready for a change. The cancer had reminded him life was too short to spend it doing nothing but working.

He'd returned to Northridge with a hefty bank account, a Maserati (his one indulgence in celebration of his remission), and the germ of an idea to start a craft brewery. He bought and renovated a house not far from his parents, and with the love and support of them and Zach, he'd recovered his stamina and energy and loved every day of his life toying with his giant chemistry set in the form of Firehouse Brews.

Not many knew about his cancer. His family, of course, and Zach. He didn't hide it, but neither did he want to be identified by it. And he didn't want his loved ones to constantly worry about him, as Zach appeared to be doing now.

"Did you tell your parents?" Zach asked, bringing Tyler back to the present.

"Yep." Tyler slid a clipboard under the bar. "Going there for dinner tonight to celebrate." His parents insisted that they not only acknowledge but commemorate each milestone to that five-year mark. He was so close. Only a few months away.

"Tell them I said hi."

"Will do. You should come for dinner sometime. They'd love to catch up with you."

"I'll do that."

"Now, what can I get you?"

"Nothing. I'm on duty in a few hours."

"You just stopped by to ask about my tests?" The thought touched Tyler.

"That, and to ask when you have a spot on your calendar to drive into Atlanta to try on tuxes. Olivia's been . . ."

"Nagging?"

Zach winced. "Nudging."

Tyler chuckled at that, shaking his head while he pulled his phone out of his pocket. He and Celeste hadn't gotten to the wedding-planning stage before he'd been diagnosed and she'd bailed on him.

Tapping open the calendar he gave it a quick scan. "I'm free Monday afternoon."

"Can't. I'm on duty. How about Wednesday after two?"

"Can do." Tyler entered the appointment in the calendar app on his phone. "Hey, maybe we can try the new brew house in Buckhead after."

"You're on. How's the investigation going?"

"Good. I have data on the economic impact to Senoia, and based on that, I can make projections for Northridge. I have a meeting with Joe Howard, Coweta County's camera-ready liaison next week, then we'll schedule a meeting with the Gwinnett County Liaison."

Zach nodded.

"I do need to discuss security with you. Get your thoughts, what the impacts would be on your station, the costs, etc. You know, once we sign on to be a camera-ready community, other opportunities may come along, and you'll be the security contact."

"Anytime. I know some of the officers have been talking about the off-duty pay opportunities this could bring, which tend to be slim-to-none around here. I think they'd be in support of it. More money in their pockets."

"Good to hear."

Zach slapped the bar with the palm of his hand. "Gotta go."

"See ya." Tyler watched as Zach made his way to the door, thinking about how much Zach's friendship meant to him. If there was one thing his bout with cancer had taught him, it was to tell the people you love how much you appreciated them, because you never knew if you'd get the chance again. "Hey, Zach?"

Zach turned, his hand on the door. "Yeah?"

"Thanks, man."

"For what?" he asked, his brow puckered in confusion.

"For being there. For caring."

Zach smiled and nodded. "You got it."

Zach, Olivia, and his family were all he had. He'd never have a family of his own.

The good news: he was still in remission. The bad news: he was sterile.

# CHAPTER FIVE

"How's IT going with you and Tyler?" Olivia asked from the driver's seat of the studio van.

They were on their way to Atlanta to look at dresses, and since she wanted Olivia to actually make it to her appointment rather than end up stranded on the side of the interstate, Kristen had recommended that Olivia drive.

Kristen's car was iffy on a good day, much less a cold rainy one like today. With Seth in New York, and her apartment and café only a block apart, she hadn't needed a reliable car. Now that Seth was home, that might change though.

"What do you mean?" Kristen returned, then winced at her sharp tone.

"Defensive much?" Olivia said, a grin on her face.

"I'm not defensive, just . . . aggravated with this whole thing."

"Uh-huh." Olivia shifted to face her at the next stoplight. "You know, you could just tell him whatever it was he did that pissed you off and let him either make it right or brush it off. At least then you could move on."

"I don't know what you mean."

Olivia blew out a frustrated breath. "Whatever."

A moment later, Oliva continued. "Or you could just have hot, steamy hate sex." Olivia's voice held a note of playfulness, but the urges her comment triggered were far from playful. More like visceral longing and naked lust.

She chalked it up to her long—very long—dry spell.

"Not happening."

"How's Seth?"

"He and Calypso are covering the café." Kristen hesitated, then continued, happy for a change of subject, "That kid. I don't know what I'm going to do with him. He came home because he misses me."

"Aw, that's so sweet. You two have a great relationship."

They did, and her good fortune wasn't lost on her. Since she'd been just nineteen when Seth was born, it was as if she and Seth had grown up together. She'd been scared to death, not only of taking care of a newborn baby, but also of raising a child. What if she screwed up? What if her lack of resources resulted in failure, or worse, a life of crime on his part?

But she swore she would do everything in her power to keep him safe, warm, and fed. And most of all loved. It wasn't always easy. They'd continued to live with her mother in the single-wide trailer she grew up in, and even though it was her mother's home, Kristen had laid down the law about smoking in the trailer and bringing home dubious men.

In the weeks leading up to her due date, Kristen had scrubbed every inch of the place, throwing open windows and doors to the fresh, chilly early-spring air, cleaning out cabinets, dumping out the bottles of cheap liquor her mother's boyfriends brought over, and making room for baby clothes, supplies, and other baby paraphernalia. To make room in her tiny bedroom for a crib, she'd crammed what furniture she'd had cheek-to-jowl against the flimsy walls.

Between working two waitressing jobs and waking nights to feed Seth, she'd been utterly exhausted the first year of his life. But he'd thrived, despite the hardships, making it all worth it. As he grew, she recognized his father's intelligence. He spoke early and began walking when he was only ten months old.

In an effort to reinforce his already sharp mind, she played classical music for him, having read an article about the correlation between the complexity of the compositions and higher brain functions. One day, when he was five, he stood mesmerized listening to one of Vivaldi's violin pieces, then after a few moments, began to air-play a violin, as if he knew what the instrument was. It gave her chills.

She pawned the TV set in her room, bought him a used violin, and asked the high school orchestra teacher for lessons. He took to the violin as if born to it, and by the age of seven, he had surpassed the orchestra teacher's skills and Kristen had to find another teacher for her son.

Turned out her smart, sweet son was a prodigy.

So, while Kristen resented Tyler's treatment of her, she couldn't regret that night—it had given her the best thing to ever happen to her: Seth.

A COUPLE OF HOURS LATER, Kristen was seated in the first bridal shop on the list, a chichi affair in Buckhead, feeling out of her element surrounded by colossal vases filled with roses in pinks, greens, and creams. An ice bucket sat close at hand with a bottle of champagne, shimmering crystal flutes at the ready. Mirror-lined walls reflected the opulence of it all from every direction.

While Olivia had apparently done her homework—she had pages marked in two glossy bridal magazines—according to an article Kristen had read on a wedding planning website, it could take weeks to find the right dress. *Ugh.* *If*—and that was a big *if*—she ever got married, a trip to the courthouse would suit her just fine.

Barely restraining a heavy sigh, Kristen tossed back the contents of her glass, the bubbles tickling her nose and making her sneeze.

"Bless you," Olivia's sisters chimed.

Champagne was a rare occurrence in Kristen's life. And by rare, she meant this was her first.

It went down easy. She'd lost count of how many glasses she'd had in the two hours they'd been here. If she didn't eat something soon, she'd be staggering out of the shop. And Olivia still had two more shops on her list. She wondered if every shop would supply a bottle of champagne.

Even after Olivia selected the dress, they still had accessories—a veil or other hair ornament, shoes, underpinnings, jewelry—not to mention the bridesmaids' dresses.

Olivia's two sisters, Alex and Satira, sat sipping champagne, looking perfectly at home in their cashmere and wool, perched on white leather chairs.

Kristen, on the other hand, fidgeted in her discount-store sweater dress and boots, imposter syndrome kicking in. She didn't belong here in this posh setting. She didn't belong in the role of maid of honor for Olivia's refined wedding. What had possessed her to say yes?

What the hell did she know about satin, brocade, chiffon, and silk? Bateau versus jewel versus sweetheart neckline? Chapel-length trains versus cathedral? Nothing—that was what. How was she supposed to help her friend select a dress for one of the biggest days of her life?

This was the fourth—no, fifth—dress Olivia had selected to try on. The others had been overblown creations with too much lace and not enough skin. Even Kristen knew Olivia needed something elegant and fine.

The door to the dressing room opened and a vision stepped out. Kristen blinked, as she heard the collective gasps from Olivia's sisters.

Olivia stood, as regal as a princess, looking every inch the ballerina in the iciest of pinks. The dress hugged the graceful curves of her body, ending in what appeared to be a chapel-length train appliquéd with the finest lace and a smattering of crystals that winked beneath the glittering chandeliers overhead. She'd pulled her chestnut hair up in a mass of loose waves, so when she turned, she revealed miles of bare skin framed with more of the delicate lace.

Kristen had never seen anything so beautiful in her life.

*Damn.* Tears clogged her throat, and her heart ached with the overwhelming beauty. Olivia emanated happiness and confidence, and for a moment, jealousy punched through Kristen's champagne-fueled haze.

"Well?" Olivia prompted, wringing her hands in front of her.

"Oh. My. God." Satira breathed, her own eyes shiny with moisture.

Alex rose and moved to take Olivia's hands. "You look beautiful beyond words."

Olivia's chin wobbled. "Thank you." Then she cut her eyes to where Kristen sat, speechless.

*Say something, McKay.* "Okay. I think we're done here."

❋

"Mom? Dad?" Later that evening, Tyler pushed through the front door of his childhood home, the smell of roasted garlic, rich tomato sauce, and the sharp tang of parmesan wafting over him. Lasagna? His stomach rumbled with anticipation.

His mom's lasagna was legendary. When he was a kid, neighborhood buddies vied for an invite to dinner when lasagna was on the menu, along with her buttery garlic bread.

"Tyler? That you?" his mom's voice carried from the kitchen.

"Well, either it's me or some hungry stranger caught a whiff of that garlic and invited himself for dinner."

When he entered the kitchen, he found his mom at the sink drying her hands on a towel. At his approach, she threw the towel over her shoulder, and reached up to cup his face, studying him.

"Mom, I'm fine." He withheld a long-suffering sigh.

"You're a little pale. Come and sit down." He resisted an eye roll as she pulled him toward the kitchen table. "I'll fix you a nice cup of hot tea."

He'd take the tea but could do without the hovering.

"Is that Tyler?" his dad's voice called from the back of the house.

*Really?* Who else did they think was in their house?

"Yes, and he's a little pale. Come tell me what you think."

Oh. My. God. "Mom, I'm fine. Just a little tired."

"Tired?" She turned to face him, her brow furrowed with concern.

What possessed him to tell her that? "Mom, my tests were clear, remember?"

"Ty." His dad came by and clapped him on the shoulder.

"Neil? Isn't he pale?"

His father made a sympathetic face. "Now, Abby, leave the boy alone. He looks tired is all."

"You think so?" She spun around so fast it was a wonder she didn't spill the tea.

Tyler groaned and shot his father a look that said *Really, Dad?* His dad shrugged in response.

Bringing the cup to him, she worried her lower lip with her teeth. Just wait until he told them they'd be getting no grandchildren from him. Time to deflect. "When's dinner ready? I'm starved!"

"Starved?" She brightened. "That's a good sign."

Ever since his remission, every time he saw his mom, she studied him as if searching for signs of relapse. As if it would be tattooed across his forehead. His shoulder blades itched with the attention. She'd done the same thing with his father since his prostate cancer diagnosis two years ago.

He got it. He really did. His parents, especially his mom, had been devastated by the news. But he didn't want them to worry about him.

"Mom, my test results were clear, remember." At least some of them were, anyway.

"I know. Can't I show my son some affection?"

After everyone was settled at the table with heaping servings of cheesy, gooey happiness, his father spoke around a mouthful of crusty bread, "So, what's this I hear about a movie in Northridge?"

Tyler filled his father in on the proposal.

"I read that book," his mom added. "How exciting to have the movie filmed here of all places! I wonder who they'll get to play Eleanor Wesley. Ooh, do you think it will be Nicole Kidman?" His mom's eyes lit at the thought. "Or maybe that pretty actress—oh, what's her name? You know, the one with the big smile."

"Well that narrows it down," Tyler's father muttered around a mouthful of lasagna.

"Jessica Chastain," his mother exclaimed, "that's the one! It has to be a redhead, because the character is a redhead." She tipped her head in thought and reached for her glass of iced tea.

"You support it then?" Tyler continued the conversation with his dad, while his mom continued her mental casting call.

"Sure!" his dad said, stopping the forkful of lasagna halfway to his mouth. "Great opportunity for the town." He shoveled the forkful in his mouth then proceeded to mop up the tomato sauce with a slice of bread.

His mom, still on the casting, continued, "And as for Samuel, they should get Hugh Jackman. He's perfect! Do you think I could meet him?"

Tyler laughed. "Mom, first, I don't know who they are casting, and second, I don't know if you can meet the actors. Maybe."

"It's all so exciting!"

"It is," Tyler agreed. "But first, we have to convince the Economic Development Council that it's a good idea."

She reached over and patted his hand. "You can do it."

"Thanks, Mom, but I'll have a little help. Kristen McKay is working with me on the report."

"Kristen?" his mom looked up at the name and her face wore a wary expression, and she *tsked*.

"What?"

"Nothing, honey. It's just I'm so glad to see her doing so well."

"Why wouldn't she be?"

"Well, you know, she lost her mother to cancer three years ago." His mom grimaced at the word cancer. "Not that the woman would have won mother of the year. But her mother's illness took a toll on Kristen. Guess Kristen was used to hardship, considering how she grew up. It's a wonder she made it to adulthood without a drug or alcohol addiction."

Tyler set his fork down and sat back in his seat. "Mom, what are you talking about?"

His mother had been a social worker by training but had become a guidance counselor at Northridge High School when he was thirteen.

"I shouldn't have said anything." She and his father exchanged one of those husband-wife looks that conveyed far more than words. She took a deep breath and folded her hands in her lap. "She didn't have an easy childhood. I'll leave it at that."

Tyler waited another moment, but didn't press it. "Okay." His mother's work with students was confidential, but his curiosity was piqued.

He knew Kristen had lived in a trailer park when they were growing up, but she'd never let on about any difficulties when they happened to be together. Her father was in prison. He'd been convicted of felony murder in a gas station robbery gone bad when she was eight or nine maybe.

Everyone knew her mother drank and smoked and entertained men—as his mother used to say—but had Kristen been abused? His fists clenched at the idea.

Even in high school she'd worked after school, waitressing at diners in the next town over. He thought it had been for spending money. All the kids he knew worked at something—mowing lawns, babysitting, washing dishes at Dominick's—for date money or to waste it on video games. But had Kristen been working to pay for food, rent, and utilities? Had it been that difficult for her?

"I hear Seth is home," his father said.

"Yeah, I met him the other day. Seems like a good kid."

"She's done a fine job raising that boy on her own." His mother offered him more bread.

"What about the father?" Tyler asked, taking another slice from the basket.

"No one knows. That's something Kristen has kept to herself." His mother took a sip of tea and set her glass down. "If he's in the picture at all, he's quiet about it."

"So Seth plays violin?"

"My, yes! They say he's a prodigy, that he'll be playing the great concert halls around the world. Who'd have guessed, little Northridge, Georgia, producing two such artists—Olivia James and Seth McKay. And now, the setting for a movie! We're moving onto the big screen."

Tyler listened with half an ear to the conversation, his thoughts instead on Kristen's difficult childhood. He wondered if Zach had known, and he wondered how he couldn't have noticed himself.

KRISTEN COLLAPSED onto her sofa and tugged off her boots. It had been a long day filled with girly activities. After settling on both the wedding dress and the bridesmaids' dresses, they'd gone out for a champagne-filled lunch at an elegant French café—she winced—the cost of which would set her back for a month.

After Olivia said "yes" to the dress, then they'd gone through a variety of veils—long and short—crystal-studded silk wedding shoes, all manner of fancy undergarments, and jewelry.

With her ice pink wedding gown—an unplanned choice—Olivia had changed her wedding colors to navy and pearl gray from the original colors of aqua and chocolate brown.

Kristen rubbed her feet. Not that she'd been on them much, but her cheap boots were *not* comfortable. She grimaced. It would be a while before she could afford even the cheapest of shoes, with the cost of her maid-of-honor dress.

But she had to admit, she'd felt beautiful in it. She'd never owned anything so . . . nice. The satiny fabric with its chiffon overskirt slipped over her skin in a sensual cascade when she'd tried it on. It had been miles too long, but then again, what wasn't on her five-foot-two-inch frame. The low-backed, spaghetti-strapped dress revealed yards of skin in anticipation of the warm summer wedding, the navy had done wonders for her skin tone and red hair, and it made her eyes stand out like two emeralds.

Mental note: wear more navy. She snorted and added a caveat—when she could afford new-to-her clothes again.

The key jiggled in the lock and her son stepped through the door. "Hey, Mom. How was Atlanta?"

"Intimidating."

He grinned then removed his coat and hung it on the peg over the door. "I've never seen you intimidated. You should try New York."

That's because you've never seen me out of my element, she thought. "How was the day today?"

"Good." He reached around to the back of his pants and pulled out the money bag from the café.

She laughed and shook her head at his hiding place.

"What? It works. With my jacket on, no one can see it."

"You're right." She took the bag from him and looked at the day's receipts. It *had* been a good day.

"Did you eat?"

"Calypso made me a ham and cheese omelet after we closed up."

"That was awfully sweet of her." Kristen made a mental note to thank Calypso.

"Yeah. I like her. We worked well together." He collapsed onto the sofa beside her. "Did you know her great-grandmother was the daughter of a sharecropper in Louisiana?"

"I did not know that. Interesting." She made another mental note to get to know Calypso better. "Want to binge something on Netflix?"

"Can't. I've got to get in some practice, and then I have calculus homework and a paper to write on the Civil War."

"Okay, honey. I've got a couple of classes to catch up on anyway. But first, I've got to get comfortable."

After changing into a pair of sweatpants and an over-sized fluffy hoody, she settled at the table with her laptop. This was her typical evening. After running some numbers on the café, she opened the university website where she was taking online business courses.

"Will it bother you if I play?" Seth asked, taking his violin out of the case.

"No, honey, I love it when you play."

With Seth making beautiful music in the background, she logged onto the site, opened the course program and clicked on the class assignment. A course or two a semester was all she could afford, time-wise and money-wise. Seth's education and training had to come first. But one day, even if that day was twenty years from now, she'd get a business degree.

She'd be the second in her family—behind Seth—to earn a college degree.

# CHAPTER SIX

OKTOBERFEST WAS a small event Tyler had started in Northridge last year to draw customers to his then newly opened Taproom, and he'd invited fellow business owners to get in on the action—and that included Kristen. Her feelings for Tyler notwithstanding, she wasn't about to pass up a chance to promote her business. She may be a woman scorned, but she wasn't stupid.

Earlier in the day, there had been wiener-dog races in Bailey Park, to the delight of kids and adults alike. No one could resist the hilarity of the dachshunds, most of whom had no idea what they were supposed to do when their owners released them for the race heats.

Now that the sun had set on the chilly fall day, The Whistle Stop Pub served up bratwurst and sauerkraut, Dominick's offered kielbasa wrapped in golden brown crust with spicy mustard for dipping, and the shops remained open beyond their usual closing time.

For her part, Kristen served soft Bavarian pretzels with hot mustard, flaky cherry strudel, hot chocolate for the kids, and authentic Rüdesheimer coffee with sugar, brandy, whipped cream, and chocolate shavings for the adults.

From the table she set up outside her door, she saw locals and visitors alike strolling along beneath the glow of the small globe string lights lining the sidewalk along Main Street, bundled up against the chilly October night, noshing on the offerings, sipping their beverages, and appearing to enjoy themselves.

The air smelled of roasting meats, yeasty beer, and wood smoke, along with the faint whiff of decaying leaves crushed underfoot. Polka music streamed through speakers mounted at intervals along Main Street.

Baskets filled with mums in brilliant golds, reds, and purples hung from the light posts, and many businesses had decorated their entrances with wreathes of fall leaves, cinnamon brooms, and husks of dried corn.

Dancers from En Pointe, Olivia's dance studio, strolled around in lederhosen, adding to the Alpine flavor of the event. They were scheduled to perform a couple of traditional Bavarian folk dances over at the amphitheater in Bailey Park later.

This year, Tyler added a photo booth with Oktoberfest-themed props, and a beer-stein race with the adult winners receiving a case of his *Weizenbier*, or German-style wheat beer, called Firehouse Dog.

"Two, please." Kristen glanced up to see a young couple hand-in-hand, eyes bright with excitement and something else . . . anticipation? She remembered those feelings. Once she'd had those same feelings for Tyler. Until he'd trampled all over her heart without so much as a by-your-leave.

She plastered a smile on her face and removed two warm pretzels from the thermal container, brushed them with melted butter and sprinkled coarse pretzel salt over them. "Mustard?"

The young man looked to his date, who nodded. "Yes. We'll share." A goofy grin spread over his ruddy face.

Before she could complete the cash transaction, Olivia and Zach walked up. She handed the change back to the young man and wished them a good evening before addressing her friends.

"Hi, guys!" They looked almost as excited as the young couple she had just served. And why shouldn't they? After seventeen years apart, they'd found one another again and were embarking on their future.

"How's business? You got two pretzels to spare?" Zach asked taking his wallet out.

"Does a baker have flour?"

Olivia observed the crowds, her hands shoved deep into the pockets of her puffy jacket. "This is amazing! What a great idea."

Zach pulled a ten out of his wallet. "Yeah, Tyler dreamed up a winner with this event. Who doesn't love pretzels and beer?" he added with a wink.

"Speaking of Tyler, how's it going?" Olivia leaned in a little conspiratorially.

Kristen grimaced and waved a hand. "Fine."

"What's this about Tyler?" Zach asked, confusion wrinkling his brow as he took the proffered pretzel.

"You know," Olivia nudged him, holding out her hand to accept her own warm pretzel, "he and Kristen are investigating what impact serving as a film location would have on Northridge."

"Oh, that. You made it sound like some clandestine spy operation."

Heat spread up Kristen's neck and into her face, despite

the chill, then she released a nervous giggle. "Pfft, hardly." She felt Olivia's narrowed eyes on her, and she cleared her throat, busying herself rearranging the pretzels in the thermal container before closing the lid.

Zach, oblivious to Kristen's discomfort and Olivia's inspection, took a bite of his mustard-smeared pretzel. "Mmm. Wow. Time for that aforementioned beer to go along with this salty goodness. Come on," he said, gesturing to Olivia. "Let's see what Tyler's got brewing. We'll come back for that cherry strudel. Save some for us."

As they turned up the street, Olivia threw another glance back at Kristen, an impish grin on her face.

Tyler had little chance to look up from the taps he'd been working, pulling beer after beer for thirsty customers. Business was good, he knew that. He hoped it was equally as good for the other businesses participating in Oktoberfest.

With the added attraction of the town being a film location for *Battle of the Heart*, this event could grow by leaps and bounds next year. Based on the number of cups he'd filled so far tonight, it had already grown since last year. Running a mental calculation, he'd have to get back to the brewery tomorrow to backfill his seriously depleted inventory. A good problem to have.

"Evening, Biermeister. What do you recommend?" Tyler lifted his head and looked into Zach's beaming face. Zach had his arm draped over Olivia's shoulder. The two must have ducked into a dark alley for a quick grope. Zach's hair was mussed, and Olivia's face bore the signs of stubble burn.

"I'd recommend you two get a room."

Zach just rocked back on his heels. "Got one. It's called our home, right, babe?"

Olivia had the grace to blush when she glanced up at Zach, then wiped a lipstick smudge off the corner of his mouth.

"Saw your parents earlier," Zach said, as he eyed a cup of beer that Tim handed off to another customer. "I'll have one of those."

"Yeah, they came by earlier. One Firehouse Dog coming up." Tyler pulled the beer and asked Olivia what she'd like.

"Do you have that lager Ladder Company?"

He handed Zach his beer then shifted the keg of lager in its ice tub, checking for volume. "You're in luck. I have some left." Drawing the beer, he took a moment to look around at the crowds. "Great night, huh?"

Olivia took the proffered cup. "It's chilly, but you couldn't ask for better weather." Tyler felt Olivia's gaze on him. "Kristen's doing the business. You should have one of her pretzels. They'd go great with your beer."

Tyler felt the hint in the comment. "Yeah? As soon as I catch a break, maybe I will."

"You got this?" Tyler asked his two employees when there was a break in the crowd half an hour later.

"Sure, man. Go." Tim nodded toward Main Street. "Take a walk. Enjoy your success," he added with a grin.

Tyler hesitated a moment then gave in. "I'll have my cell on me if you need me."

"No worries, boss."

Tyler stretched his back with a groan. He'd been bent

over the taps for what seemed like days. A stroll to stretch his legs and ease the tightness in his lower back sounded good.

Ducking into the Taproom, he grabbed his jacket off a barstool and drew it on. He'd been so busy, he hadn't noticed the cold. But the night air definitely had a bite. Not that it had kept people away.

Main Street hummed with the sounds of voices, laughter, music, and shuffling feet. A sense of pride filled him. For his hometown, for his fellow townspeople, and for himself. Northridge might be small, but it never stopped reinventing itself. It remained a thriving community because its people had vision and the determination to make that vision a reality.

He paused many times along the sidewalk to chat with folks, happy to see the growing diversity, but he had only one destination in mind: a certain café and its sexy, snarky owner.

The lively two-four time of the "Beer Barrel Polka" reached Tyler's ears. However, this version didn't feature an accordion, but rather a violin. Seth stood in front of a small crowd, tapping his foot and moving to the rhythm as his fingers and bow moved over the strings. *Who knew?*

The kid was good. He listened as Seth played the final notes of the polka, then Tyler made his way to the front of the crowd and dropped a twenty into the open violin case. Other listeners did the same, and Tyler walked away with a smile on his face.

Before he reached the café, he saw the line. Kristen's pretzels were selling like hotcakes. That pleased him. She and Calypso were hard at work doling out toasty pretzels, spicy mustard sauce, and hot drinks.

Taking up a place in the queue, he chatted with the

Kapoors, a young professional Indian couple who'd moved to Northridge from Atlanta about a year ago.

"This is amazing," Rani said, surveying the crowd. "I'm so impressed with all the activities in Northridge. We thought we'd have to drive to Atlanta for these kinds of festivals and holiday celebrations."

"Even growing up, I remember the local celebrations including Memorial Day, Fourth of July, and the winter holidays. We've just added a few more since then. Any excuse to draw a crowd," he said with a wink. As Tyler spoke, his gaze returned to Kristen. Her efficient movements, her warm smile for the customers, her command of the crush.

He wondered what it would be like to have that warm smile directed at him just once.

"Moving here has been the best decision we could have made for our new family." Aamir said, as he eyed his wife's growing belly.

"Next, please!" Calypso's voice rose above the throng.

The couple stepped up to the table, ordering two pretzels and some sort of coffee drink that looked intriguing.

Rubbing his chilled hands, Tyler thought he could use a nice hot drink.

"What can I get you? Oh."

Tyler winced at the welcome. Would Kristen ever greet him with a genuine smile and a show of friendship?

"Looks like your business is booming."

"It is, so if you don't mind, can we move it along?"

*Right.* Particularly grumpy tonight. "I'll take one of those pretzels with some mustard sauce. And what's that?" He pointed at the whipped-cream-topped coffee cup.

"It's Rüdesheimer coffee made with sugar, brandy, whipped cream, and chocolate shavings."

A hand clapped Tyler on the back. "Better give him the hot chocolate instead. Tyler and liquor don't mix."

Tyler peered over his shoulder to see Zach, Olivia behind him, licking what appeared to be whipped cream from her finger. "Mmm. That's too bad because this coffee is amazing!"

"It's her second one. She'll be up till the wee hours of the morning," Zach said with an eye roll.

"Pfft. Caffeine doesn't keep me up." She waved a hand and went back to her coffee.

"Yes it does," Zach muttered under his breath.

"That's what the brandy's for—to counteract the caffeine," Calypso supplied.

Kristen was standing hands on hips, and while Tyler couldn't see her feet, he was sure one of them was tapping in impatience.

"Fine. A hot chocolate."

Kristen drew back. "Seriously?"

Tyler rubbed his nose in embarrassment. "Yeah. Zach is right. Liquor and I don't mix. At all."

Kristen frowned. "Newsflash. You brew beer."

"Oh, I'm fine with beer. And wine. Just not liquor." He shuddered. "Something about my system. It hits my bloodstream, and it's like an amnesiac. Can't remember a thing."

Kristen stared at him, open-mouthed.

Feeling uncomfortable, he said, "Um, yeah." When she still hadn't moved, he pressed, "So, that pretzel and hot chocolate?"

"Right. Coming right up."

Kristen turned her attention to filling his order, but she kept glancing up at him, a look of confusion and—was it annoyance?—on her face.

WTH? Their hands touched as he took his pretzel from

her, and a tingle shot up his arm. She snatched her hand back, her green eyes locked on his. So, he wasn't alone there. She'd felt it too.

"Thanks." Calypso handed him his hot chocolate, the warmth of the cup a welcome respite from the cold.

"I added some whipped cream," Calypso pointed out with a wink.

He cast one more glance at Kristen before joining Zach and Olivia, who stood talking with Marshall MacKinnon.

Kristen might be able to ignore the electricity between them, but he couldn't.

Question was, what could he do about it?

"Hey, Mom."

Kristen looked up as she entered the apartment to see Seth sitting on the couch, eating a PB&J, a glass of milk on the coffee table. The kid could go through a gallon of milk in two days.

"Hey." Tossing her tote bag onto the recliner, she saw a stack of bills and a bunch of coins scattered on the table. "Where'd that come from?"

"Oh. I played polka music on the corner by The Whistle Stop. People tossed money in my violin case." He shrugged. "It came to a hundred twenty-three dollars and seventy-five cents. Sweet, huh?"

"That's great, honey. Put it in your account."

"I want you to have it. I know I'm costing you more for food." He held up the remainder of his midnight snack.

"That's sweet, but no. You earned it."

He hesitated, then nodded. "Thanks. You look

whipped. You sleep in the bed tonight. I'm good with the couch."

She put her hands on her hips and eyed her son. "Seth, your feet hang over the arm."

"So I'll curl up. Go. You're dead on your feet."

She smiled then leaned over and pressed a kiss to his forehead. "What did I ever do to deserve you?"

He grinned and shrugged. "Just lucky, I guess."

Kristen collapsed onto the bed, arms wide, as she heaved an exhausted sigh. She hadn't even bothered to remove her clothes.

It had been a great night. She hadn't tallied the numbers yet, but she knew the day's sales topped any of her previous days in business. Ever. And, as much as she hated to admit it, she had Tyler Kincaide and his brilliant idea to thank for it.

She turned her head to look at the clock. *Ugh.* One o' five a.m. She had three and a half hours to sleep before she had to be back at the café to bake the day's pastries, cookies, and cinnamon rolls. Rolling onto her side, she tucked her hand under her cheek then revisited the conversation with Tyler. *Pfft.* If you could call the few words they'd exchanged a conversation.

Tyler had said liquor gave him amnesia. And Zach had backed that claim up. Could that explain why Tyler behaved as if their night together seventeen years ago had never happened? She knew he'd been drinking that night. Hell, they all were.

She'd only had one beer. She'd seen enough drunks in the form of her mother and her mother's boyfriends to last her a lifetime. She didn't drink more than a beer or two at a time to this day—or the occasional glass of wine—but no liquor.

What had Tyler been drinking that night? He'd appeared to be feeling good, not knee-walking drunk. There had certainly been liquor at the party. Jack Daniels. Rum. Vodka. And some Tequila. She seemed to recall someone with moonshine as well.

She closed her eyes, trying to remember. God knows she'd been watching him that whole night, waiting for him to notice her. Hoping for a goodbye kiss before he left for Princeton. But all she could remember were the cups being passed around. Who knew what had been in them? She'd only pretended to take a drink when pressured by her former fellow classmates.

And when did Tyler learn about this reaction to liquor? Was it the morning after that night? Or had he known based on some previous experience?

Groaning, she reached up and turned off the lamp. Too tired to do anything more than pull the blankets up over her, she closed her eyes, but sleep was nowhere in sight.

All she could think about was whether she had hated Tyler all these years for something he never even remembered? And whether her feelings of inadequacy colored her memories, making her believe one thing when the truth was another.

But she'd left a note. *An unsigned note*, a voice reminded her. "Yeah," she muttered, "because I didn't think I needed to sign my name."

Even so, it might explain why he didn't have any suspicions about Seth. How could he see the resemblance in Seth if he had no recollection of their encounter? And the reason he'd asked what he'd done to piss her off. But it didn't explain why he never returned her phone calls. And with that reminder, she recommitted herself to her dislike of Tyler Kincaide.

# CHAPTER SEVEN

TYLER GLANCED at his phone as a news story popped up on the screen. The flu was taking its toll on the Atlanta area, with hundreds diagnosed. A few had even died. The flu season had hit early and with a vengeance.

Zach must have seen the same story on his phone. "Olivia and I got our flu shots about two weeks ago. You got one, right?" his expression told Tyler he knew how important it was for him to get his.

"You know it." He'd never bothered in the past, figuring he was young and healthy. Why did he need a flu shot? Then cancer. The disease and the treatment weakened his immune system, which put him at higher risk of serious, even life-threatening complications from the flu. He'd been getting a flu shot every year since.

Kristen cleared off the remains of Marshall's breakfast from the bar.

"How about you, K?" Zach asked. "You get your flu shot yet?"

Her brow furrowed, then she shook her head. "Never been sick a day in my life. Why should I get a flu shot?"

"Because there's currently a flu epidemic raging in Atlanta, and it's only a matter of time before a visitor walks in here carrying it?" Tyler chided.

She waved her hand as if shooing away a fly, then headed for the kitchen.

Zach shrugged. "You can lead a horse to water . . ."

"But you can't flog it." His gaze lingered on Kristen's ass, clad today in snug jeans, her feet stuffed into the ever-present fuzzy boots as if she lived in Alaska.

Zach laughed. "You two. I swear. Just take her to bed and get it over with."

"What are you talking about?"

Zach snorted. "Sure, play dumb. But everyone knows you two have the hots for one another. All this arguing is just foreplay."

Tyler shifted in his seat. "I think all this wedding planning has softened your brain." He polished off his chocolate croissant and pushed the plate aside. "You ever notice how Kristen dresses like a blizzard's coming?"

Zach looked in the direction of the kitchen where Kristen had disappeared. "She hates to be cold," he suggested, shrugging.

"It's like sixty degrees outside, yet she's wearing a thick sweater and fuzzy boots." It had been an unusually warm week for fall.

"There were many times when she was growing up that she and her mom didn't have heat. It left her with a sensitivity to the cold, I guess."

"Why didn't they have heat?"

"Couldn't afford it." Zach's words were matter of fact and made Tyler shiver, despite the warmth of the café.

Tyler thought back to his mother's words about Kristen's childhood and wondered, once again, how he hadn't noticed.

"Beans 'n Books, this is Kristen."

"Just the person I need to talk to."

Kristen shuddered at the voice on the other end of the phone.

At her silence, her father prodded, "Hello?"

"How did you find me?" She rubbed the space between her brows.

"The internet. And a prison buddy who was just paroled," he replied. "Seems like you're doing pretty good for yourself. I'm glad to hear it."

"What do you want?"

"Forgiveness."

"And I want a million dollars. We don't always get what we want."

"You never were very forgiving," her father muttered into the phone.

Just as she reached out to slam the receiver into its cradle, his voice rose. "Wait! Don't hang up."

She held the phone to her ear as if she half expected it to explode. "Give me one good reason not to."

"I'm dying."

She huffed out a disgusted laugh. "I can't believe even you would stoop that low."

"It's true. It seems I pickled my liver." He laughed at his own joke, but the laugh turned into a smoker's cough, deep and wracking. If he didn't have liver disease, he'd likely die from emphysema, COPD, or cancer like her mother. As soon as he was capable of breathing again, he continued, "Cirrhosis. End stage."

"You've been in prison twenty-six years and you've never once contacted me. Even when I was little, you never checked up on me or Momma. Didn't even call or write when she died." A sob caught in her throat, then the anger kicked in again. "You don't *deserve* forgiveness."

"You're likely right. But before I go to my grave I'd like to try to make things right."

"Well, good luck with that."

Just before she hung up, she heard him say, "I'm just saying, things aren't always what they seem."

"Problem?"

Kristen's head shot up to see Tyler standing at the coffee bar. *Great.* "No. Just a pushy telemarketer." She didn't intend to share her sob story with Tyler.

She stomped off to the solitude of her office, leaving Calypso at the counter.

That her father was in prison wasn't a secret. The whole town knew. Her father's trial and conviction had been covered in the local papers and TV stations. His accomplice, who'd actually shot the clerk, had received the death penalty, and after eleven years behind bars had finally been put to death. Her father, on the other hand, had been serving a life sentence in Phillips State Prison in Buford, Georgia.

She'd never visited him. And to her knowledge, neither had her mother. The less she had to do with him the better.

She sank into the creaky office chair as if the specter of her father sat on her shoulder.

As the years passed, so had the negative attention she and her mother had received. Out of sight, out of mind, and all that.

And now, he'd contacted her out of the blue thinking she would just roll over and forgive him for what he'd done. For leaving her and her mother to fend for themselves. For humiliating them.

Well, Hell could freeze over. Forgiving that man would be the last thing she ever did.

A COUPLE OF DAYS LATER, Tyler entered Beans 'n Books for his meeting with Kristen armed with data that was burning a hole in his laptop. He'd pulled data from Coweta County where Senoia, Georgia, was situated.

Senoia, location for many feature films including *Fried Green Tomatoes* and *Driving Miss Daisy*, and the block-buster TV series *The Walking Dead*, had been generous with economic data showing the impact for their similarly sized community. Fans of the TV series had flocked to the town in the hopes of catching the filming, meeting their favorite characters, and serving as extras. There was even a store in the town dedicated to all things *Walking Dead*.

Taking a seat at a table directly in front of the coffee bar so Kristen would see him, he heard her before he saw her. A coughing Kristen tottered out from the storeroom, the crook of her elbow pressed to her mouth.

She stopped when she saw him and dropped her arm. "Oh. Is it that time?" She pressed a tissue to her reddened nose with her other hand and sniffed.

"You're sick."

"Boy. Nothing gets by you, does it?" She swayed a little like she stood on the deck of a rolling ship instead of on terra firma.

Even sick, she couldn't ditch the sarcasm.

He rose and approached her as if approaching a wild animal. She cringed when he reached out a hand to touch her forehead. "You're warm."

"Tell me something I don't know."

"You need to go home."

"Can't," she choked out before another coughing fit hit her.

He scanned the café. "Where's Calypso?"

"Called out sick." She wrapped her arms around her waist.

"And Seth?"

"Lake Lanier with a friend."

"Ah." He just gazed at her. "Did you get your flu shot?"

"No," came her grumpy reply.

"Well, you can't stay here. One, who wants to come into a café only to be exposed to your germs? And two, you need bed rest."

"And close up the café?" The horrified look on her fever-flushed face said it all.

He folded his arms over his chest, considering. "I could stay. Take care of things."

She shook her head. "What about the Taproom? Besides, you don't know anything about making coffee."

"Tim is manning the taps this afternoon, and while I don't know anything about making a cup of chichi coffee, at least patrons can get a cup of self-serve, an afternoon Danish, or the latest bestseller."

She stood her germ-infested ground.

"They'll understand," he prodded. "Much better than carrying the Typhoid Mary moniker for giving the whole town your crud," he joked.

She folded her arm over her mouth and sneezed—three times without pause—and he stared at her, brow lifted.

Her shoulders slumped, and she blew her nose on the tissue. "Okay. Fine."

"Sit. I'll get your jacket and your bag. Office?"

She nodded and pointed to the back of the café. That she hadn't argued told him how bad she felt.

He surveyed the microscopic space that served as her office. A wood desk that looked like it had been rescued from the school district's surplus sat against one wall, a ratty office chair in front of it, a flannel-lined denim jacket draped over the back, and a metal utility shelf rounded out the furniture inventory.

He pulled the jacket off the back of the chair and found a canvas tote bag tucked beneath the desk. "Jesus. What does she carry in this thing?" he muttered as he hefted it onto his shoulder.

When he returned, he found her sitting at the table where he'd set his laptop, her head lying on the wood surface. Note to self: disinfect the tabletop and laptop.

She rose and before she could take her jacket, he helped her into it and handed her the tote bag. "What do you have in this thing, bricks?"

"Mace," she said with a smirk.

"Seriously?"

"I carry cash. You bet I'm serious."

"Good to know. Can you get home okay?"

"Yeah, I only live . . ." she stopped abruptly, "yeah." She shuffled to the door then turned back. "Don't burn the place down."

"I'll do my best."

She gave him a warning look and left.

# CHAPTER EIGHT

KRISTEN GROANED in frustration when she heard a knock at her door. Couldn't she just be left alone to die in peace?

"Go away!" She croaked, then coughed with the effort.

"No."

*Tyler? WTH?* Closing her eyes, she gritted her teeth. Maybe if she didn't answer he'd give up and leave.

As if reading her mind, he continued, "I'm not leaving until you open this door."

She struggled to her feet, cursing when she tripped over the blanket she'd wrapped around herself. Jerking open the door, she glared at Tyler. At least, she thought she did. It was difficult to tell exactly what her eyes were doing, they hurt so bad. "Do you have a death wish?"

Something flashed in his eyes, then he had the temerity to chuckle.

"Wait, how—how'd you know where I live?"

"Zach."

*Zach.* Curse him.

Of course. He was the only one who knew—primarily

because he'd helped her move her meager belongings in a year ago when Seth was accepted into Juilliard's Pre-College Program. Not even Olivia knew where she lived.

"Why are you here?" Try as she might, she couldn't resist leaning her head against the door. Her noggin felt as if it weighed a hundred pounds.

"I brought soup," he held up a grocery bag, "along with some orange juice for vitamin C, soda crackers for nausea, popsicles for a sore throat, and cough drops. I also brought the day's receipts." He presented the bank bag. "Ben Porter says get well soon. I think he's sweet on you, by the way."

Ben Porter was an eighty-five-year-old widower who, like Marshall, preferred a splash of coffee with his cream and sugar. "Ben is sweet on any female who happens to be in his presence at the time."

She took the money from Tyler, and as tempting as all the rest sounded, there was no way she was letting him in. He didn't need to see her shabby apartment.

She'd done nothing but save her money since she set her sights on having her own business, then continued after she got it up and running. And with Seth in New York, where she lived didn't really matter all that much. She snorted. She grew up in a shitty single-wide trailer that leaked when it rained and shook when the cold winter winds blew. She was used to living in a dump. Why change now?

But one day. One day, when (not if) her business was a success, she'd have a tidy little American Craftsman in a nice neighborhood. Even if it was a fixer upper. She'd have a home someday. And it would be all hers. Well, and the bank's for the thirty years it would take her to pay it off. And Seth would have a room whenever he returned from concerts in Budapest, Paris, or Salzburg.

She held out her hand to take the bag. "Thanks." Then she shivered and a cough rattled through her, leaving her exhausted.

"Come on." Tyler gently put a hand on her shoulder and moved her backward into her apartment.

Dammit. She didn't have the strength of an ant. Check that. Ants were pretty damn strong. What was weak? Kittens. Newborn kittens. Yeah. She didn't have the strength of a newborn kitten.

Okay, now she was blabbering inside her fever-soaked brain.

The next thing she knew, she found herself tucked up on her thrift-store couch wrapped in her Walmart blanket, a steaming cup of chicken soup in her hands, and a hot man frowning down at her.

His cool hand touched her forehead then her cheek, and she shivered at the touch.

"Jesus, Kristen, you're burning up."

"You're not too bad yourself," she muttered over the fragrant steam of chicken. *Ugh.* Did she just say that out loud?

He released a short laugh. "Delirious too." He went hands on hips. "Do you have a thermometer?"

She made a face that said *are you for real?*

"That would be a no. Well, let's go." He held out his hand, and she eyed it.

"Go? Where? In case you haven't noticed, I'm not exactly up for a night on the town."

"To the urgent care center. You need Tamiflu."

A jolt of panic shot through her. She couldn't go to a clinic. She didn't have insurance, and she sure as hell didn't have the money for the visit, much less the prescription. She sunk lower into the couch, willing it to swallow her. "No."

He studied her face a moment, then as if deciding it wasn't worth the battle, he shook his head. "Okay, how about aspirin or Tylenol?"

"Tylenol. Generic." She lifted a shaky hand and pointed. "Bathroom. Medicine cabinet." She winced, wondering when she'd last cleaned the bathroom she and Seth now shared. Not that anyone could tell—the sink was permanently stained a rusty brown from the previous tenant's hair dye.

She drank the soup and sighed at the salty, savory taste. *Mmm.*

He returned a couple of minutes later, the bottle of acetaminophen and a glass of water in his hands. "Take two." He opened the childproof cap as if it was a pop top and, tossing out two capsules, held his hand out to her.

She set aside her soup and gave him a sullen look from beneath her lashes. "Bossy." She accepted the pills and the glass, then tossed them back with a gulp of water.

"Now finish your soup. It's good for what ails you."

He placed the bottle of pills on the ancient metal TV tray that served as an end table.

Obediently, she took another sip and sighed again at the warmth as it glided down her throat. "You shouldn't be here," she croaked. "You'll get sick."

"No I won't. Unlike you, I got my flu shot."

She rolled her eyes then regretted it when it felt like they were going to escape from their sockets and roll across the floor. She didn't bother telling him she couldn't afford a flu shot. *And now instead of a forty-dollar flu shot it would end up costing you more,* a snotty voice in her head chided.

He perched on the ratty recliner that had been her mother's and waited while she finished up the soup. When she handed him the empty cup, he asked if she wanted more.

She gingerly shook her head.

He plucked the cup from her fingers, then she heard water running in the kitchen sink and the unmistakable clank of a pot. "You don't have to do that," she croaked, irritated that Tyler Kincaide was here at all, seeing how she lived, much less cleaning up her 1970's harvest gold kitchen with its chipped Formica countertops.

"No worries," he called.

A few minutes later he stood in front of her again, hands in the pockets of his jeans. Jeans that hugged his parts like they were made for him.

"Thanks," the word stuck in her throat. "For this. For minding the store. I'll be fine, so goodnight." She shivered and pulled the blanket closer around her.

He moved to the sofa where she was lying, then bent to pick her up blanket and all, making her squeak in surprise. He settled back on the sofa, her chill-racked body in his arms. "Sleep."

"Did I say you were bossy?"

"Yes."

"I was wrong. You're not bossy. You're highhanded."

He chuckled, warm and low, and she could feel the laugh right to her core.

Tucking the blankets around her, he tightened his grip and the warmth of him against her relaxed her aching muscles, easing the shivers, and she released an involuntarily sigh. Exhausted, she laid her head against his chest and closed her eyes. His cologne, warm and spicy, filled her head as she drifted off to sleep.

Sometime later, she woke thinking someone had poured

a bucket of water over her. Wet tendrils of her hair stuck to her cheeks and neck. Sweat pooled where her body met something hard and warm. *Ugh.*

Then she remembered with a startled gasp and sat up.

"What?" Tyler's equally startled expression met hers.

"Oh." Great. She'd just sweated all over Tyler Kincaide like a construction worker in July. "Oh God, I'm so sorry," she said, as she peeled the damp blanket off his equally damp T-shirt.

Without so much as a grimace, he reached up and palmed her cheek. "You're fever broke. Good."

If she hadn't felt like the underside of a mud-covered hog, she'd have returned the gesture. His face was so close to hers she could make out blue-green flecks in his hazel eyes.

He held up a finger in admonition. "But you should take the acetaminophen every four hours for the next twenty-four hours just to make sure it doesn't come back."

"Right. Thank you, Dr. Kincaide." She made to rise, but his arms tightened around her like steel bands. "Where are you going?"

"Well, if you must know, I have to pee."

He winced and released his grip. "Um. Right." Rising, he brought her with him then placed her on her feet. She raked him with her gaze, from his sweat-dampened shirt to the splotch on the front of his jeans. God, she didn't, did she?

Reading her expression, he chuckled. "No. It's just sweat."

"God," she groaned. "Why didn't you wake me? That's so gross."

"You needed your fever to break, and you were sleeping so soundly, I didn't want to wake you."

She shook her head then made for the sanctuary of the bathroom.

After relieving her full bladder—you'd think with all that sweat, she wouldn't have anything left—she splashed water on her face. When she caught her reflection in the medicine cabinet mirror, she groaned.

Her hair was matted to her head, especially the side she'd had pressed up against Tyler's rock-hard chest. Her face had lost its fever-flush, but her eyes had raccoon circles beneath them . . . and was that a blanket crease across her cheek? *Good grief.*

Her mouth tasted like something died in it. Four days ago. She smacked her lips and grimaced in revulsion. Pulling out her toothbrush and toothpaste, she gave her teeth a thorough scrubbing. She craved a shower, but that would have to wait until Tyler left. No way was she getting naked and showering with him in the next room. She leaned against the sink, exhausted from her efforts. Why had he stayed? For that matter, why had he come?

When she got back to the living room, he'd neatly folded the blanket, organized the pile of papers on the coffee table, and fluffed the pillows on the sofa.

Wrapping her arms around herself, she eyed him. He needed to go. As grateful as she was for his kindness, she felt the first chinks in her armor where he was concerned, and she couldn't afford to let him in. She'd made that mistake once. She wouldn't make it again.

"Well, thanks for everything." She lifted her hand then dropped it. "You, uh, you probably want a shower after I, uh," she grimaced, and circled her finger in the general direction of his crotch, "sweated all over you."

He scratched the bridge of his nose and looked down at

his crotch with a chuckle. "Yeah. Hopefully no one will think I had an accident."

Her gaze followed his and she swallowed hard, her mouth suddenly dry.

He continued, and she pulled her gaze away to meet his eyes, a flush creeping up her neck that had nothing to do with a fever. "No worries. You would have done the same for me."

"No. Probably not." She laughed to soften the blunt statement.

His mouth lifted at the corner as he reached for his jacket.

"Take it easy, Kristen. You're not out of the woods yet. When does Seth get home?"

"Tomorrow night."

"If your barista can't cover for you tomorrow, let me know. I'll help out."

She folded her arms across her chest as he stepped to the door. "You've done plenty. Besides, you don't know how to make a French press."

He turned, his hand on the open door. "No, but I follow directions well."

The door closed behind him with a soft click, and she sank to the sofa, her legs giving way.

TYLER DESCENDED THE EXTERIOR STAIRCASE, zipping his jacket against the October chill, his thoughts still on Kristen.

When she had opened the door to his knock, she'd been flushed with fever, her eyes glassy, her long hair hanging in tendrils from a messy bun, her smokin' hot body covered by baggy sweatpants and a terrycloth robe. She'd looked . . . pitiful.

As an afterthought, he'd wondered where Seth slept. In the bed? On the couch? Wondered why she'd rented a one-bedroom apartment. But then again, maybe she hadn't expected him to be living with her again for a semester. Or more.

While it wasn't the same, he remembered the days after his chemo when he felt like one of the "walkers" from *The Walking Dead*. When he thought it might be easier to die. To let the cancer take over and eat him alive.

He'd had no one, really. While his co-workers had sent him get-well cards and cheerful text messages, he hadn't had anyone to lean on, to take care of him when he felt like he'd had the shit kicked out of him. His mom came to New York, of course, but she couldn't move up there for the full six months of his treatment. She had her hands full with his father. His father came, but then he had his own treatments to deal with. His younger sister Megan and younger brother Joshua came but they had lives and families of their own. And of course, Zach came when he could get away.

He should have had Celeste. After all, they had been engaged. But she'd shown her true colors shortly after his diagnosis.

Sighing, he shoved his hands in his pockets turning his footsteps to his truck parked in the alley by Kristen's piece-of-shit compact. He peered through the driver-side window at the interior of the car with its cracked dashboard, split seats, and drooping headliner. She really needed a new car.

His mother had said she'd had a tough time growing up, and apparently not much had changed. He wondered how Kristen managed to raise Seth, start her own business, and send her son to Julliard. Clearly she'd sacrificed for Seth and her business. No wonder she'd come down with the flu. She needed to take better care of herself.

Knowing what it was like to be sick and in need of a caregiver, he couldn't leave Kristen to fend for herself, even though he knew she'd get her back up about it. She'd fought him at first. That she gave in at all told him just how bad she felt.

Rubbing his forehead, he groaned. And he'd been a pervert, despite her illness.

When he'd picked her up to place her in his lap, she'd smelled of coffee beans, vanilla cream, and the honey-lemon cough drops he saw on her coffee table. And when he'd held her in his arms while she slept, he couldn't fight the yearnings for more and his imagination took flight.

Kristen, naked beneath him, whispering his name as he licked and nipped her skin from neck to toes and back again.

Kristen, her fingers clutching his hair as he kissed her mouth until they were both breathless.

Kristen, face aglow in the aftermath of their pleasure.

He'd gotten the odd sensation that he'd been there before. Like *déjà vu*. But no. He definitely would've remembered taking Kristen to bed. There would be no forgetting that. Just wishful thinking on his part.

What he still couldn't figure out was why she harbored such animosity toward him. He was a nice guy. He didn't kick puppies or yell at children. He wasn't a player. He didn't steal, or lie, or cheat. So what was her deal?

He glanced back up at the now-dark window of her shabby apartment. She deserved so much more. By all accounts, she'd done a fine job raising her son. And over this last year, he'd watched her nurture her business, working long hours, dedicating herself to its success, and sacrificing to make her dream come true. On top of being a mom.

And succeed she would. Or had, for that matter. She was smart, resourceful, and driven. He really liked that about her.

Now if he could just figure out how to make her like something—*anything*—about him.

# CHAPTER NINE

Two days later, still exhausted from her battle with the flu, Kristen entered the café mid-morning to find it doing a brisk business, and her barista recovered and handling the crowd with ease. Calypso had been a good hire, Kristen acknowledged, even though her salary was taking a bite out of the café's skimpy profits.

The baked goods sales had taken a hit while Kristen had been laid up. Calypso could whip up a mean cuppa joe, but she wasn't a baker. That would have to be her next hire when she could work it into the budget. Kristen rarely got sick, but if nothing else, her bout with the flu had shown her she wasn't invincible, and she couldn't let her business take another hit like this one.

And with a reluctant nod at Tyler's I-told-you-so lecture, she'd be getting a flu shot from now on.

"Welcome back," Calypso murmured as she added steamed milk to a café latte.

"Thanks. Glad to be back." Eyeing the patrons, Kristen lifted her apron from its peg, slipped it over her head, and gave it a quick tie around her waist.

"Seth back?"

Kristen nodded. "Last night." Thank God he'd been gone. That's all they needed was for him to get sick. "What do we need?"

Calypso thrust her chin at Mat Anderson. "He's waiting on an espresso, and Brenda is waiting on her usual."

"Got it." Kristen made quick work of the espresso for Mat and tried not to roll her eyes at Brenda's nonfat frappe with extra whipped cream and chocolate sauce. *Really?* That's like ordering a diet soda to go with your iced cinnamon roll.

While Calypso served the orders, Kristen circled the seating area, picking up stray napkins, empty coffee cups, and plates, wiped down the tables and arranged the chairs.

Tyler had texted her last night to see how she was feeling, if Seth was home, and if she'd needed anything. She could only assume he got her number from Zach because she definitely hadn't given it to him. Even so, the unexpected kindness had touched her more than she'd have liked to admit.

She couldn't remember the last time someone took care of *her* for a change. It felt . . . damn good.

She'd followed his instructions, taking the acetaminophen every four hours, eating more of the chicken soup, and drinking the orange juice. In all honesty, he'd been a lifesaver. There had been little food in her apartment because she'd put off going grocery shopping since Seth was going to be gone for the weekend.

Spotting a customer, she headed in his direction to see if he needed assistance finding a book. That's another hire she should consider. Maybe a high school book nerd in need of a part-time job.

After helping the customer, she straightened the

shelves, re-shelved some books lying on one of the tables, and adjusted a display of books on the history of Georgia. She'd been so focused on the café part of her business that she'd been neglecting the bookstore side. It was really a small piece of the revenue, but it had potential to be so much more.

She kept an inventory of local authors, and she'd been toying with the idea of inviting authors for book signings, providing a venue for book clubs, and maybe holding monthly reading salons. A local writers group already met in the café once a month on Wednesday evenings.

She froze, her hand suspended over a copy of *Battle of the Heart* when another idea struck her. *Holy café au lait.* She couldn't believe she hadn't thought of this sooner. If the Town Council approved Northridge as a film location for the movie, she could invite Jordan Raven for a book signing. Here. In her little café!

Her head swam with the possibilities! People would come from all over to meet Ms. Raven. It could really put her business on the map and position her as a location for future book signings and author events.

And, of course, she'd bowl them over with her gooey cookies, delicate croissants, spicy cinnamon rolls, and fresh-roasted coffee.

Energized by this idea, she renewed her determination to work with Tyler on the proposal and convince her towns-folk that opening Northridge to the filming would serve everyone in the community. Suddenly exhausted by her meager activity, she collapsed into the armchair.

She'd get right on that—as soon as she fully recovered from the flu.

❄

After a busy morning at the brewery—one of the boil kettles had gone out—Tyler finally found the time to drop by the café and check on Kristen. He found her still a little pale but much better than the last time he'd seen her. The bell over the door alerted her to his presence, and she glanced up from her cleaning.

"Hi," she said, and if he hadn't known her better, he might've missed the shy note her voice carried.

"Hi." He walked over to the coffee bar, hands in his pockets against the chill of the rainy day. After the front passed through, it promised to be a cold night. "How are you feeling?"

"Better, thanks."

"You look better." As soon as the words were out of his mouth, he wished he could take them back.

"Gee, thanks," she said with a smirk on her face.

"Not what I meant." He felt the heat rise in his face.

She waved him off with a laugh. "I have a mirror. I know what I looked like the other night."

Beautiful, he thought. You always look beautiful.

"What can I get you?"

"Oh. Nothing. I just wanted to check in, see how you were feeling."

A funny look skittered across her face. Surprise? Disbelief?

She put aside her cleaning wipes and, tucking her hands into the pockets of her apron, regarded him. "Tyler, I want to thank you for what you did for me the other night. I really appreciate it."

The heat of embarrassment over his poor choice of words bloomed into a warmth of pleasure at her appreciation. Waving off her gratitude, he said, "Anyone would have done it. I just happened to be the one who knew you were sick."

"No, not anyone," she muttered. "Let me make you an Americano, and I think I have a lone cinnamon roll left after the morning rush. It's the least I can do."

"I won't turn down one of your cinnamon rolls. They're worth the extra mile I have to run to work them off."

As she busied herself making his coffee and heating the cinnamon roll, Tyler took a seat at the counter. The café was quiet, with only a couple of people sitting at the tables and another browsing the books in the back. The scent of the warm cinnamon roll reminded him that he'd missed lunch working on the boil kettle.

She slid the plated cinnamon roll onto the counter and set a cup of coffee next to it.

"Thanks!"

He dug into the sweet, spicy warmth and observed her as she returned to her cleaning, this time with a can of Bar Keepers Friend and a scrubber. As she scoured the stainless-steel sink, tendrils of hair came loose from her messy bun, and he longed to pull her red hair from its constraints and run his fingers through it. He knew from the other night how soft it felt to the touch. Like satin. *Jesus*, he had it bad.

"Don't overdo it," he cautioned. "You don't want to relapse."

She straightened up, arching her back, making her breasts thrust against the black apron and making the steaming cup of coffee printed on it stand out.

"Yes, Dr. Kincaide," she said with an eye roll. She flipped on the water and grabbed the sprayer nozzle to rinse the sink. Finished, she moved to the counter and picked up his now-empty plate, but before turning away, she asked, "How do you know so much about treating an illness?"

"Oh, well, I guess I listened to my mother when she took care of us when we were sick."

A smile ghosted across her face. "She taught you well."

He couldn't help but think there was more to that statement. "Yeah, she did." He stood and reached for his wallet.

"No."

He glanced up at Kristen in confusion. "What?"

"No charge," she said with a shrug.

At his hesitation, she continued, "Just my way of saying thank you."

He still felt uncomfortable not paying, but this small gesture was the closest thing to friendship that Kristen had shown him in a long time, so he'd take it.

THE NEXT DAY, Kristen found it difficult to concentrate with Tyler sitting at one of the café tables waiting for her to clean up after the morning rush. His laptop sat open in front of him, and his fingers clicked on the keys typing something.

Zach sat a few tables back, with one of his deputies going over some document in front of him.

She'd sent Calypso to the storeroom for more self-serve coffee cups and lids, while she wiped down the counters and put cups, saucers, plates, and utensils in the dishwasher.

The bell over the door tinkled and in walked a tall blond guy in a dark suit. After glancing around, he turned his feet in the direction of the coffee bar. As soon as he pulled up a stool at the counter, she recognized him. The years had not been kind to Jonah Miller. He'd developed a paunch and appeared to have lost the rangy muscular build he'd had as a teenager, along with a good bit of his hair.

Jonah had been a senior in high school when she was a junior. He'd always considered himself the big man on campus, but most people saw him as the big jerk on campus.

One afternoon after school in her junior year, Kristen had been leaving cheerleading practice when he'd cornered her outside the girls' locker room, backed her up against the wall, and groped her.

The school's star tight end became an octopus—his hands everywhere at once. Her breasts, her ass, between her legs, all while he stuck his tongue down her throat.

The door to the gym slamming shut stopped any further molestation. He'd just grinned at her and winked, then shrugged. "I thought that's what you trailer-trash girls liked."

She lived with a single mom in a rundown trailer park, so of course she must be a slut. She'd wanted to throw her gym bag at him, but Coach Patterson came out of his office then stopped to give them a look. "What's going on here?"

"Nothing, Coach," came Jonah's chipper reply. "Just offered to carry Kristen's bag to her car, but she said she's got it." He'd turned and winked at her, a smarmy smile lifting the corners of his cruel mouth.

"Excuse me. I'd like to order." His annoyed voice pulled her from her dark memories.

Recognition registered in his eyes when she approached him.

He snapped his fingers. "Kristen, right?"

"Yes." Knots the size of fifty-pound bags of flour formed in her stomach. Why couldn't she have escaped his notice? Why couldn't she have gone to the storeroom and left Calypso here to wait on him? She despised feeling this way.

Like she deserved his condescension because she grew up in a trailer park.

"I thought that was you." His gaze roamed over her body, stopping at her breasts before returning to her face, leaving her in want of another shower. "Can't forget that hot body. You still look great."

Not bothering to thank him for what she was sure he felt was a compliment, she asked, "What can I get you?"

"Your phone number, to start," he said with a snicker, giving her another leer.

"Sorry, that's not on the menu."

He laughed, but there was an edge to it. "I'm here from L.A., a few days visiting my folks, thought maybe we could hook up. Just like old times."

"First, I don't 'hook up,' and second, we didn't have any 'old times.' Now, if you'd like a coffee, I can get that for you, but otherwise I have things to do."

He leaned over the counter, and it took everything she had not to retreat. "Now come on, McKay the Lay, I'm just trying to have a friendly conversation. I'm sure your boss wouldn't appreciate you running a paying customer off with your rude behavior."

"Don't you dare call me that," she gritted out.

He reached out and grabbed her wrist, squeezing. "That's your nickname, isn't it? I mean, you earned it, right?"

The grip on her wrist hurt, but no way in Hell would she let him know that. "Let go," she picked up a fork off the counter with her free hand and held it up, "or I'll stab you with this fork."

He released her wrist but didn't move his hand.

"Now, get out," she kept her voice low, not wanting to draw the attention of the other customers, and especially not Tyler. She couldn't bear him witnessing this humiliating encounter.

He sat up. "No. I don't think I will. Where is your supervisor? I'd like to make a complaint."

With some deep-seated satisfaction she hadn't felt in a long while, she drew herself up, crossed her arms over her chest, and said, "You're looking at her."

His eyes widened then narrowed. "Fine. So you're a manager here. I'd like to speak to the owner."

"I repeat, you're looking at her."

Before he could respond, Tyler walked up behind Jonah and clapped his hand on the man's shoulder. To witnesses, the encounter might appear friendly, but Kristen could see the anger in Tyler's eyes and the slight wince from Jonah when Tyler squeezed the tender area where neck met shoulder.

"Problem here?" Tyler's hazel gaze fixed on hers.

"No, Jonah was just leaving," she said, her calm voice belying the butterflies in her stomach. The last thing she needed was a brawl in her café. "He didn't see anything on the menu that suited him."

"Well, Jonah, don't let me keep you," Tyler said, his tone friendly as he released his hold on the man.

Jonah stood and spun to face off against Tyler, but as the few customers in the café turned to watch, he thought better of it. He gave Tyler the once-over, then looked back at Kristen, quickly making the assumption they were together.

"Who wants sloppy seconds anyway?"

Before Kristen could even react to the insult, Tyler's fist made contact with Jonah's jaw, sending him sprawling to the floor.

Seth walked in just in time to see Tyler deck Jonah.

"Dude, nice right-cross." His face wore a look of teenage awe.

Tyler shook his hand, wincing in pain before bending over Jonah's prone form to haul him to his feet by his arm.

Jonah's hand cradled his jaw, and he jerked his suit jacket back into place. "You're going to regret that."

"Doubt it," Tyler said.

"I plan to file a police report."

"Go for it," Tyler said, lifting his free arm in the direction of Zach, who'd witnessed the entire incident. "There's the Chief of Police."

Zach waved, then stood and approached the men.

"You saw it all. Do something."

"I did. And what I saw was a man coming to the aid of a woman you not only manhandled, but insulted."

Jonah's flaccid face turned red. "I'll sue."

"You always were an ass, Jonah," Zach said. "Go see your parents. While I'm sure they'll be happy to see you, the rest of us could do without your company."

Zach addressed Kristen, "You want to trespass this guy?"

She nodded.

"Don't set foot back in here while you're visiting, or I'll be hauling you off to jail."

Jonah's gaze skittered from Kristen to Tyler, and then Zach. "I knew I left this punk-ass town for a reason."

He strode to the door, but with a last glance back at Kristen, he muttered "Once trailer trash, always trailer trash."

KRISTEN HELD the dishtowel-wrapped bag of ice on Tyler's

hand. He wasn't gonna lie, it hurt like a mother. Jonah's jaw was as hard as his head. It had been a long time since he'd punched someone. And he'd be happy to go another long time without doing it again.

"Why did you do that?" Kristen asked, her eyes on his face.

"He's an asshole. He deserved it."

"I won't argue with you there, but I had it under control."

"Maybe. But I couldn't just sit there and let him harass you. Hurt you."

He reached out with his good hand and drew her free hand toward him, flipping it so the underside of her wrist was facing up. Bruises the size and shape of fingertips were developing.

"You need ice too." He pulled her hand next to his so that the ice covered both their hands.

Zach had gone to pick up Olivia for an appointment in Atlanta—something about a cake-tasting—Calypso's shift was over, Seth had gone home to do homework, and the customers had left, leaving the two of them alone in the café.

"No one talks to you like that," Tyler said, and meant it. He was aware of Kristen's reputation in high school. He didn't know if it was true or not, but he didn't care one way or the other.

Looking down at their ice-covered hands, Kristen just shook her head. "It's nothing. I'm used to it."

"No." He lifted her chin and made her meet his gaze. "No one," he reiterated.

"Tyler, there's always going to be someone from my past who's going to still think of me as trailer-park trash, as McKay the Lay. I'll always be that girl to everyone in town."

He winced at the moniker. Assholes. Every one of them.

"You know what I say? Fuck 'em. They don't deserve the time of day from you. You blow me away, Kristen McKay. I watch you work with such efficiency, and I see how you manage Calypso, teaching her, correcting her, while not making her feel criticized. I see you with Mr. Berg, your patience with his forgetfulness, your kindness to Mrs. Sprigs when she asks for your advice about which book to read for her book club."

He skimmed his fingers along her cheek. "And you're wrong. Everyone in town sees you for what you are—a successful businesswoman making a positive impact on the town and its citizens."

She leaned across the table, touched him beneath his chin, and he felt it down to his toes. "Thank you." She pressed her lips to his in a soft, sweet kiss, but he wanted more.

Changing the angle of the kiss, he cupped the back of her head with his free hand and coaxed her mouth open with his tongue. A moan of pleasure rose from her throat, and the kiss went from a smolder to a raging fire in three-point-four seconds. She rose from her seat and, without breaking the kiss, straddled him.

Her fingers gripped his hair as her tongue played with his.

Fuck the ice. He shook it off his hand and lifted it to run his hands along her ribs, just to the underside of her breasts and stopping there. The desire for more left him dizzy and breathless. But this wasn't the time or the place. Not here in the middle of the café where any passerby could see.

Just one more taste, and he'd stop.

❄

So LONG. It had been so damn long since she'd felt the touch of a man. And this wasn't just any man. This was Tyler Kincaide. Her kryptonite. And the man who broke her heart. The man who used her and set her aside.

At that bitter reminder, she pushed away from him, seeking to regain control of her traitorous body and her breathing. She climbed off his lap, cheeks burning with shame. "You should go."

"Kristen—" His face held a mixture of desire, tenderness, and confusion.

"Please." She wrapped her arms around her waist and turned toward her office and the refuge it offered.

He hesitated another moment, then she heard the scrape of his chair and his footsteps as he made his way across the wood floor, the sound of rustling clothes as he put his jacket on, then the soft tinkling of the bell as the door opened and closed.

The silence of his departure was deafening.

# CHAPTER TEN

"Rack 'em," Olivia said, as she selected a pool cue from the rack.

Olivia had invited Kristen out for a girls' night and to talk over wedding plans while Zach and Tyler took Seth to Atlanta for an afternoon Falcons' football game.

The evening had started with bridal magazines and Olivia's wedding board on her Pinterest page over at The Whistle Stop Pub, but had moved to a new poolroom—she supposed it should be called a billiard room— called On Cue that opened up in the old VFW hall one block off Main Street.

Kristen didn't know how they did it, but they'd managed to remove the decades-old odor of stale beer, filthy ashtrays, and cigarette and cigar smoke. They'd gutted the place in the renovations, which had helped. They'd done wonders with the VFW hall. Where smoked-stained walls had once stood, rich hardwood gleamed. And in place of the torn linoleum were beautifully worn pine floors, apparently recovered from an old warehouse.

The daughter of two two-pack-a-day smokers, she

despised the smell of cigarette smoke. And unlike many of her friends in middle school, no amount of peer pressure could get her to smoke. She'd inhaled enough secondhand smoke at home, thank you very much.

As Kristen gathered the balls from the pockets and placed them in the rack, she surveyed the large open room.

The place boasted only six pool tables, leaving room for rich leather sofas and chairs in intimate seating arrangements defined by area rugs, the soft light from brass floor lamps casting a warm glow on the rich browns of the décor and the emerald green felt of the tables.

Games were underway at a couple of the other tables, but it was early yet. A corner bar served beer, wine, and snacks. Between dinner, a glass of their cheapest house wine, and some billiards, Kristen would be living off Kraft mac 'n cheese and Ramen noodles the rest of the week so she could feed Seth healthier alternatives.

"It's been ages since I've played pool," Olivia was saying as she chalked her cue. "I sucked then, but I'm sure I'll suck even worse now."

"Good, that means I'll kick your ass."

Olivia laughed. "I think you've wanted to do that since high school."

"Maybe," Kristen said with a shrug. "I was a nasty little bitch back then."

"Back then?" a very male voice said from behind her.

She stifled a groan. She didn't need to turn around to know who it was. Tyler. How'd he know where they were?

Apparently reading her mind, Olivia held up her phone with a look of chagrin. "I texted them when we got here."

*Great. Perfect.* She hadn't seen him since 'The Kiss,' and at the memory her face heated and her pulse skipped like a stone across water.

"How was the game?" Olivia asked, her eyes alight with happiness.

"Falcons won," Zach replied with a grin.

"Where's Seth?" Kristen asked.

"We dropped him off at your place. He said something about practicing a new piece."

"How about boys against girls?" Zach asked, leaning over to kiss Olivia on the mouth.

"Sounds like a plan," Tyler said, a smirk on his face, "but we should make it interesting."

Olivia stood, hip cocked, one hand on her cue stick standing on its end. "Interesting how?"

"You know, a bet of some kind." Tyler walked over to the cabinet where the cues were stored and began testing them out.

Zach rocked back on his heels, a mischievous look on his face. Before he could put voice to those thoughts, Kristen stopped him with a raised hand. "No. No sexual challenges, since you're the only couple involved."

"It doesn't have to be the same bet. Olivia and I can have one bet." He smacked his fiancée on the ass. "You and Tyler another. Maybe, I don't know, loser could mop the winner's floor or something."

She felt Tyler's eyes on her. "I'm sure we can get more creative than that."

When she faced him, he went hands on hips, and she could practically see the cogs grinding in his head.

"If you lose—and you will—you have to go to Senoia with me next weekend."

"Senoia?! You're—you're out of your mind." No way in Hell she could spend several hours cooped up in a car with Tyler. The incident in the café had been a close call, one she didn't plan to repeat. And the sad truth was she didn't know if she had the discipline to resist him anymore. "I have a café to run."

"And a capable assistant manager," Tyler returned.

Olivia rubbed her hands in glee. "Now this is getting interesting."

She groaned and threw her head back to look at the beamed ceiling. "Why?"

"Because the committee asked us to work on this together, so we should both go to Senoia to meet with the marketing coordinator.

"And what do I get if *I* win?"

"Name it."

She stood, tapping a finger against her lips in thought. She'd been thinking of painting the café restrooms, and maybe updating the fixtures, but the labor costs were out of her budget. Now, if that labor were free . . .

"If I win, you have to paint the café restrooms and install new fixtures."

She expected him to balk, so he surprised her when he said, "You're on."

TYLER FOUGHT BACK A GROAN. What had possessed him to make the bet? He had no qualms about his billiard skills, but his concentration was taking a serious hit. Every time Kristen bent over the table to make a shot, he had to adjust himself.

And there was no good—or should he say bad?—angle. When Kristen leaned over the table to line up a shot, either he got a boob shot or an ass shot. The V-neck blouse she wore offered him a clear view of cleavage and the full round tops of her breasts. The tight jeans, on the other hand, offered him a tantalizing view of her tight, round ass. Both led to thoughts of things other than his next shot. Like Kristen bent over the pool table, that now jean-clad ass bare under his roving hands. Or a fully naked Kristen moving beneath him as he . . .

"Are you going to take your shot or what?" Zach asked, a hint of humor in his voice.

Busted by his best friend, who clearly had no doubt as to where his mind had drifted, Tyler felt the heat rise in his face.

Since the kiss in the café, Tyler had wondered what thought had entered her mind that made her pull back from him, flipping the switch from heated passion to cold disdain. He shook his head. He'd give anything to be able to read her mind. Then he thought better of it. His ego might not be able to take it.

If he could only figure out what it was he'd done to Kristen to make her dislike him. She'd never tell him, that's for sure. But he'd made progress that day. Until they'd kissed, that is. Then she'd shut down on him again. He'd just keep tearing down her walls with kindness. By the time they presented their report to the EDC, come Hell or high water, he'd make her like him.

There were only two balls left on the table aside from the eight ball. One was solid—the ladies'—and the other stripes—the guys'. All he had to do was sink the stripe in the side pocket, then the eight ball was lined up and ready for the corner pocket. Easy peasy.

He walked around the other side of the table, past Kristen, the fresh scent of her filling his senses. At his approach, she'd backed up to give him room. Now he could swear he felt the heat from her, and he resisted the urge to twitch under the weight of her frustrated glare.

Yeah, it looked like she'd be joining him on his road trip. The thought refocused his attention and he lined up his cue for the simple tap in. He didn't know how it happened, but his cue slipped, sending the nine ball careening off the bumper and out into the middle of the table.

Zach groaned, as Olivia and Kristen gasped.

Still bent over the table, he closed his eyes in disgust.

"What the hell, dude? How could you miss that shot?" Zach threw up his free hand in annoyance.

Gritting his teeth, Tyler finally stood and tried to shrug it off. "Should have chalked my cue."

Zach snorted. "Is that what they're calling it these days?"

Tyler shot him a warning glare.

"You're up, Kristen," Olivia prodded, a note of glee in her voice. Of the two of them, Kristen was clearly the better player. She should be able to knock the two balls in for the win. Which meant he'd be playing handyman.

She bit her lip and, hefting her cue, presented him with another torturous boob view then tapped the four ball into the corner pocket. She cut him a glance, both relief and triumph on her face. The eight ball shot was a piece of cake. Straight into the corner pocket.

Lining up her cue, she put a little too much on the cue ball, sinking the eight ball but sending the white ball into the pocket right behind it.

She'd scratched on the last shot of the game.

Zach gave a whoop of surprise then grabbed his bride-to-be and whispered something in her ear, making her blush.

Kristen stood, hand on her cue stick, a look of utter astonishment on her face.

He couldn't resist. "I'll pick you up Saturday morning at eight."

Monday evening, Tyler strode out to his truck in the brewery parking lot, anxious for a hot shower and an even hotter meal. It had been a long day.

Before he reached his vehicle, strains of a violin reached him. It sounded like it was coming from the direction of the abandoned button mill next to its sister building, now Olivia's dance studio.

The volume increased the closer he got to the dilapidated structure. He and Zach used to play in the old mill, so he walked to the back, where he knew the doors hung from their hinges, and squeezed in. He burrowed deeper into his jacket. The air was cold and damp inside, and the mill smelled like rust, rotten wood, and bird shit.

The sounds from the violin floated in the cavernous space of the mill, rich and resonant. Seth was seated on an upturned crate, his eyes closed, the instrument tucked beneath his chin as nimble fingers flew along the neck and the bow glided across the body.

Tyler couldn't put his finger on the tune. Not that he was a classical music *aficionado*, but he could at least recognize the more popular pieces. Even so, he recognized Seth's skill. The kid was not just good, he was phenomenal.

The piece ended abruptly, leaving the notes to echo in the space. Seth opened his eyes and caught Tyler standing there. "Hi."

"Hi." Tyler approached the kid, taking in the condition of the old mill. It had been at least two decades since he'd set foot in here. The building still managed to hang in there, though there were more broken windows than he remembered and a few more birds' nests in the rafters.

His gazed returned to Seth. "You practice here often?"

Seth shrugged as he wiped the chin rest with a cloth and placed the violin in the case. "Since I was about fifteen. I like the acoustics."

"How long have you been playing?"

"Since I was seven."

"I didn't recognize the piece. Bach? Vivaldi?"

"McKay," Seth said with a grin.

"You? Wow, that's impressive. Truly."

"Thanks."

"No wonder you got a scholarship to Juilliard."

"They say I'm a prodigy." It was said without conceit.

"What do you think?" Tyler asked.

Seth shrugged. "I think I'm good." He closed the case and flipped the latches. "But Joshua Bell is great."

"He's also got more experience. You'll get there."

"I guess." He rose from the crate and stretched. "You like classical music?"

"Yeah. I've been known to listen to classical music from time to time. Especially when I was studying. I see mathematical equations in my head when I'm listening to Bach, Beethoven, Mozart, or Chopin."

"Dude. And I thought I was a nerd."

Tyler laughed. "Yeah. I guess that's pretty nerdy."

"Nah." At Tyler's look, Seth relented. "Okay, it's nerdy. Did you know Einstein was also an accomplished pianist and violinist?"

"Yeah. Math and music go together like peanut butter and jelly." A cheeky grin split his face as he bent to pick up his backpack and violin case.

"You good at math too?" Tyler asked, kicking a rusty bolt across the worn and dirty wood floor.

"Math, science, music. They seem to be my special jam," Seth said with a shrug.

"Everybody needs a special jam." He shoved his hands into the pocket of his jeans.

Seth directed his feet toward the door Tyler had come in through.

"Did you walk here? You need a ride home?"

"I won't turn one down."

Tyler blew on his fingers as they made their way to the sagging doors. "How do you play in this cold?"

"My fingers get pretty warm when I play." Seth preceded Tyler through the gaping doors.

Outside, Tyler drew alongside Seth and pointed to his truck in the brewery parking lot across the street. Night had fallen, and the air held the promise of a cold, clear night.

"Mom said you used to work in New York."

"I did."

"Why'd you move back to Northridge?"

Without getting into the sordid tale, Tyler just said he missed Northridge.

"Yeah. Me too."

"You don't like New York?"

"I thought I would, but it's too noisy. I can't think. I can't hear the music inside my head over the blaring of sirens and horns. I know Juilliard is the best place for me, and I appreciate the opportunity, but . . . I like the peace of Northridge."

Taken aback, Tyler remained quiet a couple of beats. "Not too many kids your age would miss a town the size of Northridge—choosing it over the big city of New York and all it has to offer."

"I just want to play my violin."

"You said you hear music in your head. You mean Bach, Vivaldi, or original music? Your music?"

"I hear original music. Notes and arrangements float through my thoughts and I have to jot them down."

"What an incredible talent you have. Do your time in New York, learn everything you can about your craft, make it big, and then you can live anywhere you want."

"That's the plan," he said with a grin. "That, and take care of my mom."

Kristen could use someone to take care of her. She worked too hard. Though he had a feeling that Kristen wouldn't sit back and let someone pamper her.

They'd reached the truck and climbed in. Tyler cranked up the heat and threw the vehicle in reverse, backing out.

Seth took his phone out of his pocket. "Damn," he muttered.

"Problem?"

"No. Just later than I thought." He shoved the device back into his pocket. "I get lost in my music and lose track of time. I'd planned to have dinner ready for Mom, so she could study for an exam."

"Exam?" What the hell?

"Yeah. She's been taking online classes for the past few years. She's working on her business degree. We have a mother-son challenge going—who's going to graduate from college first. My money's on Mom. She's only a few credits shy." His fingers tapped out a rhythm on the console like he was practicing his fingering for a musical piece.

I'll be damned. So that's what Kristen does in the evenings that keeps her up until midnight, even when she must get up again at four-thirty in the morning to bake. And

he's added to her burden by roping her into this film location investigation.

He groaned.

"You okay?"

"Huh? Oh yeah, just been a long day." But not as long
as Kristen's.

# CHAPTER ELEVEN

The following Friday, Kristen opened the door onto
the frigid night and hauled the bags of trash out to the
dumpster in the alley behind the café.

Her breath fogged in front of her, and she shivered in
her fleece jacket. Hurrying to finish her chore, she tossed
the bags over the top then folded her arms across her chest,
shoving her hands beneath her armpits.

God, she was exhausted. And cold.

Then she heard it, a soft mewing sound, almost like a
baby's. She stopped, head cocked, waiting for the sound
again. Just when she thought she'd imagined it, she heard it
again, coming from behind a stack of empty crates from
Pints and Paints. An eerie sound, both heartbreaking and
frightening.

In the dim glow from the alley light post, she made her
way over to the crates and knelt down, her heart racing with
fear. What if it was a rabid raccoon? Or maybe a feral
tomcat?

*Mew.*

There, tucked into the very corner she could just make out the shape of a tiny ball of matted fur. Holding her breath, she reached out to touch the kitten, afraid it might bite her. She'd never had a pet growing up and knew nothing about how to handle a situation like this. She lightly stroked the fur on its back, amazed at the downy feel of it.

The creature shrank back and hissed at her, but otherwise didn't try to get away or defend itself. "Where is your mother?" she asked the little guy. The only response she received was another pitiful *mew*, and her heart was toast.

Slipping off her meager jacket, she held her breath a moment, then in one swift move scooped up the critter, and with her teeth chattering, sought the warmth of the café, the kitten cradled against her body. She could feel it shivering beneath the jacket and tears stung her eyes. *Poor thing*.

Still carrying the precious bundle, she stepped behind the counter and opened the fridge, taking out a container of cream to pour into a bowl then thought better of it. It was already chilled to the bone. Better to warm it first.

One-handed, she opened the twist cap, poured some cream into a saucer, and popped it in the microwave for twenty seconds. Removing the saucer, she set it on the counter and tested the temperature with her pinky. Perfect. Warm, but not hot.

Squatting, she placed it on the floor and carefully unwrapped the fur ball, setting it on the floor in front of the warm cream. The kitten staggered over to the dish on shaky legs then hesitated for only a moment before it began lapping up the treat.

Kristen carefully sank to her bum on the floor, watching, her heart breaking at the little guy's predicament. Cold, abandoned, and alone.

Stifling a sob, she fought to suppress the memories of nights at home alone with nothing in the house to eat and no electricity for heat because there was no money for either. On those nights, her mother went out to sell her body to put food on the table.

She reached out a tentative hand and stroked the creature's scrawny back. It didn't protest, too hungry to care about the big scary human touching it. The thing couldn't have weighed more than an eight-ounce bag of coffee.

It finally drank its fill, the little belly protruding on both sides. It took a few hesitant steps, exploring its new surroundings. In the light, she could see it had orange stripes with white "socks" and a white tip on the tail.

Shaking her head, she wrapped her arms around her knees, laid her head on them, and heaved a sigh. "What now?"

The last thing she needed was another mouth to feed, vet bills to pay, and supplies to buy. And what did she know about caring for something so small and helpless? She could barely take care of herself and Seth.

Tired of its exploration, the kitten tentatively made its way back to her. When it finally reached her, it stepped onto the puddle of her jacket, promptly curled up into a ball, and began purring.

*Okay then.*

She'd take the thing home for the night. But that was it. Tomorrow she'd take it to the local animal shelter. They'd feed it, check it for medical problems, and find it a good home. Better than the one she could offer.

She went to her office, and picking up the day's receipts, shoved them into her tote bag before returning to the bar. She gazed down at the kitten, sound asleep on her jacket, then bent to scoop it up and gather it close against her chest. It would be a cold walk to her apartment without her jacket. And damn, she hated being cold.

As an after-thought, she plucked the container of cream off the counter and tucked it into her tote bag. The little guy needed nourishment after all.

Making her way to the door, she set the alarm, flipped off the lights, locked up behind her, and went out into the night, her tiny bundle nestled against her, trusting and warm, as the first snowflakes began to fall.

CINNAMON.

Dammit. The last thing she intended to do was name the thing. Once it had a name, that was it. And yet Cinnamon had popped into her head unbidden.

"Are you a boy or a girl?" she asked it, having no idea how to tell.

Already dead on her feet and with at least two hours of homework ahead of her, she eyed the creature with a groan. She had to get up in the morning, run to the café, bake the morning's offerings, come back to the apartment, shower, and dress for her dreaded trip to Senoia with Tyler.

Even so, the kitten clearly needed a bath. The fur was sticky and matted in places from what looked like motor oil. She recalled seeing TV commercials about using dish soap on birds who'd been caught up in oil spills. Maybe that would work on the kitten.

Gathering towels, a washcloth, and dish soap, she questioned her sanity once again. Plugging the drain in the kitchen sink, she placed a folded bath towel in the bottom and filled it with a couple of inches of warm water.

Pleased with her efforts, she turned and gazed down at Cinnamon with her hands on her hips. "You're not going to like this, but trust me, you'll feel a whole lot better when you're clean. Then you can take it from there."

She plucked the kitten off the kitchen floor, again amazed at its diminutive size, then, taking a deep breath, lowered it into the water. To her surprise, it didn't make a fuss, only looked confused by its predicament.

"Okay, McKay, be quick about it." It could decide against the treatment at any moment and rebel. "Plus, I have other more pressing tasks to complete, like putting together a bank deposit, entering today's sales data, and finishing the business calc section on properties of definite integrals. Riveting stuff," she muttered to the kitten.

A few minutes later, its towel-dried fur standing out like it had been struck by lightning, Cinnamon wobbled off into the corner of the kitchen and squat, leaving a puddle of urine on the floor.

"Right." Grabbing a roll of paper towels, Kristen bent to wipe up the mess. At least it was just pee. She shuddered in revulsion. She had to come up with a litter box and fast. When she turned around, Cinnamon was gone.

How'd something so small and wobbly move so fast?

She checked the living room. Nothing. The bathroom. Bedroom. Dining-room-slash-office. Still nothing. Now in a panic, she circled her tiny apartment, willing herself to calm down. *I mean, it's not like it could have escaped, right?* It was too small to get up on the furniture, so wherever it was, it had to be at floor level.

But there were so many places a creature that small could get stuck. And maybe hurt.

"Here, kitty, kitty. Here Cinnamon. I have a nice bowl

of cream for you." She set about pouring said cream into a saucer.

*Mew.*

She whirled, following the sound. "Meow for me again, baby."

*Mew.*

The living room. Following the growing number of meows, she found her . . . him . . . it behind the sofa, tail-side out, trying to back up. Kristen laughed despite herself. "There you are."

Reaching in, she managed to get it out, then grimaced at the dust bunnies clinging to what had been clean fur. She really needed to vacuum behind the sofa.

Running her hand along the kitten's fur, she managed to remove the puffy debris. The vibrations coming from the animal's little body filled Kristen with a calm she hadn't known since the nurse laid a newborn Seth on her chest. And just like that day, when the kitten settled into her as if it trusted her with its life . . . she lost her heart.

Cinnamon curled into her, its warmth a welcome respite from the cold outside. Speaking of warmth. She shivered then moved to check the thermostat. They were expecting a light dusting of snow that night, with temperatures in the low twenties.

Sixty-two. She listened for the low rumble of the furnace. *Nada.* Then she banged her fist on the ancient analog thermostat as if that would help, startling Cinnamon. *Great.* Nine o'clock on a Friday night. Her landlord would never get someone out to fix it until Monday.

At least she still had hot water (she hoped) to shower, and she had an electric blanket on the bed. Seth would be warm.

As if conjured from her mind, Seth's key rattled in the

lock, and he stepped through the door. "Brr. It's damn cold out there."

"Hey, baby. Unfortunately, it won't be much warmer in here tonight." At Seth's questioning look, she continued. "The furnace is out."

"Well, that sucks." Then his attention strayed to the orange fur ball in her arms.

"Who's this little guy?" He moved to stand next to her and held out a finger to stroke the kitten's fur.

"Or girl. Cinnamon."

"You never let me have a pet growing up," he said, scowling at her

"Because we couldn't afford one."

"And now we can?" He bent down to examine Cinnamon's sleeping face. "It's so cute!"

"No, we can't really afford one now, either. But I couldn't leave it outside to freeze or starve to death, now could I?"

Seth's gaze lifted to hers with a grin. "You're such a softy." He took the cat from her arms with his big beautiful hands and settled on the couch with it on his lap. "So, we're keeping it?"

"I'm keeping it. You're going back to New York in January."

He grimaced but didn't argue. "What about the furnace?"

"We'll never get it fixed tonight, so bundle up. You sleep in the bed with the electric blanket. I'll put on a few layers and sleep out here."

"No, Mom. You hate to be cold. You sleep in the bed. Besides, I've spent a winter in New York, so my blood's thickened up," he said with a cheeky grin. At her look, he continued, "I insist. Besides, I'll have this little guy, or girl, to keep me warm."

"At least take a hot shower before bed. I'll take one when you're done."

Seth placed the curled-up kitten in the corner of the couch, gave it one last stroke, and headed for the bathroom.

She owed her son so much more. She swore he'd never spend a night without heat like she did growing up. At least this wasn't due to unpaid bills, but still. She wanted better for him. And if his violin teachers were right, he'd have it. He'd be famous and live the kind of life she could only dream about.

She cleaned up the kitchen from Cinnamon's bath and made a supply list for tomorrow.

Ugh. Tomorrow.

She'd nearly forgot—she owed Tyler that trip to Senoia. Hours alone in the car with him. Just the two of them. How could she put physical distance between them in the space of a truck cab? It was getting more difficult to put mental and emotional distance between them.

Seth came out of the bathroom wearing sweatpants, a sweatshirt, and socks, followed by a blast of steam that felt good on her chilled body.

"Night, Mom," he called before crawling onto the sofa, gathering a couple of blankets around him, and tucking Cinnamon into the curve of his body.

Unable to resist, she sat on the sofa next to him, brushed the damp hair off his forehead, and smiled down at her beautiful, kind son. Life had handed her some shitty circumstances, but Seth made up for all of them—past, present, and future. Her heart swelled with love for him.

"If you get cold, you wake me up, and I'll switch with you."

"No worries, Mom." He yawned, then sighed and closed his eyes.

Resigned to spending a cold night huddled in bed, she rose and turned her steps toward the bathroom, and with her thoughts returning to Tyler, she knew she wouldn't be getting to sleep anytime soon.

# CHAPTER TWELVE

THE NEXT MORNING Tyler knocked on Kristen's door, blowing into his cold hands to warm them. He'd love a cup of Kristen's coffee right now.

Just as he raised his hand to knock again, the door flew open to reveal Kristen bundled up in a thick sweater, knit cap, and gloves. "Oh, you're ready."

"Not exactly. My heat's not working."

"What the hell? Did you call someone?"

"I left a message with Tony, but he's out of town and hasn't been able to get in touch with anyone."

"That's bullshit. It's freezing in here." He strode into the apartment, despite her look of annoyance. "Thermostat?"

She pointed to the wall by the TV.

"Jesus, Kristen. It's fifty-four degrees in here."

"Thanks. As if I can't read the thermostat myself. I'm fine. Seth's fine." His gaze followed hers to the lump of blankets on the couch. "I took a hot shower and I've got on several layers of clothes. Let's go."

"We'll swing by the hardware store and pick up a

ceramic heater."

"No. We don't need a heater. We're fine. I'm going to be gone most of the day today anyway, Seth will be in the café, and it will be fixed tomorrow." She crossed her arms and wore a belligerent expression he'd come to know well.

"Well, let me at least check the furnace before we go. It might just be the ignitor. We can pick up any parts while we're out." He reached up and touched her nose, and she jerked back as if stung. "Your nose is so cold I'm surprised it hasn't fallen off yet."

"Don't be ridiculous."

"I'm not the one without heat refusing to buy a heater."

A look of panic crossed her face then disappeared. "They're a fire hazard," she said, her hand brushing off his suggestion.

He studied her a moment then said, "Fine. But I'm still going to check out the unit. If it's simple to repair, there's no reason to spend another night in a cold apartment. And if it's not a simple fix, you and Seth can stay at my house."

Kristen blanched then shook her head as if a bee were buzzing around it. "No."

He gazed at her a moment, trying to get a read on her. With her rigid body, tight mouth, and pugnacious chin, he knew he wouldn't win this one.

He shrugged. "Suit yourself." Stubborn-ass woman. Maybe it would be a simple fix and this would all be moot.

As they pulled onto I-85, Kristen had to admit, it had been a nice day. Not only the weather, which had been cold and sunny, but Tyler's company had been . . . pleasant.

Oh, who was she kidding? It had been more than pleasant. She had to hand it to Tyler, if the rumors were true, he'd been wildly successful in New York, but you'd never know it simply looking at him.

She cut her gaze to him beneath her lashes. He had on worn cords, work boots, and a flannel shirt over an olive green Henley that brought out the green flecks in his eyes. His fleece-lined denim jacket had been tossed into the backseat of the truck cab.

At one point today, he'd gotten ahead of her on the sidewalk when she'd stopped to admire a gift shop's window display, and when she glanced up, she'd been graced with a lovely view of Tyler's fine ass nicely cupped in his brown cords. He had an ass to be admired, no doubt about it.

And now, seated in the toasty truck cab, she realized she was warmer here than in her apartment.

The meeting with the marketing coordinator in Senoia had been fruitful. Surely, armed with that information, she and Tyler could convince the council this was the right decision. They had to. That's all there was to it. Failure was not an option. She had too much riding on this. She'd already put plans into motion for Jordan Raven's author appearance by contacting her literary agent.

After the meeting, she and Tyler had walked along the charming Main Street, visited the shops, and spoken to the owners or managers to get their take on their experiences serving as a film location for multiple feature films and TV shows.

It wasn't all good. She got that. But for the most part, even those reluctant business people said that in the long run, it had been the right decision.

They'd finished their visit with a late lunch at one of the cafés and topped that off with a shared slice of decadent pecan pie. For some reason, sharing that slice of pie, their forks sometimes tangling in their zeal to snag the next sweet, gooey bite had felt . . . intimate.

She cut a glance at him out of the corner of her eye. He drove the truck with the same easy manner with which he did just about everything. Confident but not arrogant. Efficient but not controlling.

Could she be wrong about Tyler? The more time she spent with him, the harder it was to reconcile this Tyler with the one who'd had sex with her and never spoke to her again.

Her heart thudded heavily in her chest when she thought about the secret she was keeping from him. Was it fair to keep the knowledge of his child from him?

Probably not. Yet she couldn't bring herself to tell him. At least not yet. She needed more time to determine whether he would try to take Seth away from her. After all, he still had a year before he reached adulthood. Maybe seeing how she lived—the fact that she had no heat—he'd think Seth was better off with him instead. She couldn't let that happen.

"So tell me. Did that suck?"

Startled by his comment, she stared at him a moment. "What?"

His expression unreadable, he clarified his question. "Did spending the day with me suck?"

Still trying to unscramble his question, she shook her head to clear it, then eyed him. "I—why would you say that?"

He flipped his blinker on to change lanes and glanced in his side-view mirror then shrugged. "It's clear you don't like me—though I don't know why—so I just wondered if being with me today had been a hardship."

She ignored his statement about her disliking him and

pondered the question a minute. If she were honest with herself, the answer would be no. Far from it. But should she admit that to him?

"It wasn't a root canal," was all she could come up with.

He barked out a laugh. "I guess I'll take what I can get."

Her phone buzzed, and she exchanged a text with Calypso, who reported they'd had a good day and that Seth had gone to a friend's for dinner. That was a relief. Kristen had been concerned about leaving the café for an entire day. She needed to trust her own abilities to read character. Calypso had been a good hire. Now she had to trust her to handle things in her absence. She sighed. Trust, like forgiveness, was not an easy thing for her.

"Everything okay?" Tyler interrupted her musings.

"Yeah." She stashed her refurbished early model iPhone into her purse and sat back in the seat.

"We'll stop at the hardware store on the way back and pick up a new ignitor for your furnace."

"You don't need to do that."

"I know I don't, but you and Seth need heat tonight and it's an easy-enough fix."

Kristen bit her lip to keep from arguing. Seth did need heat. And so did Cinnamon. And so did *she*. *Dammit*. It was supposed to get into the low teens, much colder than the night before, and she'd nearly froze her ass off when she'd climbed out from under the electric blanket this morning. And what the hell? He'd already seen her low-rent apartment. Twice.

"Any other stops while we're out?"

"No. I'm good." She needed pet supplies, but she needed to get the hell out of the warm, intimate confines of Tyler's truck. The heat in her own car died long ago, so riding with the heat making her feet cozy warm in their knock-off Uggs and the seat heater toasting her buns, she thought she could get used to this.

Then there was the warmth from the man behind the wheel. She could practically feel the heat rolling off him. The woodsy scent of his cologne or soap filled her head with visions. Dangerous visions she could not, *would* not, explore. Not again.

When Tyler had suggested that she stay at his house if the furnace couldn't be fixed, she'd panicked. There was no way in Hell she and Seth could stay in Tyler's house. Her brain said no, but based on the electricity in the truck cab, her body hadn't gotten the message.

"How much is an ignitor anyway?" Kristen asked as they walked along the aisles in the home improvement store. It seemed a casual question, but she worried her bottom lip, and there were creases between her brows.

Tyler shrugged. "Probably less than twenty bucks. You should tell Tony to reimburse you for it. You're saving him money in labor costs, after all."

Kristen's shoulders visibly relaxed, and she nodded, confirming Tyler's suspicions that she lived on a tight budget. He'd offer to pay for it, but it would be useless— she'd never accept. He'd have to satisfy himself with the fact that it was an inexpensive part and that she and Seth would at least be warm tonight.

They turned down the aisle, and he scanned the various parts before finding the one he needed. "Here you go."

She took the ignitor, frowning. "This is it?"

"Yep." He gazed at her as she rolled the piece over in her hands. Her flaming red hair hung down her back in a thick plait, tendrils drifting loose and curling around her face. A sudden longing to pull it loose and run his fingers through it hit him like a bolt from the blue.

He'd asked her if being with him sucked. He could definitely say being with her had not sucked. Not one bit. The quiet intimacy of the drive, the fresh scent of what he assumed was her shampoo surrounded him in the warmth of his cab, and he'd had to resist drawing in a deep, lung-filling breath.

Kristen wouldn't wear a heavy scent. It didn't suit her carefree attitude. And, given her financial situation, she couldn't afford expensive perfume. The clean scent of lavender pleased him far more than some of the expensive cloying scents many women in his former profession wore after business hours.

"Ready?"

He mentally shook himself and found her regarding him, puzzled. *Right.* How long had he stood there staring at her, his mouth watering, his fingers itching to touch her?

"Sure. Hey, you said you wanted to paint and update the café bathrooms. Want to look while we're here?" Any excuse to spend more time with her, he thought.

Emotions flitted across her face: confusion, consideration, then finally disappointment. "Thanks, but I haven't budgeted for the labor costs involved. I mean, I can wield a paintbrush, but I'm not sure about new toilets and sinks."

"I'm happy to help."

"You won the bet, remember?"

He shrugged. "I'm still happy to help. Zach and I could knock out the project in a day."

"You'd do that?"

"Why not? What are friends for?" He left that hanging

out there, hoping she'd confirm that relationship, but she didn't. She didn't deny it either, so maybe that was progress.

"I guess it doesn't hurt to look."

She preceded him up the aisle and he took advantage of the situation to admire her fine ass, displayed to perfection in the snug black leggings she wore, and he resisted the urge to reach out and give it a squeeze.

He winced, and surreptitiously adjusted himself. It was going to be a long, uncomfortable trip back to town.

KRISTEN WAITED, impatient. Tyler had his head in the closet housing the furnace, muttering a curse when he banged his head.

"Jesus. Could they have shoved this unit into a smaller space?"

A knock sounded at the door.

"That'll be the pizza," he said, his voice muffled inside the closet.

*Pizza? Was she supposed to pay for that?*

As if reading her mind, he continued, "I already paid with the app."

Kristen gritted her teeth. So far he'd insisted on buying her lunch and now dinner, on top of driving round-trip, fixing her heater, and committing himself to updating the bathrooms. She didn't want to be beholden to anyone, much less Tyler. She opened the door and was just about to tell him she wasn't hungry and he could take his pizza home, when the scent of pepperoni and cheese wafted up from the box the delivery boy handed her. "Thanks."

*Okay. So maybe one slice of pizza wouldn't hurt.*

"God, that smells good!" She jumped when Tyler

stepped up behind her and leaned over to inhale the spicy scent of cured meats. He wiped his hands on an old towel she'd given him, then she heard the familiar rumble of the furnace and nearly leapt with joy.

"You fixed it?"

"Of course." He looked affronted at her question. "I said I would. Now let's eat."

Setting the box on her table-slash-desk, she shoved some papers aside and went to the kitchen to get plates and napkins. When she turned, she bumped into Tyler who stood at the sink washing his hands, making her almost lose her grip on the plates.

Tyler set his still-wet hands on her hips, catching her, and her breath backed up in her chest. "You okay?"

She nodded, but his eyes had dropped to her mouth. Ooh boy. *Danger, Will Robinson.* For a heartbeat, she considered . . . then stepped back and he released her. Danger averted. Then why the disappointment? "Yeah, I'm starved. Let's eat."

"Good day today." Tyler lifted the lid on the pizza box and held out his hand for Kristen's plate.

She hesitated a moment, then handed it to him. He slid a slice onto the plate and handed it back to her, capturing her gaze with his. She murmured a thank you, and he turned his attention back to the pizza, selecting his own slice.

"What do you mean?" She muttered around a bite of food.

"We have some great testimony from the good citizens

of Senoia, you and Seth aren't going to freeze to death tonight, and you managed not to kill me."

She snorted. "Yeah. So far anyway." She eyed him, and he laughed.

"Why do you think that is? That you managed not to kill me?"

"No alibi. Everyone knew we were spending the day together."

"Good point. I'll keep that in mind for the future."

Tyler spied what appeared to be business calculus notes on top of the pile of papers on the table and remembered his conversation with Seth. How did she do it all? He glanced over at her, seeing the shadows under her eyes. She did it by not sleeping, that's how.

Before he could comment, tiny pricks of pain in his calf distracted him from his intended question. What the hell?

Tyler twitched as if shocked.

Kristen looked down to see Cinnamon climbing Tyler's denim-clad leg. She couldn't blame the little critter. She often wanted to climb him like a tree herself.

He dropped his pizza slice on his plate, his brow puckered in surprise as he looked down and inspected his leg. "Well, what have we here?" He bent to pluck the fur ball off him and held it up in front of his face, eye to eye. "Where did you come from?"

"I, uh, found it. In the alley. Behind the café." She shrugged, trying to appear nonchalant. "It was freezing and I couldn't very well leave it out there, now could I?" wincing at the defensiveness in her tone.

His gaze shifted from the kitten to Kristen, and the warmth she saw there unnerved her.

"I never saw you as an animal lover." Tyler tucked the kitten up against his chest with one hand then picked up the pizza slice with the other.

If her heart hadn't melted to the consistency of hot caramel before, it did then. Cinnamon clung to Tyler's chest, as if its claws didn't hurt a bit, purring loudly enough to wake the dead. *Lucky cat.* "I'm not. At least, I never have been. But what was I going to do? Leave it to starve or freeze to death?" She reached for another slice of pizza. What the hell. It was here, she might as well eat.

"Are you keeping it?" He glanced down at the thing and the kitten sniffed Tyler's chin, making him laugh.

Her stomach did a backflip at the sound.

"Yeah."

"Did you name it yet?"

"Cinnamon."

Tyler plucked the kitten from his chest, eyeing it, then nodded and put it back, where it snuggled right in again. "Perfect." He took a bite of pizza, chewed it thoughtfully a moment, and—be still her heart—rubbed his scruffy jaw against the downy fur. "Boy or girl?"

"Don't know. I thought Cinnamon would work either way."

"We can figure it out after dinner."

"What do you know about sexing kittens?" she asked with a note of skepticism.

"Nothing. But I'm sure we can find something online."

She snorted then held back a giggle.

"What?"

"You, uh, you have fur on your face." She circled her finger in the general direction of his jaw. Cinnamon's fur had caught in his two-day-old scruff, making him look like the Wolfman.

He grinned at her, and before he could take action, she reached over and plucked the cat hair from his face, her fingers burning where they touched his skin.

The grin faded from his face and he went very still, his eyes holding hers, the only sound in the room Cinnamon's purring. Try as she might, she couldn't pull her gaze from his. He reached up and, wrapping his big, warm hand around her wrist, held the palm of her hand to his face, then his gaze zeroed in on her lips, momentarily stealing her breath. "Thank you."

When she finally regained her senses, she gave herself a mental shake. "For what?" She tugged at his hold and he released her.

"For spending the day with me, for having dinner with me. For not killing me." The last he said with a soft smile tugging at the corners of his lips.

Her eyes flitted to his mouth. A mouth she would very much like to kiss right now.

"I should be thanking *you*. For making me go with you. For driving. For fixing my furnace. For dinner." Then she shrugged. "And for not giving me a reason to kill you."

He chuckled at that, and she felt it deep in the pit of her stomach. "You're welcome. For all of it." He held her stare a moment more then, reaching for his phone where it had been laying on the table, swiped it awake. "Now, let's see if we can figure out whether Cinnamon is a he or a she."

"Um, I don't mean to be rude, but I have an early wake-up tomorrow."

"Even on Sunday, huh?"

"Time waits for no one, and no one likes to wait for their coffee and breakfast. Some of our townsfolk like to stop by for a muffin and coffee before church." She gathered up the dirty dishes to carry to the kitchen as she rose.

Tyler followed her, carrying the now-empty pizza box and the bottle of wine.

Without seeing him, she sensed his presence, but she tried to ignore the heat of him. Setting the dishes in the sink, she flipped on the tap.

He flipped it off. "Kristen."

She swallowed hard at the gruffness in his voice. A voice thick with desire. Sucking up her courage, she lifted her eyes to his and drew in a breath at the heat she saw there.

His gaze flickered to her mouth, making her heart stutter in her chest.

His big, warm hand went to her hip, drawing her toward him. "I had a really nice day," he muttered, his mouth inches from hers. If she lifted up onto her tiptoes, she could press her lips to his.

"I think we've established that already. I did too."

"I'd like very much to kiss you."

*Yes, please,* her body said. *Hell no,* her brain said. *Stupid brain,* her body said. *Don't listen.*

She didn't. Reaching up, she cupped the back of his neck and tugged his mouth down to hers.

The kiss started out soft, warm, and sweet, but came to a rolling boil in seconds as his tongue coaxed her lips apart to tangle with hers. Moaning, she leaned into the hard planes of him, a sudden desperation taking hold.

They both came up for air, panting as if they'd run a marathon.

*Tell him*, a voice said. *Tell him, now.* "Tyler, I—"

"Mom! Guess what!"

She and Tyler sprang apart like an atom splitting. She cut a glance at Tyler. His hair showed the aftereffects of her fingers, and he wore a guilty expression.

They were so busted.

"Uh . . ." Seth's gaze bounced between the two of them. "Am I interrupting something?"

*Jesus.* "No. Tyler was just leaving."

"Uh-huh." He broke into a grin, so like his father's she wondered how Tyler didn't recognize it.

"You had some news?" Kristen prompted, glad for the deflection.

"Yeah, Joshua Bell is playing in Atlanta. Can we go?"

Kristen bit her lip. She'd do anything for her son, but since money didn't grow on trees, tickets to Joshua Bell were likely out of her reach. She eyed Tyler then said, "We'll talk about it later."

"But, Mom—"

"It's late. Why don't you jump in the shower and get ready for bed?"

Seth released an annoyed teenage sigh. "See ya, Tyler."

"Night, Seth."

As Seth headed for the bathroom, he sang under his breath, "Kristen and Tyler sittin' in a tree, K-I-S-S-I-N-G."

She laughed despite herself and glanced up at Tyler, who rubbed his nose, an embarrassed flush on his face.

"Good night, Tyler," she said.

"Night."

He slipped on his jacket, bent to give Cinnamon one more rub, then left.

She collapsed against the kitchen counter for support. What the hell was she doing?

Playing with fire, that's what.

And when you played with fire, you often got burned.

Close call. He felt a little like a horny teenager who'd just been caught making out by his parents.

Zipping his jacket against the cold, he strode to his truck. He'd started the engine before he left the apartment and sighed at the warmth in the cab. He looked up at Kristen's apartment, the window aglow with light, and palmed his face with a groan.

God, that kiss!

He'd wanted more. So much more! And he would have sworn there for a minute, while she'd held her soft palm to his cheek, that she'd wanted more too.

Her soft curves, lush lips, and warm body had been so right against his. Flashes of . . . something—recognition maybe—flitted through his lust-fogged brain. Like his body knew hers on some elemental level.

He glanced down at his crotch. The bitter cold had done nothing to chill his desire. It had been over a year since he'd last been with a woman, and his body protested the sudden loss of the opportunity presented to it. But with any luck, more such opportunities with Kristen would present themselves.

He put his truck in drive and headed down the quiet streets of Northridge toward his cold, lonely bed, but happy in the knowledge that she, Seth, and little Cinnamon would be warm and cozy tonight.

# CHAPTER THIRTEEN

A couple of days later, Tyler laid out three event tickets on top of the coffee bar.

"What's this?" Kristen eyed the tickets in surprise.

Tyler shrugged. "Tickets to see Joshua Bell. I hope you didn't buy them yet."

*Yet? Ha.* As if she could afford them.

She slid the tickets back in his direction. "Tyler, this is way too much."

"Seth is a brilliant violinist—he should get a glimpse of his future." Tyler slid them toward her once more.

Her breath caught. The thought of her son becoming the next Joshua Bell filled her with pride. And a little fear. But she couldn't just take these tickets. She caught a glimpse of the face value and nearly choked. Orchestra seats. And she sure couldn't buy them either.

"Thank you, but we can't." She slid the tickets back across the bar to him.

"You mean you won't." Placing his fingers on the tickets, he slid them back to her.

"Tyler." Grasping his wrist, she tried to push them away again, but couldn't budge him.

"Kristen."

She rolled her eyes at their idiocy. "I can't afford to repay you."

"Who says you have to? They're a gift."

At her continued defiance, he sighed. "Okay. If you feel you must repay me, how about this? Coffee and a cinnamon bun for the next two weeks, no charge."

"Pfft. That wouldn't even come close to what these tickets cost." She pointed at the tickets for emphasis.

He shrugged and leaned across the counter, saying for her ears only, "I can think of another form of payment." He wore a sexy grin, and though she should feel insulted by the insinuation, she couldn't argue with the flurry of butterflies that took flight in her belly at the thought.

Nevertheless, she shoved his shoulder. "You wish."

He put his mouth to her ear. "Oh, I more than wish. I crave. I dream. I yearn."

She shivered at the tickling of his breath against her skin, and the thoughts his words conjured sent her pulse into overdrive. Then she caved like a cheap suitcase. "Okay. Fine."

Tyler popped up, grinning like a fool. "Fine you'll repay me with sexual favors? Or fine you'll take the tickets?"

"I'll take the tickets, but I'll repay you with coffee and cinnamon rolls."

"I'll take what I can get. I'll pick you both up Saturday at four-thirty. Dinner then the show." Tucking the tickets into his jacket pocket with one hand, he slapped the coffee bar with his other. "Don't be late."

❄

"Man, that was amazing! Did you see his fingering on Vivaldi's *Concerto alla rustica*? Brilliant! I have to go home and practice. And that Stradivarius! The purity of sound is unlike any other."

Seth practically fizzed in the back seat of Tyler's Maserati. The kid extolled the virtues of Stradivari versus Guarneri but hadn't batted an eyelash over the car. Most guys Seth's age would have a week-long hard-on over this car. Not Seth. He reserved that for violins.

Their return trip to Northridge was filled with Seth exclaiming over Joshua Bell's technique, his music selection, the twelve-year-old guest artist from Dahlonega. "I would give my right arm to play with Joshua Bell."

Kristen snorted. "If you gave your right arm, you wouldn't be *able* to play with Joshua Bell."

"You know what I mean." Tyler caught his eye roll in the rearview mirror.

Tyler didn't know Seth that well, but he thought this effusive side of the quiet, thoughtful kid was probably rare.

While Seth jabbered on about the concert, Tyler cut a glance at Kristen to see a soft smile grace her lips. She must have felt his eyes on her because she looked over at him and mouthed, "Thank you."

Those two words touched him to the core. "My pleasure." He reached across the console and lifting her hand to his mouth, he pressed a kiss to it, then released it to downshift for the upcoming exit.

For a moment, Tyler could almost believe they were a family. His family.

But that would never be. Maybe, over time, when he'd come to accept his sterility, he could adopt a child. He gave himself a mental snort. First he had to find a woman.

Kristen laughed at something Seth said, and Tyler's chest tightened. Maybe he already had.

NOT USUALLY ONE TO count her chickens before they hatched, but a planner just the same, Kristen sat at her dining table-slash-desk reviewing her notes on the off-chance that Jordan Raven, the bestselling author of *Battle of the Heart*, would agree to a book signing.

She'd already made up her mind that even if the film location fell through, she'd invite her to come. The film location would be the perfect tie-in, but it wasn't a deal breaker to her mind.

On her to-do list—if Ms. Raven agreed—a press release, social media strategy, website update, and flyers all over town. Then there were the plans for the event itself. A thorough cleaning of the café and bookstore and the bathroom upgrades would be priority number one.

In her mind, she saw the café's exposed brick walls, the hardwood floors, and the bookshelves in the back. She tapped the pen against her lips as she considered the space and where Ms. Raven should sit and what setup would work best. Plenty of her most-popular baked goods, as well as some other enticing offerings. Maybe The Whistle Stop Pub would like to cater.

Of course, Ms. Raven would need a room at the 1885 B&B, unless she preferred to stay in Atlanta. She winced at the cost of that.

She'd need to increase her inventory of the book in the days leading up to the event. Maybe Ms. Raven's agent would be able to give her an idea about how many to order. And she'd need additional help behind the coffee counter and with the books. There was no avoiding the fact that this venture was going to cost her. She only hoped it would pay off. Maybe she could enlist the help of her friends.

She pondered that thought a moment. Her friends. Not just Zach anymore, but Olivia and her stepmother Jenny, Marshall, and of course Tyler. Her support system. Her network. When had that happened? When had Kristen McKay, loner and single mom, become Kristen McKay, joiner?

Cinnamon mewed and rubbed against Kristen's ankles. And pet owner and cat lover?

She bent to scoop her up and onto her lap. Cinnamon settled in, her purr so loud it vibrated through Kristen's body.

"You're getting fat," she said, as she stroked the cat's soft fur, earning her a clipped *meh*.

"I guess that comes from not knowing where your next meal is coming from when you were young," she muttered to the cat, who blinked up at her, her little orange face a mask of pleasure. Kristen knew that feeling all too well. "You're lucky I found you," she said, rubbing her nose in Cinnamon's fur.

Cinnamon meowed as if to say, "You're lucky you found me too." And she'd be right.

A WEEK LATER, Kristen bit her lip as she parked her car in the parking lot outside Tyler's craft brewery. She had this overwhelming need to see him. To share her news with him.

But . . .

Would he welcome the interruption, or would he resent her dropping by in the middle of his work day?

A year after Tyler returned to Northridge from New York, he'd started his craft brewery just outside of town, located in what was once a red-brick and masonry firehouse, and aptly named it Firehouse Brews.

She gazed through the fine mist forming on her windshield at the red-brick two-story building. He'd maintained the original late-nineteenth century architecture. The glass and wood double-doors that covered the bays where fire engines once awaited the call were painted a deep gray to match the stones that formed each arch. The same stones accented the three tall windows on the second floor. A brass plaque on the building, like those on the buildings downtown, declared it the "Old Northridge Firehouse, 1890."

Through the windows on the top half of the doors, she could see huge gleaming stainless-steel kettles and piping. An old-fashioned painted sign that read FIREHOUSE BREWS hung beneath the roof lintels. Two enormous tanks flanked the building, Firehouse Brews and its nineteenth-century horse-drawn fire engine logo adorning them. A restored version of the same fire engine stood to the left of the building.

"All right, McKay, you can't sit in your car all day." Pulling her jacket tight around her, and tucking her hair beneath the hoodie, she braced herself for the raw, wet cold. Stepping through the doors and into the warmth of the brewery, she shivered at the contrast in temperatures.

Huge metal cauldrons lined one side of the exposed brick and masonry walls. Gleaming concrete floors, clean enough to eat off of, reflected the overhead lighting two stories up. Tyler had removed the second story floor to make room for the massive tanks, pipes, and coils that filled the room.

Two men stood at the back of the brewery, iPads in

hand, tapping away. They wore work boots and protective glasses.

Neither of them was Tyler.

His truck had been parked out front, so she knew he was here somewhere among the metal sculptures that made up the brewery. The air hummed with the sound of machinery— a constant, orderly sound that permeated her skin and sank into her bones.

A man in worn jeans, work boots, a brown Henley, and safety glasses came out from behind a tank and stopped short at seeing her.

"Kristen? What are you doing here?"

She winced inwardly at his words. She wasn't welcome. Before she could make an excuse to leave, Tyler stepped into her, took her by the shoulders and kissed her on the mouth.

"I'm glad you came."

"You are?" Her insides melted in relief.

"Yes. I could use a little break. I've been working on a new recipe all morning and it's alluding me. Everything okay?" His eyes held a note of concern.

"Yes. More than okay." She took a deep breath. "Jordan Raven's agent has agreed to an author appearance and book signing at Beans 'n Books," she held up a finger, "Provided Northridge is selected as the filming location for the movie."

"That's great news!" He picked her up and swung her around before placing her back on her feet. As he did so, she slid inch by slow inch down the length of his body, and her breath caught in her throat.

Clearly, he wasn't unmoved by the contact because his eyes darkened to a deep mossy green, and his hands glided down, palming her ass. "And as for the proviso, it's a mere formality. The EDC and the Town Council are both going to see the wisdom of it, especially after we wow them with our presentation."

"I'm not one to count my chickens before they hatch."

"Fine. Then I'll count them for you. We should celebrate. Dinner. My house."

She hesitated a moment.

"I promise to make it worth your while," he said, nuzzling her ear, sending shivers along her spine.

She sighed and leaned into him. "Fine."

"Good," he said, pulling back, a boyish grin lighting his features. "How would you like a tour?"

"I'd love that."

# CHAPTER FOURTEEN

Pleased that Kristen had sought him out to share her news, he wrapped an arm around her waist and steered her toward a room covered with industrial-plastic vertical blinds. He tried to see the room as Kristen would, with its stacks of what would look like flour sacks to her lining the wall on pallets.

"Basic beer consists of barley, water, hops, and yeast. This is the grain room, where we mill the malted barley, wheat, and rye to the style of beer to be brewed." He reached into one of the open bags and took out a handful of dark grains and held them to Kristen's nose.

"It smells a little like coffee."

"Good nose." He tapped the tip of her nose with his forefinger. "The darker the barley is roasted, the stronger the coffee smell. It gives coffee notes to the beers brewed using dark-roasted barley." He tossed the grains back into the bag then reached into another one. "These are lightly roasted. They taste like the inside of a malted milk ball." He held a grain out to her. "Taste."

Rather than taking it from his fingers as he'd expected,

she leaned in and wrapped her lips around his fingers, sucking the grain into her mouth, and white-hot lust shot down his spine.

Crunching on the barley, her mouth lifted at the corner in a knowing smile.

"Tease." He laughed and kissed her, tasting the barley on her tongue.

Before he could reach out an arm to her, she skipped out of his reach and said, "So, what's next?"

He shook his head at her flirtation, so contrary to the outright loathing she'd displayed earlier this month, and continued. "Once the grains are turned into grist, they are transferred through this pipe," he pointed to a pipe along the wall, "into the mash tun via an auger."

Holding back the heavy flaps in the doorway for her, they exited the room and entered a vast space that held enormous stainless-steel tanks joined with pipes. Gauges, taps, tubing, and other paraphernalia decorated the tanks. The air hummed with the sounds of the machinery.

"Just like the ingredients, the basic brewing process is simple. Mashing, lautering, sparging, and fermenting. These tanks are the mash tun, the boil kettle, and the fermenter." He pointed to each.

Stopping in front of a giant stainless-steel barrel with pipes and gauges, he patted it. "Next comes the mashing and lautering. The grist is then mixed with hot water in the mash-slash-lauter-tun to create the mash at a target temperature between a hundred forty-nine to a hundred fifty-five degrees Fahrenheit. The natural enzymes of the malt convert starches into sugars, which creates a sweet wort—the liquid extracted from the mashing process."

He looked at her for a moment to see whether, one, she was still interested and, two, to gaze at her beautiful face.

She nodded, intent on his lecture. "The lautering process begins by recirculating the wort to set the grain bed, then sparging—adding more hot water—to rinse the sugars out of the mash until sufficient wort is collected." He pointed to a bin. "The spent grains go to local livestock farmers for their animals."

"During the lautering process, the wort is heated in the boil kettle, reaching a boil by the time sufficient wort has been collected. While the wort is vigorously boiling, hops are added to impart bitterness, flavor, and aroma. We use pelletized hops in the actual brewing, but we keep these to show folks taking a tour." He dug his hands into a small wooden barrel, filling them, then turned to her. "These are the hops. Smell."

He held his hands out to her nose and she bent to sniff. "Hmm. They smell . . . earthy . . . nice." A wayward tendril of her hair tickled his hands, and he resisted the urge to drop the hops and touch the silky red strands. When he got her all to himself, the first thing he would do is pull her hair loose and run his fingers through it.

Refocusing his attention, he continued. "Different hops have different scents. Some have floral, citrus, or fruity notes. Some have none at all. Hops are only harvested once a year, and in the U.S., that's in October. What that means for my business is that I have to place my hops order a year in advance."

"Yikes! I can't imagine placing my coffee order a year in advance. How do you predict the quantity?"

"Good question." He dropped the hops back into the barrel and dusted off his hands. "You base it on past sales of the various beer types—what were the most popular. Since we only have a year's worth of data, we don't have much to go on, only instinct."

"At the end of this cycle, the burner is turned off and the wort is separated from suspended solids using the whirlpool technique. The whirlpool creates a vortex which causes most of the hops to separate from the liquid. Like a centrifuge." He gazed down at her. "Bored yet?"

She shook her head. "No, I love this stuff. Go on."

"Okay, don't say I didn't give you an out. Wort cooling happens at the heat exchanger on its way to the fermentation vessel. Hot wort is pumped in one side of the heat exchanger while cold liquor is pumped in from the other side. The heat from the wort is transferred to the cold liquor flowing in the opposite direction, which is recovered for cleaning and use in the next brew. The temperature of the cooled wort is typically sixty-six to six-eight degrees Fahrenheit, while the recovered water is typically about one hundred sixty degrees. Oxygen is added to the wort during run-out to the fermenting tanks. The water which is used to cool the hot wort is recycled into the process as hot water used in the mashing stage."

He took her hand in his and towed her along to a series of enormous conical tanks.

"These are the fermenting tanks. We've got thirty- and sixty-barrel tanks here," he turned and pointed to gigantic tanks, "and those big guys are one-hundred-twenty-barrel tanks."

Feeling bold, he wrapped an arm around her waist. When she didn't pull away, he relaxed, barely repressing a sigh of contentment. "This is where the yeast is added. After cell growth, the yeast then begins breaking down the sugars in the wort to form alcohol and $CO_2$. During this process, the tank is kept at a constant temperature to regulate healthy yeast growth and proper fermentation. Once the most active stage of the fermentation process is completed, the temperature may be raised to allow the yeast to consume unwanted byproducts, and some styles are dry hopped—more pelletized hops are added to increase hop aroma. The beer is then cold crashed to thirty-three degrees before being moved into a bright tank."

"Here," he took a miniature plastic cup out of a dispenser hanging on the wall and held it beneath a tap on one of the thirty-barrel tanks. A cloudy liquid filled the cup. "This has only been fermenting a day. You can see how cloudy it is. It's filled with live yeast."

She held the cup to her nose. "It smells like yeasty bread."

"Go ahead, take a sip."

Holding the cup to her lips, she took a tentative sip. "Tastes like beer, but it's pretty bitter."

"Yeah, it's over-hopped at this point. This will level off during the fermentation process."

He took the cup from her fingers and brought it to his lips to taste. Based on his experience, this yeasty bitter liquid would make the perfect IPA. Tossing the cup into a trashcan, he continued. "The energy the yeast obtains during fermentation allows it to multiply itself four or more times. This allows us to harvest the yeast for use in future brewing. We maintain our own yeast cultures. One of my employees maintains our yeast lab, ensuring the purity of the culture." He pointed toward the back of the building to a windowed room filled with beakers, a centrifuge, test tubes, and other paraphernalia one would find in a chemistry lab.

"Kind of like a baker maintains her own starter for sour dough bread," she interjected.

"Yeah. Brewing beer is more akin to baking than cooking. It's very precise."

"Something we have in common."

"Yeah." He pulled her close, his mouth inches from hers. "Chemistry is another thing we have in common." His mouth claimed hers, and he tasted the hops and yeast from the beer as his tongue tangled with hers. Desire went from zero to sixty in a matter of milliseconds. Her arms lifted to his neck as she attempted to plaster herself against him.

"Ahem."

They shot apart and looked in the direction of the voice.

"Sorry." A chagrined young man rubbed his nose, his face flushed with embarrassment. "I, uh, I'm just checking the tanks."

"Ricky Cregg, this is Kristen McKay."

"Yeah, hi. I come to your coffee shop."

"For a double shot with a splash of vanilla syrup." She laughed.

"That's right!" He grinned.

"Ricky is our quality control manager. He checks the tanks daily, tastes the brew, checks the $CO_2$ levels, and makes notes on these clipboards you see hanging on the tanks. I was just giving Kristen a tour. We'll just let you get to it. Next up is the bright tank." Wrapping his arm around Kristen's waist, Tyler led her to another tank at the end of the line.

"How many employees do you have?"

"Right now we're at twenty-four, that's including the Taproom, but I'm looking for an assistant cellarman."

"What does that person do?"

"They do packaging, kegging, moving and palletizing kegs, cleaning kegs inside and out, scrubbing tanks, floors, and everything else."

"Sounds like fun," she said, her voice heavy with sarcasm.

"Yeah, it's a tough job. Made tougher in the summer because the production area is not climate controlled, so it can be pretty warm with the heat generated from the equipment."

"It's toasty now, though."

Knowing how much Kristen hated the cold, Tyler was happy for the warmth.

"So, where were we?"

"Bright tank," she prompted.

Impressed by her level of attention, he nodded. "Right. Once in the bright tank, the beer is force-carbonated using a $CO_2$ stone then conditioned. 'Conditioning' is the process where the beer matures to the ideal state for consumption. At this point, the beer is then transferred into kegs, cans, or bottles for distribution."

He steered her over to the canning line. "We package the beer into half-barrel kegs, one-sixth-barrel slim kegs, seven-hundred-fifty-milliliter bottles, and twelve-ounce cans."

"Besides your taproom and other Northridge businesses, where do you sell your beer?"

"We only sell in Georgia, primarily in North Georgia, but we're expanding to South Georgia as well."

"Sorry. I get carried away." He shoved his hands into the pockets of his jeans and shrugged, a diffident smile on his face.

"No, I enjoyed it." And she had. Once, she took a tour of a coffee-roasting house in Atlanta and had been equally fascinated by the process and the pride that went into the work.

"How'd you get into this?"

He shrugged, hands still in his pockets. "I'm a science and math nerd. I like chemistry."

"Tyler Kincaide, you are far from nerd status."

"Oh yeah? Why's that?" He stepped into her personal space, filling her vision with strong, broad shoulders and a firm chest.

She set her hands on that chest and almost groaned with the heat of him beneath her palms.

"I don't know too many nerds capable of making a woman see stars when he kisses her."

"I make you see stars?" He wrapped his arms around her waist, hauling her against him.

"Mm-hmm." She lifted her face to his, hoping he would take the hint.

He did.

Claiming her mouth with his own, he kissed her senseless. But his hands stayed put, much to her dismay.

"Hey, boss! I'm heading home."

She pulled back, but Tyler didn't release her.

"See ya, Dave. Have a good night." His eyes never left Kristen's face.

"You too," Dave called.

"Oh, I plan to," he said with a grin that turned her insides to Jell-O.

"COME HOME WITH ME. We can order pizza and some wine and . . . talk. You'll be home in time to see Seth before he goes to bed," Tyler said.

Kristen lifted her green gaze to his, studying him. In that moment his happiness seemed to hang in the balance.

He wanted her in a way he'd never wanted any woman. And not just physically. He wanted to know what made her tick, what made her tough and resilient. What made her such a great mom to Seth.

He'd never know the joys of fatherhood, but it didn't keep him from admiring her dedication to her son. She wore her motherhood like a bad-ass superhero wore a cape. And it made her sexy as hell.

"Talk?"

"If that's all you want to do. But I'm not going to lie, I want to do more with you than talk." He stepped back from her, not wanting to pressure her with the evidence of his desire for her. "I'll leave it up to you. You know where I live. Either way, I'm stopping by Dominick's for a large pepperoni and mushroom pizza, then I'll be home."

He called to one of his employees. "Good night, Gina! I'm heading out. Lock up when you leave."

"Will do!" came a disembodied voice from the location of the grain room.

He ushered Kristen out of the brewery and into the cold darkening evening and over to her car. He bent to kiss her, tender and quick. "I'll either see you later or tomorrow. Your choice."

And then he walked away, leaving her to make her decision. The desire to look back pulled at him, but he kept striding toward his truck. Climbing into the cab, he pressed the starter button, backed out of the parking lot, and finally glanced into his rearview mirror.

She stood where he'd left her, by her car, staring after him.

He had no idea what she would do, but he sure as hell hoped he'd see her standing on his front porch after he got home.

# CHAPTER FIFTEEN

Kristen didn't know how long she stood rooted to the spot by her car door, watching the tail lights from Tyler's truck disappear around a bend in the road, but when she came back to herself, she was chilled to the bone.

Dropping into the driver's seat, she leaned her forehead against the steering wheel. What should she do?

She knew what she *wanted* to do, but what *should* she do?

She'd been down this road before, and it hadn't worked out too well. Unless she counted Seth, in which case, though it had been tough at the time, Tyler had given her a gift. But emotionally, could she handle it? Could she handle another broken heart at the hands of Tyler Kincaide? Because she knew damn good and well, she'd never be able to just have sex with him. She'd give him her heart.

But first things first. She had to tell him about Seth before things went too far. Before she could fall for him again, only to have him hate her when he learns the truth.

Next thing she knew, she found herself standing on his front porch, palms sweaty in the cold night air. "This is crazy." Her breath came in short, rapid pants, as if she'd run to Tyler's house instead of drove. She knocked on the door, her foot tapping restlessly.

The door flew open, and there he stood, a welcoming smile on his face. "You came."

She nodded, her mouth suddenly dry, and all thoughts of confession fled.

"Come in."

He'd just closed the door when she turned and pushed him up against it, her mouth reaching for his. He obliged, pulling her against him as his mouth devoured hers. He reversed their positions, pressing her into the door, the raised panels pressing into her back. She didn't care. There was only one thing uppermost in her mind. Tyler naked, his skin against hers, his mouth and hands on her body. Her mouth and hands on his.

He broke the kiss then studied her face. "I guess this means you want to do more than talk too?"

In response, she snagged him around his neck and drew his mouth back to hers. One of his muscular thighs found its way between her legs, and she moaned at the contact. His lips and tongue blazed a trail down her neck, as his hands tugged aside her turtleneck sweater. Damn the cold weather!

"Take me to bed," she muttered as he nibbled her earlobe, sending shivers along her spine. "Take me to the couch, the floor—I don't care, just take me."

He palmed her thighs, lifting her legs up and around him, and strode deeper into the house. She didn't know where he was taking her and she didn't care. Next thing she knew, her ass hit the soft give of a mattress, and he followed her down.

His bedroom then.

That thought flew from her brain as his big, warm hands slid beneath her sweater and up the sides of her ribs. God! It had been far too long. He might not even get her naked before she came.

Her hands found their way beneath his Henley, and she nearly cried with the pleasure. The skin of his back was smooth and warm, the muscles bunching and rippling beneath her touch.

"Kristen," he whispered. "I want to see you. All of you." He lifted the hem of her sweater and pulled it up and over her, the turtleneck snagging around her head.

"Jesus," she muttered from beneath the heavy knit, then giggled at the absurdity.

He chuckled then gave it another tug, yanking it free, grinning down at her, his hazel eyes dancing with amusement. Then his gaze traveled south, and amusement quickly turned to desire.

Kristen was lying before him, her creamy white skin glowing in the lamplight by the bed. Her breasts threatened to spill from her bra, and it would be fine with him if they did. They rose and fell with each shallow breath.

Straddling her, he lifted her head and took the clip from her hair. Spreading the gorgeous red strands out across his comforter and her bare shoulders, he ran an open hand down her chest, over her breasts, and along her exposed belly, stopping at the waistband of her jeans before skimming back up. Praising the creator of the front-clasp bra, he flicked it open and her breasts were bared to him.

"Beautiful."

"My turn." She grabbed the hem of his shirt and pulled it over his head. "That's how you remove a shirt," she said, humor in her voice.

"Hey. I wasn't wearing a turtleneck."

She froze, her gaze landing just below his right clavicle.

"It's a—"

She brushed her fingertips over the raised scar. "A port scar. I know what it is."

"That's right," he said, remembering. Her mom.

She propped herself on her elbows and kissed the scar, her lips like the wings of a butterfly against his skin. He closed his eyes against the emotion that welled up inside him. The few women he'd been with since Celeste had chosen to pretend the scar didn't exist, but not Kristen, and her straightforward approach left him feeling both vulnerable and trusting.

He tilted her chin up and captured her mouth with his again, guiding her back down to the mattress. Her breasts pressed against his bare chest, their nipples hard, and he had to taste her.

Taking a tawny nipple into his mouth, he sucked hard, taking pleasure from the moan that rose in her throat. He directed his attention to the other breast, as his hand skimmed the smooth flesh of her belly. Faded stretch marks evidenced her pregnancy. He reached the button on her jeans and flicked it open. Gliding the zipper down, her hips rose to meet his hand, yearning for his touch.

Right back atcha', he thought. As anxious as she was to be touched, he was to touch her. Sliding his hand inside the open fly and into her panties, he nearly wept at the warm wetness of her. His eyes on her face, he stroked her. The flush covering her cheeks and neck, the stubble burn on her breasts from his unshaven face, filled him with a desire to mark her.

Bending, he clamped his teeth into the tender flesh of her belly and she hissed out a breath that quickly evolved into a sigh. He watched as the red mark rose on her skin.

She twisted and turned on the bed, her hips rotating to meet his hand. "Tyler, please, now!"

She didn't have to ask him twice.

Reaching into the nightstand drawer, he drew out a condom. Making quick work of his jeans and boxers, he rolled the condom on then directed his attention to removing the remainder of her clothes.

She was lying on his bed, her glorious red mane spilling around her, the patch of hair between her legs a deep russet.

He leaned over her, bracing himself on his arm. "Open for me," he whispered into her ear. He drove into her, and his world focused on nothing but where their two bodies were joined.

Tyler filled her. Clasping tight onto his back, she opened herself to him. As he thrust into her, he whispered into her ear. "God, Kristen, you feel so damn good. So beautiful. So fucking sweet." The words became incoherent, as he lost himself in her, but those first few phrases lifted her.

He braced himself above her on one elbow then raised her hips with the other, driving into her deep and hard.

She felt the tension building in them both, knew he was getting close, just as she was. "God, Tyler!"

"I've got you, baby. I've got you."

And before she could respond, the explosion rocked her

to her core, shooting up her spine and down her legs, leaving her limp and shaken. He groaned one last time and collapsed onto her, his breath harsh but warm in her ear.

They were lying there, a tangle of limbs, as their breathing returned to normal. Only then did he rise to discard the condom, and she all but whimpered at his absence.

"When?" Her voice came soft and tentative.

"The year I turned thirty."

"Hell of a milestone birthday."

"Yeah. Wondered if it would be my last birthday, much less my last milestone birthday."

After inhaling a few slices of Dominick's pizza, he'd lit a fire in the brick fireplace in the living room and spread out blankets on the floor, where they laid entwined and sated after their second round of lovemaking.

"What kind?"

"Hodgkin lymphoma."

"And?"

"And I'm now almost five years out. My last check-up was all clear." Except for the *little* problem of my sterility. But he wasn't ready to share that bit of news yet.

She nodded. "Good. I'm glad to hear that." Her fingers traced a pattern across his chest, raising gooseflesh. "How did you find it?"

"January of that year, I developed a persistent cough that I couldn't shake. No fever, no congestion, just a dry cough. Then came the chest pain. I brushed it off as soreness from the cough. It wasn't until I noticed a steep drop in my stamina, especially during a run or weight workout, that I sought a medical opinion."

After a battery of tests, including bloodwork and chest X-ray, followed by a CT scan, the news he'd received shook his world.

Cancer.

He recalled sitting in his doctor's office, letting the words about chemotherapy and radiation, side effects, and survival rates wash over him as his brain struggled to comprehend his diagnosis. He didn't get sick. He sure as hell didn't get cancer. He wanted a second opinion.

His doctor had been gracious, agreeing that a second opinion is never a bad idea.

Hearing the diagnosis a second time didn't make the shock of it any easier.

Realizing this was his *life*, he'd delved into everything he could find on the disease, the treatment, and the prognosis. He lived in a city with some of the top cancer centers in the world. Surely this would be to his advantage, he had thought.

"Telling my family had been the hardest part. My mother and sister cried. My father simply told me I'd beat it, and my brother echoed those sentiments. I knew my family would be by my side through it all. Through the six months of chemo, followed by another two rounds of radiation. Through the hair loss and weight loss, the nausea and vomiting, the extreme fatigue, the blood transfusions, the hospitalizations, and the abandonment of my fiancée— they'd been there in one way or another. As had Zach."

"Wait. What?" Kristen rose to her elbow and stared down at him, eyes wide and mouth agape. "You were engaged . . . and she *left* you?"

"She dumped me, while I was in the hospital, no less.

She came into my room all teary-eyed and said this wasn't what she'd signed up for, and when I wouldn't take the ring from her, she set it on the bedside table, kissed me on the forehead, and walked out without a backward glance."

"Jesus," Kristen said under her breath.

"In Celeste's defense, she'd watched her father unsuccessfully battle pancreatic cancer and had dealt with its aftermath. On some level, I got that she didn't want to go through it again." But dammit. They had been about to take vows that they would love one another in sickness and in health. Even so, as much as it had hurt, it was better she'd left *before* they were married.

When his own father had been diagnosed with prostate cancer, his mother would never have dreamed of leaving him. That's what marriage was supposed to be. Through thick and thin. For better or worse.

Kristen snorted with a note of derision. "Is that why you returned to Northridge?"

"Yes. After my cancer was declared in remission, I took a long hard look at my life and decided I no longer wanted the long hours and stressful work environment. I'd faced my own mortality and a change was in order, so I moved back to Northridge to recover and rethink my career."

Now, after follow-up visits every three months for the first two years, then every six months for three years, he'd almost made it to the all-important five-year mark.

He'd manage to escape the hearing loss, pulmonary fibrosis, and chronic respiratory issues that often came after treatment for Hodgkin's, but the one thing he had not escaped—sterility.

And because of that, he owed it to any woman with whom he might be forming a relationship to address the fact that if their biological clock demanded children, he wasn't their guy. At least Kristen already had her son, so maybe it wouldn't be as important for her.

He pulled her back down into his arms, giving her a squeeze. "I'm glad you came by the brewery today."

"I really enjoyed the tour today. Thank you for sharing what you do."

He shook his head, chagrinned. "You're just saying that."

"No, really. I enjoy learning new things. I once took a tour of the coffee-roasting house in Atlanta that supplies my beans. It was fascinating."

"Tell me about it."

She sat up, a frown on her face. "Really?"

"Sure. Why not?"

"Well, okay. But don't say I didn't warn you." She laid back in his arms. "Well, before the beans arrive at the roasting-house in Atlanta, they're processed in their home countries to increase revenue to coffee-producing countries like Ethiopia, Costa Rica, Haiti, and Ecuador."

He fiddled with her hair, enjoying the silky feel of the red locks between his fingers. How long he had yearned to know how they felt between his fingers, along his bare chest, between his thighs . . . and now he knew. Heavy as satin, soft as a feather. The flicker of firelight lit it in burnt reds, brilliant golds, and warm umbers.

"I'm boring you, aren't I?"

He mentally shook himself. "No." Quite the opposite in fact, he noted, as his body rose to the occasion. Again.

"At the roasting house, the coffee's sorted. At smaller operations, this is done by hand. In larger operations, the bags of green coffee beans are dumped into a hopper and screened to remove debris."

He liked how her green eyes lit up as she warmed to her topic.

"The green beans have little to no taste. It's the level of roasting that brings out the flavor—light, medium, medium dark, and dark. Kind of like your barley."

"I like mine dark roast."

"I know," she said with an eye roll. "I've pretty much memorized my regular customers' preferences."

"Even mine?"

"Even yours." He liked the flush that covered her cheeks when she admitted that. "Then the beans are weighed and transferred by a conveyor belt to storage hoppers, then to the roasters."

She rolled onto her side and propped herself up on her elbow. With her free hand, she began running her fingers along his chest, up and down, up and down.

He bit back a moan of pleasure.

"Initially, the beans are heated by the roasting machine. But at some point the beans begin heating themselves, so adjustments have to be made. Kind of like the yeast when it starts producing $CO_2$," she said, remembering his comments earlier in the day.

Speaking of heating themselves . . . he closed his eyes in ecstasy.

THE FIRE at her back warmed her bare backside, while the man at her front warmed lots of other places.

"When they've reached the desired roast, they're dumped from the roasting chamber and air-cooled with a draft-inducer."

A soft snore rose from the man beside her. "You've got to be kidding me," she muttered.

Next thing she knew, she was on her back and two hundred twenty pounds of hard male were on top of her. He looked down at her, his eyes sparkling with mischief. "Just kidding."

"You brat," but her words held no heat. She wiggled, situating him perfectly between her legs, and he groaned.

Leaning his forehead against hers, he sighed. "You fascinate me, Kristen McKay."

She froze. "No, I don't."

He rose onto his elbows and she could feel his gaze on her face. "What did I say?"

She looked away. "I'm just Kristen McKay from Northridge, Georgia. I've never been any further than Atlanta my whole life. How could I possibly fascinate anyone, much less you?"

"You have a bad habit of underestimating yourself." He brushed the hair off her forehead, kissing the now-bare skin, his lips warm and comforting. He rolled off her, and she felt bereft of his heat and weight. Before she could complain, he wrapped his arms around her.

"Kristen, you are so smart, and you work so hard. You get up at four-thirty in the morning, when the rest of the world is sound asleep, to make food to feed the hungry folks of Northridge. You study reading trends to fill your bookshelves with the most relevant reads, everything from local authors and books on local history to national and international bestsellers. You provide a quiet, welcoming place for visitors and citizens alike to catch up on email, study for exams, or write the next great American novel. You rescue kittens and support your community. But most importantly, you raised a terrific human being."

As he spoke, tears backed up in her throat and guilt threatened to choke her.

"You're putting yourself through school, running a business, and raising your son. You've sacrificed so much to accomplish your dream. It hasn't been easy for you, but nothing worth having ever is. I could learn so much from you. I already have. So don't ever underestimate yourself."

Her heart had cracked open and all the self-doubt and negative voices spilled out. A sob rose in her throat, and she covered her mouth to keep it from escaping.

No one. Not a single living soul had ever told her these things. No one. Until Tyler.

She had to tell him. She knew that. But not yet. Because when she did, Tyler would never want to speak to her again.

Kristen reluctantly pulled her jeans on and stepped into her knock-off Uggs, dreading the cold, damp air of the misty night. This had been a pleasant interlude, but she had a son waiting at home and a paper due tomorrow.

"Don't you think it's about time we went on a date?" Tyler's question interrupted her thoughts.

"A date?"

"Yeah, you know, two people, dinner, maybe a movie. A date."

She'd just had sex—three times—with Tyler, but the thought of a date with him filled her with panic.

What did she know about dating? She couldn't recall dating in high school, much less after having Seth. The closest thing she came to dating was grabbing a pizza with Zach before Olivia moved back home.

And the guilt returned. Ten-fold. She should tell him now, before this went any further.

Sensing her reticence, he drew her close, his still-bare chest pressed to hers. "I want to treat you. You deserve it."

But with his arms around her, did she really want to ruin this wonderful evening? This . . . *détente* of sorts? The scent of him filled her and she caved. "Yes. I'll go on a date with you."

*Kristen McKay, since when did you become a coward?*

# CHAPTER SIXTEEN

"Too bad we don't wear the same size shoe," Kristen muttered as she eyed a pair of red-soled Louboutins. Poor she might be, but she did love shoes.

"This brings back memories of me seeking your advice when Zach asked me out for my birthday." Olivia sighed dreamily as she scanned her closet for something Kristen could borrow for *her* date with Tyler.

"No. Don't even go there. It's nothing like that."

"And why not? You know you want him. And you know he wants you." She shrugged as if it were all a foregone conclusion. "Stop fighting it. And him."

*Too late for that piece of advice.*

"Ooh! This." Olivia held up a luxurious emerald green cashmere sweater dress. "Perfect! It'll look smashing with your red hair, peach skin tone, and green eyes."

"It will also be too tight and too long." Kristen folded her arms across her chest.

"Tight is good." Olivia held the dress up in front of Kristen. "And it looks like it will hit just below the knee. Sexy, but without being blatant."

"I'm not trying to seduce Tyler." She already had. Well, let's be honest, she'd attacked him is what she'd done.

"Uh-huh." Olivia held Kristen's gaze in a game of chicken, and Kristen flinched.

"I slept with Tyler," Kristen blurted, as she studied the dress.

"Well," Olivia slapped her hands on a shelf stacked with gorgeous cashmere sweaters. "It's about damn time. Wait." Her brow furrowed. "Wait. You haven't been on your date yet."

Kristen shook her head. "No. I mean, yeah, I slept with him last week, but . . . I meant that I slept with him once before that. The night before he left for Princeton." She bit her lip, wondering if she should have kept that second part to herself. But now that it was out there, she was relieved to have told someone.

"Oh. *Oh!*" Olivia sank onto a bench in the spacious walk-in closet, draped the dress across her lap, and propped her elbow on her knee, her chin in her hand. "Come on. Spill it."

"You got any more of that red wine?"

"Sure. Help yourself." Olivia pointed to the bottle on the dresser where she'd set it earlier.

Kristen poured herself a healthy serving then took a gulp to bolster her courage. Sharing her deep, dark secrets wasn't in her DNA. Taking a seat next to Olivia, she took a deep breath and shared the whole sordid tale.

"You remember the party at Billy Bing's house?"

"Sure. It was a bit on the wild side." The understatement of the year.

Thanks to some older friends, the alcohol flowed freely, and it wasn't long before most of the partygoers were drunk, especially Tyler. Kristen, on the other hand, hadn't drank much. She'd seen what happened to her mother when she drank, and Kristen didn't want to lose control.

"Well, I found myself dancing with Tyler, his arm wrapped around my waist, doing his best imitation of dirty dancing."

Olivia snorted at the vision that likely conjured of Tyler, the cute math nerd dirty dancing.

"He had his thigh between mine, and he was nibbling at my neck, and, well . . . he was the first guy who didn't look at me like I was just a piece of ass."

"Oh, Kristen." Olivia reached out and squeezed her hand, and her eyes stung with emotion from the genuineness of the gesture.

She shook her head. "Anyway, we left and went to Tyler's house." His parents had lived in a modest three-bedroom house a few doors down from the party.

They'd walked hand in hand, Tyler murmuring sweet things in her ear—not the usual trashy sex talk from the few other guys she'd been with—how pretty she was, how much he liked her, how her hair smelled like strawberries.

They sneaked through his darkened home to his basement bedroom. His parents had renovated it for him, so he had his own bath, kitchenette, and living area, leaving the two other bedrooms to his younger brother and sister. There, in their own private sanctuary, better than anything Kristen had ever had, she'd given herself to him.

"I had the breakfast shift at a diner over in Doraville, so after he fell asleep, I left." In the wee hours of the morning, not wanting to wake him, she'd left and walked the two and a half miles back to her mom's trailer.

"Did you leave a note?"

"Yes." She still remembered exactly what she'd written:

*Thanks for everything. Call me tomorrow.* "I didn't sign the note. I didn't think I had to."

"What happened?"

"Nothing. Tyler left for New Jersey the next day and I didn't hear from him again."

"Oh, honey." The look on Olivia's face said it all. "Okay. First, why haven't you said something to him?"

"Because I was hurt. And angry. And not a little ashamed. Maybe he thought I was just another fuck. McKay the Lay strikes again."

Olivia choked back a cough. "Tyler? You should know better. He doesn't have a player's bone in his body."

Kristen sighed. "I see that now."

"And as for your 'reputation,'" Olivia made air quotes around the word, "that wasn't true, was it?"

Kristen lifted a shoulder, uncomfortable with the question. "Did it matter? I was trailer trash, so everyone assumed . . ."

Olivia lifted a hand. "You'll get no judgment from me. And," Olivia continued, "Tyler can't handle liquor."

"I didn't know that then."

"No. You wouldn't have. But you know now. Have known since Oktoberfest. Why not talk to him about it then?"

The discomfort of confronting the lies she'd built up in her head made her face flame with heat. "Pride?"

"You have to tell him."

"But what if he's horrified that I threw myself at him? What if he thinks I'm a slut?"

"Oh please," Olivia said in exasperation. "Like he'll think you're a slut for sleeping with him seventeen years ago."

Kristen watched as realization dawned on Olivia's face.

"Seth?"

The wine Kristen had guzzled to give her courage now felt as if it would make a return visit. Swallowing hard against the bile in her throat, all she could do was nod. Heat suffused her face and suddenly the voluminous closet was too close. She sprang to her feet and stepped out into the bedroom.

"Kristen," Olivia's graceful hand landed on her shoulder, delicate as a butterfly. "Honey, you have to tell him."

Kristen's eyes filled with tears. "I know." She also knew this would be a touchy subject for Olivia, who grew up not knowing who her father was. It wasn't until her eighteenth birthday that she'd found out he'd died a year earlier. It had created a rift between her and her mother for many years. Then, just earlier this year, she'd found her half-sisters on a DNA site and finally learned the truth about her father.

Tears burned the back of Kristen's throat, and Olivia wrapped her arms around her, pulling her into a hug. Kristen sniffed and Olivia released her to snatch a Kleenex out of the box on the dresser.

"Why didn't you tell him at the time?"

Kristen huffed out a laugh. "I tried. I left messages with his roommate at Princeton. He never called me back."

Olivia stepped back then picked up her own glass of wine. "Well, that certainly explains your anger. But he deserves to know now."

"I know, I do. It's just, can't I just enjoy this a little longer?" Her emotions, which she always managed to hold in check, had been so close to the surface these last few weeks. She twitched under the weight of Olivia's stare and sighed. "Because when I do—bye-bye, Tyler."

Olivia glanced down at the dress still in her hands and then back up at Kristen. "You don't know that."

"Oh please," Kristen echoed Olivia's earlier sentiment. "We both know Tyler will never trust me again."

"If he cares about you, he will. Now, are you going to try the dress on or not?" Olivia held up the green cashmere dress.

Kristen looked away. Dammit! "Oh, all right. I'll try it on."

She tried to snatch the dress out of Olivia's hands, but Olivia pulled it back. "You have to tell him. Promise me."

# CHAPTER SEVENTEEN

Sᴉᴛᴛɪɴɢ across the candlelit table in an intimate little French bistro on the outskirts of Atlanta, Tyler couldn't take his eyes off Kristen. With the candlelight catching strands of her hair, turning them to molten gold, she looked beautiful —if not a little uncomfortable—in the sleeveless bottle green sweater dress she wore.

When he'd removed her coat in the restaurant, he couldn't help but notice the way the cashmere knit hugged her every curve, stopping just below the knee to reveal shapely legs displayed to perfection in those high-heeled ankle boots so many women favored. He'd thoroughly enjoyed the view as she'd preceded him to their quiet table in the corner.

Her hair hung in waves past her breasts, surrounding her in a mass of fiery red. He'd never seen her hair down, at least not in public. She always wore it up—in a ponytail, a messy bun, or a braid. The look softened her features and amped up her already off-the-charts sensuality.

The waiter approached to take their drink order. "Wine?" Tyler asked her.

"Um, sure." He'd never seen Kristen seem so unsure of herself. She fiddled with the silverware then finally took the linen napkin and laid it across her lap.

"Red or white?"

She looked up startled. "Oh, um, red."

"We'll have a bottle of the Merlot."

The waiter left them to peruse the menu. The restaurant served a delicious four-course *prix fixe* menu with two choices for each course. He considered the herb and lemon poached artichokes appetizer and the warm goat cheese salad followed by the cassoulet. And for dessert, he couldn't resist the crème brûlée taster. Decision made, he set aside his menu and considered Kristen, whose face bore a look of bemusement, as she chewed her lower lip.

"See anything you like?"

She closed her menu and flashed him a tentative frown. "I can't decide. I'll just have what you're having."

"Great. Snails, oxtail soup, and beef tongue it is."

"What?" She squeaked, her eyes growing round as an owl's.

He chuckled. "I'm kidding. I'm having the artichokes, salad, and cassoulet."

A relieved smile lit her face. "Oh. Okay. Sounds delicious."

"You should do that more often."

"Order the same dinner?"

"No, smile. It looks good on you."

A blush tinged her cheeks. Another look he'd rarely seen on her. Until they'd made love, that is. Then he'd seen that peach blush suffuse her from face to breasts. He twitched in his seat, becoming uncomfortable with the result of those thoughts.

The waiter returned with the bottle and served the wine before taking their orders.

At his departure, Tyler lifted his glass in a toast, hoping Kristen would follow suit. She did, lifting her glass, along with an inquisitive brow. "What are we toasting?"

"Feature films, economic development, book signings, and . . . friendship."

FRIENDS? Is that what they were?

Kristen took a sip of the wine. She was no connoisseur, but it was definitely better than any wine she'd ever tasted. She took another sip then set the glass back on the linen-covered table.

Recalling her conversation with Olivia, she knew she had to tell Tyler the reason for her animosity all these years. Like Olivia had said, if he truly didn't remember, and apologized, then maybe they could move forward with friendship, if nothing else. And if he did remember, and didn't apologize, then fuck him.

Regardless, she had to tell him about Seth. She winced inwardly at her cowardice.

But not yet. *Please.* She wanted to enjoy this rare evening out while she could. Maybe pretend for a little while that the man across from her admired and respected her, even thought her beautiful and . . . smart. Something few people thought when considering Kristen McKay.

A C-student, she'd graduated high school by the skin of her teeth. She hadn't thought an education, even high school, would do much to advance her life. Unlike many of her classmates, college didn't seem to be an option in her future at the time.

She was destined to be a waitress working for two-dollar tips at the local diner, or a hair dresser like her mother, toiling over the hair of people in her same boat—eking out a living, so what good were straight A's?

For something to do in the awkward silence that followed the toast, she picked up her glass again, and glancing around at the other couples in the dimly lit bistro, she felt out of place alongside their intimate body language, whispered words, and seductive smiles. She took a sip and set the glass down again, nervous and unsure of what to do next.

The chic hostess escorted a voluptuous young woman wearing an eye-poppingly low-cut dress and her date to seat them at the table behind them, and it struck her once again, her lack of experience in the world of dating. The couple couldn't be much older than their early twenties, and here she was some ten years older going out on her first real date, as nervous as a teenager.

Apparently the voluptuous young woman was seated facing Tyler, because she saw his eyebrows lift in consternation, and then he pointedly looked elsewhere.

Shifting her gaze to the surroundings, she admired the simple, clean elegance of the place, the white linen table-cloths, votive candles, and gleaming silverware. She'd never been anywhere so . . . upscale. Feelings of imposter syndrome rose to the, surface making her fidget in her chair.

Tyler leaned across the table and, with an impish grin, whispered, "Do you have to pee?"

A snort escaped, followed by a giggle. "No." She appreciated his lightening the mood, reminding her that just because they were in a fancy restaurant didn't mean she had to be all stiff, formal, and uncomfortable.

"Relax. Stop squirming and enjoy yourself."

Nodding, she lifted her glass for another drink. Over the soft murmur of the other diners, she heard the waiter asking the young couple what they would like to drink. The young man sang the praises of Argentinian reds, instructing his date on the ins and outs of red wine. She could just imagine the dignified waiter's reaction to this pompous dissertation and smiled.

Apparently, Tyler had heard it too, because he shook his head with a soft laugh. Then his gaze held hers. "I don't think I told you how beautiful you look."

She shook her head. "You don't have to tell me that."

"I know I don't. But it's the truth."

The heat rose in her face. "Thank you."

"The chef would like to present this *amuse-bouche*," their waiter said, as he placed a small plate in front of each of them displaying what appeared to be a small cheese puff.

She looked up at the waiter a little confused. She hadn't ordered this, had she?

"It's complimentary. A free appetizer if you will." Tyler popped the puff into his mouth.

"Oh." Kristen followed suit, and nearly whimpered as the flavors of warm gooey brie and raspberry burst from the flaky pastry.

"Good, huh?"

"Delicious."

The rest of the meal awakened Kristen's senses. The sights, smells, and tastes were tantalizing. Such simple foods that carried such intense flavor.

After a lifetime living on Hamburger Helper, Ramen noodles, macaroni and cheese, and canned vegetables, this was like entering a whole other world she never knew existed.

The sweet, light, airy crème brûlée they'd had for

dessert had been orgasmic. It had taken every ounce of her self-control to hold back the moan when she took her first bite.

"We'll have a glass of port, please," Tyler told the waiter when he came to clear the dessert plates.

The waiter nodded and left to do Tyler's bidding, and a comfortable silence descended at their table.

"Sir," the waiter intoned at the table behind them, "are you still working on that tart?"

Startled at the waiter's unintended double entendre, Kristen lifted her gaze to Tyler's and couldn't hold back a laugh. Covering her mouth, she snorted, as Tyler chuckled, his chest heaving with the effort to hold back his outburst.

They finally caught their breath, but it didn't last. Every time their eyes met, they both snickered like two kids. Even after their delicious port arrived, they continued to titter at the waiter's unfortunate word choice.

Tyler reached across the table for her hand and began to stroke the back of it with his thumb. Little tremors of pleasure set the otherwise quiescent butterflies in her stomach into motion. "Thank you."

Surprised, she blurted, "For what?"

"For joining me tonight. For agreeing to go out with me. For looking so beautiful."

"After this sumptuous and very expensive dinner, shouldn't I be the one thanking you?" she replied, his thumb continuing its back and forth motion across her hand, reminding her of what else his brilliant hands could do.

"It was my pleasure." His gaze held hers captive. "What are you doing tomorrow?"

❄

SHE STIFFENED at his question and withdrew her hand. "What did I say?"

Placing her hand in her lap, she shook her head and her gaze skittered away. "I have to go somewhere tomorrow. All day."

"Okay." He eyed her body language. Where she had been relaxed, she was now strung tighter than Seth's bow. "Kristen, I'm not trying to pressure you, if that's what you think."

Releasing a sigh, she turned to look at him again. "I'm sorry. It's just that . . ." this time she drew in her breath, "I'm going to Buford—to Phillips State Prison—to visit my father." Her shoulders hunched, the tension in her neck visible.

"I didn't realize you maintained a relationship with him."

"I haven't. He called. A few weeks ago. Said he was dying. This will be the first time since he was arrested that I've seen him." Her voice was flat, devoid of the emotion one wouldn't expect from a child whose parent was dying.

Tyler sat back with a groan. On one hand, he hoped for Kristen's sake that the man wasn't toying with her. On the other, dying in prison was a shitty hand. "Would you like me to come with you?"

Her eyes lifted to his in surprise, but then she shook her head. "No. I'd rather not air my family's dirty laundry in front of you."

"I don't have to come in. I can just drive you."

"No. Thank you. This is something Seth and I have to do on our own."

"So, this will be the first time he's met Seth," Tyler said, stating the obvious.

"Yes. I talked to Seth about it and he said he wanted to meet him."

"Well, if you change your mind, let me know."

"Thank you."

"Thank you—for sharing. For opening up. It means a lot to me."

Her eyes appeared to glow with unshed tears. Damn. He hadn't meant to upset her. "You ready?" At her nod, he rose and held out a hand to her. Accepting it, she stood and picked up her purse, but before she could move away, he wrapped an arm around her waist, pulled her to him, and pressed a kiss to the top of her head.

He could have sworn he heard a sniffle.

## CHAPTER EIGHTEEN

THE NEXT DAY, Kristen hovered in the doorway of the prison's visitor room, struck by the changes in her father. Twenty-five years changed a person in the best of circumstances. Twenty-five years in prison even more so. And her father's illness had taken its toll on top of that.

There was no denying his liver disease. Sickly yellow skin hung on his thin frame, and as she approached the table and he blinked up at her, she could see the jaundice in his eyes. Guess he wasn't playing her for a fool after all.

Family members filled the cold institutionalized room, visiting other prisoners, the hum of their voices punctuated by the occasional burst of laughter.

He rose from his seat at the round plastic visitor's table, and she could see the effort it cost him. "Kristen." He nodded, then his gaze cut behind her where Seth stood. "Who's this?"

She suppressed the shudder in her breath and signaling to Seth to step forward said, "This is Seth. Your grandson."

"My—" his eyes shot to her face, "grandson?"

"Yes." Her voice was barely a whisper.

"Seth, this is your grandfather, Jerry."

Seth, her sweet, polite son, stepped forward and held out his hand to shake. "Sir."

He took Seth's outstretched hand into his own frail one, the withered and wrinkled snake tattoo slithered down his arm. Her father's eyes filled with tears, and a tired smile crossed his features. "Well, I'll be damned. Good-looking kid."

"You would have known that, but you never bothered." The bitterness rose in her chest again, swamping any feelings of sympathy for him.

Jerry sank back into the plastic chair as if his legs would no longer support him and released a heavy sigh. "I understand your resentment. Really, I do. And I know I have a lot to make up for. I only hope you'll let me." He lifted his gaze to hers and held it, unflinching.

"We'll see. In the meantime, get to know your grandson while I get some coffee." She pointed to the coffee pot in the corner. "I'll be right over there."

KRISTEN BEAT a rhythm on the steering wheel, glancing over at her son whenever it was safe to take her eyes off the road, wondering what he was thinking. Had it been a mistake to bring him to meet his convicted felon of a grandfather?

"Would you like to stop for dinner at Sweet Tomatoes in Duluth?"

"Sure," he muttered.

Unable to take it any longer, she asked, "What did you and your grandfather talk about?"

Seth shrugged. "What I like to do. My violin playing. School. Just . . . things."

Though generally quiet and introspective, she sensed a disquiet in her son. "Seth, honey, did I do right by bringing you to meet Jerry?" She couldn't think of him as Dad or Grandad.

He finally turned to look at her. "Yeah, Mom. You did. It's fine. I just have a lot of questions."

"That's fair. Shoot."

His mouth lifted in a smile. "Well, my questions are more for him. Questions I didn't think to ask when I was there."

"Like what?"

"Like whether he missed watching you grow up. Watching me grow up. What life is like in prison. Things like that."

Silence descended, then within the constraints of the seatbelts, he shifted in his seat to face her. "Did you know he took up painting in prison?"

"No, honey. I don't know anything about what the last twenty-five years of his life have been like." And don't really care.

"Why didn't you want to see him? I mean, I understand you were probably hurt and angry over what he did, and you and Grandma being left to struggle. But, was it worth losing a relationship over? Is forgiveness that difficult?"

Kristen fidgeted in her seat. At first, she swore she would never forgive him. He'd made a choice that removed him from their lives, and though he would never have won Father of the Year when he had been around, he had at least kept the wolves from their door with his job as a long-haul truck driver.

As she grew up, she only thought of him when she and

her mother didn't have enough to eat or when there was no heat, and she'd been filled with anger and resentment toward him. After she'd had Seth, the only thing she could focus on was keeping a roof over their heads, food on the table, and the utilities on. She didn't have the luxury of time to reflect on her broken relationship with her father.

Then her mom got sick, and she resented him all over again. Resented him for leaving her to face her mother's illness and subsequent death alone.

"It's complicated."

"Is it?" Seth asked with a note of skepticism in his voice.

She had no response to that, and at her silence, Seth returned his attention to studying the scenery flying past at sixty miles an hour, leaving her to wonder if she could forgive her father, if only for Seth's sake.

A few days later, Kristen knocked on Tyler's door, dilapidated laptop in hand, to go over the notes for the PowerPoint presentation she was putting together for the EDC. Just yesterday, her used commercial fridge went on the fritz, resulting in a repair bill she wasn't expecting and the bad news that she'd likely need a new one in the next few months. She'd asked the guy if he could find her another used refrigerator.

She shifted on her feet, anxious to get started, and had just raised her hand to knock again when the door swung open. All thoughts of unexpected bills fled. Tyler filled the doorway clothed in nothing but a towel, his wet tousled hair dripping on his broad bare shoulders. She swallowed then licked her suddenly dry lips. "Hi."

"Hi." He followed the line of her gaze, which had

landed squarely on his naked abs, then chuckled. "Sorry. I thought I could manage a quick shower before you got here. Come in."

He stepped back and she brushed passed him, inhaling the scent of his soap or shampoo. She watched a runnel of water as it rolled down his chest. Maybe she should just catch that with her tongue. You know, to help him dry off.

"Ahem. My eyes are up here," he said, humor in his voice.

"Right." Heat suffused her face. "So, why don't you, um, get dressed, or . . . something." Dammit. She sounded like she'd just sprinted to his house from her café.

He chuckled. "Make yourself at home. I'll be out in a minute."

She followed his departure, admiring the tight ass wrapped in navy terry cloth. "Get a grip, McKay. You came here to work, not to jump Tyler's bones. Focus." Setting her computer on the dining room table, she wandered around his living room, picking up family photos and putting them down, running her hand over the back of the massive leather sofa, and otherwise exploring Tyler's things.

The last time she was there, she'd been too distracted by Tyler's other, um, things, to notice his home. It was the classic American Craftsman with lots of natural wood, leaded glass, and built-in shelves. The brick fireplace with its enormous wood mantel served as the room's focal point.

She shivered when she recalled the things they'd done in front of that fireplace.

The sound of a cell phone came from the direction of his bedroom, then she heard the soft murmur of his voice. Deciding he might be a few minutes, she pulled up a chair at the table and opened her laptop then clicked on the notes for their presentation.

Her phone buzzed with an incoming text. Thinking it might be from Seth, she took it out of her jacket pocket to see it was from the repairman. A buddy's father was closing his restaurant and had a two-year-old Arctic Air two-door refrigerator/freezer. She nearly gagged when she saw the asking price.

"Problem?" Kristen sat at the table with her head in her hands. He hoped it wasn't bad news about her father.

Her head flew up in surprise, then she signed. "No . . . yes. No."

"Okaaay." He approached the table and set a hand on her shoulder. The tension there worried him. Placing his other hand on her other shoulder, he began to knead the golf-ball-size knots there.

She groaned and dropped her head, giving him better access to her tightly corded neck.

"Damn, Kristen. You're wound tighter than a torsion spring." She rolled her neck and tendrils of her hair brushed the backs of his hands. It reminded him how her hair felt between his fingers, the silky feel of it across his bare chest, and the tumble of it on the pillow. A tightening in his groin reminded him it had been a week since he'd been inside her, learning all her sounds and pleasure spots, and he longed to be there again. *Down boy.* Right now, he needed to find out what was wrong and figure out how to help.

"What's wrong?"

She huffed out a laugh devoid of humor. "Name it. My fridge decided to stop working, my car needs a new radiator, Seth needs knew shoes, Cinnamon needs vaccinations. My business and I *need* the economic boost the film location approval could provide. This is not just a nice idea. I need it to become a reality." The desperation and passion in her voice went straight to his heart.

Before he could speak, she rose from her seat and paced into his living room. "When Seth was gone, I was living on Ramen noodles and mac 'n cheese for God's sake. I've scrimped and saved and tightened my belt so much I squeak. I live in a shithole. My car is one road trip away from the junkyard. When I buy clothes," she held up a finger for emphasis, "which is hardly ever, I buy them at church bazaars and consignment shops. I have jeans older than Seth. I don't know how much longer I can hold on, and I'm tired. So tired. Catering for a film crew, attracting fans of the book—I need this." She rubbed her temple as if she had a headache.

He followed her into the room. "But from the looks of things, your business is a success. Breakfast attracts a good crowd. The café is frequented by townies and visitors alike. You have fantastic reviews on Yelp, your social media, and your website. You now have a book club and a writing group who meet there once a month. You've created a warm, welcoming environment. What am I missing?"

She threw up her hands. "It's show. It's all show. You know the whole adage 'if you want to be successful, you have to look successful'?"

"And the four- and five-star reviews? Are those for show?"

"Well, no. At least I hope they're real."

He hated to see her fear, but he loved that she felt safe opening up to him. And he wanted to help. But he knew she would never take money from him or anyone else. Maybe he could assess her books, see if he could find ways for her to cut expenses without cutting the quality of her product.

"Okay. We all need this location agreement. But in the meantime, why don't we go over your business expenses and see if there are places you can cut back."

She gnawed on her lower lip, her hands shoved into her back pockets, thinking.

Rather than prod, he waited for her to make up her mind, hoping she would trust him.

"Okay."

"Okay?"

"Yes." She nodded.

Kristen returned to her laptop, and he took a seat next to her as she opened a file folder that contained subfolders from the years since her café had opened. Clicking on the current year, icons for each month appeared. Impressed by her organization, Tyler bit back a smile. His accountant father would be proud.

After opening the September file, Kristen rotated the screen in his direction. He scanned the numbers in the Excel spreadsheet, which included the typical expenses for a business like Beans 'n Books—coffee supplies, baking supplies, paper goods, books, utilities, some social media advertising, rent, a payment to Patti Cotton, the previous owner of the bookstore, Calypso's salary, and Kristen's salary.

He noted Kristen's salary was half what she paid Calypso. He also noted she had a small business loan.

The anxiety rolling off Kristen was palpable, and he caught the nervous bounce of her knee beneath the table. Scrolling down the document, he stopped when he got to the net sales column. Then sat back in shock.

※

Kristen fidgeted in her seat. It was as if she'd revealed her bank account to someone, and in doing so, also revealed her lifelong economic struggle. Having sex with Tyler for the first time after seventeen years was easier than this. She felt more naked and exposed here than in his bed.

He sat back, and unable to stand another moment, she said, "Say something."

"This is your net sales for September?" he pointed to the number in the column.

"Yes." Her stomach roiled. She knew it. He was shocked at how bad her business was doing. How close she was to going down the tubes.

"And last month's?" he continued.

"About the same." Her voice sounded small to her own ears, and her lips felt numb and tingly. "But I had the added expense of repairs to my oven."

"The previous months? How comparable were they to this month?"

She shrugged. "About the same, give or take a few hundred dollars or so. Net sales are going up, but only marginally."

"And after you pay your expenses, what do you do with the net proceeds?"

"I either put them back into the business in the form of improvements or new equipment, or I move it into a savings account." She twisted her hands in her lap. "Why? Is it worse than I thought?"

"Well, let's put it this way, you can certainly afford to pay yourself more than you're paying your one employee. In fact, you could probably hire another employee or two *and* pay yourself more." He moved to look at her. "Kristen, with numbers like those, your business is already a success."

"But—" She shook her head, confused.

"No buts." He turned and took her by the shoulders. "Listen to me, your numbers are those of a healthy, growing business, not one about to go under."

That can't be right. Maybe she's not explaining things correctly.

He released her then scrolled back up through the document. "Some things to consider . . . start paying toward the SBA loan principal to pay it off sooner. You can afford it, even if it's only a hundred dollars a month. You could also afford to pay Patti more toward that principal if you want."

Still unable to believe what she was hearing, she sat biting her lip until his thumb and forefinger pulled it out from between her teeth. "And one more thing . . . buy yourself and Seth a nice juicy steak every now and then. You've earned it."

An hour later, Kristen clicked save on the presentation file. "What we discussed doesn't change anything." The presentation was coming along, but it still needed a few tweaks. "I'm determined to win over the EDC and get approval for this location agreement."

"I'm with you." He sat back with a sigh. "Why don't we see if Seth wants to meet us at Dominick's for pizza?"

Every time Tyler mentioned Seth, Kristen's innards tied themselves into knots. She'd promised herself she'd tell him after the presentation, and no matter how much it would hurt, she would accept the consequences of her actions.

"He can't. He's meeting with a violinist from the Atlanta Symphony Orchestra who has agreed to work with him until he returns to New York in January."

"All right. I have a better idea. Why don't I order

delivery from Dominick's and," he leaned over and nuzzled her neck, nipping at her tender flesh, making her shiver, "see if we can find some way to entertain ourselves."

"What do you have in mind?" She tilted her head, giving him better access to the desired spot. "No, let me guess—Gin rummy. No, wait, Monopoly." She snorted with laughter at her own joke.

"Strip Monopoly." He skimmed his hand down her arm, then back up.

"Mmm. Wait." She sat back. "How do you play strip Monopoly?"

"Instead of cash, players use items of clothing to buy property or pay rent." Taking her by the arm, he hauled her onto his lap then slid a warm hand beneath her sweater, settling it at the curve of her waist.

She wrapped her arms around his neck, enjoying the feel of his arms around her. That wasn't the only thing she enjoyed, she thought, as she squirmed against his erection, making him groan.

"Keep that up and you can forget about the pizza."

She wiggled again. "Oh yeah? Why is that?"

"Because, woman, I'm going to lie you down and have *you* for dinner."

"Promises, promises," she muttered against his neck and wriggled again.

"All right. That's it. Don't say I didn't warn you." He rose from the chair with her in his arms and carried her to the hearthrug like she weighed no more than a child.

As soon as he planted her butt on the floor, he pulled her sweater off in one swift move, then to her surprise and chagrin, blew a raspberry on her belly. She squealed and fought to curl into a ball, but he pressed his mouth to her stomach again and blew another raspberry. "Stop!" she choked out around a giggle.

His only response was to do it again. "Why?"

She laughed and squealed, gasping for breath. "It tickles!"

"Doesn't tickle me a bit." Another raspberry.

Her gales of laughter left her breathless and dizzy, as she writhed against him.

He stopped long enough to say, "I love the sound of your laughter," then his mouth struck again before he glided up her body to plant a kiss on her lips.

She struggled beneath him, irritated that she secretly enjoyed the weight and warmth of him. "Get off me."

"Who knew you were so ticklish," he said, before pressing another kiss to her lips.

In a vain attempt to maintain her guise of annoyance, she bucked her hips once more, trying to dislodge him. "Get. Off," she ground out.

"Oh, I plan to. But ladies first," he said with a wolfish grin.

# CHAPTER NINETEEN

TYLER ROSE and rolled over to lie next to her, and as he gazed down at her, all the playfulness in his eyes fled. His eyes darkened to a deep blue pool in the dim light of the room. "You have no idea how beautiful you are, do you?" Not waiting for a response, he dropped his head and kissed her long and thoroughly, his tongue tangling with hers, stealing her breath and sending her pulse into overdrive. She arched up, wanting his hands on her.

She slid her hand down his back. When she hit the waistband of his jeans, she slipped her hand inside, reveling in the feel of his warm, firm ass. She gave it a squeeze and he moaned into her mouth. Reaching back, he took her wrist, removing her hand from his pants. Breaking the kiss, he pressed his lips to the inside of her wrist, sending a shiver down her spine, then lifted her arm above her head. "Ladies first, remember?"

"But—"

"No buts. Lie back. I want to love you from the top of your head to the tips of your toes."

Said toes curled inside her fleece-lined boots at the thought.

"First, let's get you out of these clothes."

"Can I at least help?" she asked, then bit her lip.

"You can do more than help. Undress for me." He sat up and propped himself on this elbows.

Feeling a little self-conscious, but anxious for his hands and mouth on her, she sat up and shed her sweater, followed by her bra. Tyler's sharp intake of breath spurred her on, as she toed off her boots then wiggled out of her jeans and panties in one move.

"Take your hair down."

Reaching up, she pulled the hairband from her ponytail, then shook her hair out. Completely naked, she laid back on the plush rug. His gaze raked her, leaving tendrils of heat behind, as if he'd touched her with his warm, calloused hands.

Despite her high school reputation, she had limited experience with men, especially since Seth was born, but she could honestly say no one made her feel the way Tyler did. Sexy, beautiful, and above all desirable.

He emitted a deep growl then rolled to his side and, brushing aside her hair, nuzzled her neck, nipping and kissing. His mouth, hot and wet on her skin, shot heat straight to her belly. As promised, he worked his way down her body, his hands skimming, his tongue grazing, until she writhed and whimpered with need. "Please, Tyler," she intoned. "Please."

"I plan to please, baby. Don't worry."

When he took a hard nipple into his mouth, she almost came undone. Fingers grasping his hair, she arched into him. He focused his attention on her other breast, paying homage to it before continuing his southbound tour of her body.

He nipped at the tender spot behind her ankle and she cried out. Who knew her ankles were so sensitive? On his return trip up her body, he parted her thighs, scraping his coarse stubble along the tender skin. She gasped at the delicious abrasive sensation on her delicate flesh. He settled himself there, draping her legs over his shoulders.

His tongue caressed her and she nearly came out of her skin. "Tyler. Oh, Jesus, Tyler!" She twisted beneath him as the first contractions of her orgasm unfolded. With a shuddering cry, she exploded into a million tiny sparks.

Tyler stroked her thighs as she floated back down to earth, limp and boneless. Pressing one last kiss on her heated flesh, he crawled up her body and grinned down at her as only a self-satisfied male can. "Pleased?"

She rolled her eyes. "You know I am." Reaching up, she palmed his face and lifted her mouth to his, tasting herself there. She shifted, reversing their positions so he laid on his back beneath her, her breasts pressed flat against his chest. "Your turn."

Kristen's hair fell around them in a fiery red curtain as she bent over him, her cheeks flushed, her lips swollen from his kisses. He'd never seen anything so beautiful in his life. She skimmed her hand down his chest, making short work of the buttons on his flannel shirt, but his thoughts were several steps ahead, yearning for her touch, her hands on his bare skin, her mouth caressing him.

Peeling back the shirt, she lowered her mouth to his nipple, licking and sucking, giving him the same treatment he'd given her just minutes before. "God, Kristen, you're killing me!"

"Turnabout is fair play," she said with a smug grin, before returning to her exquisite torture. Writhing, he hissed out a breath as her teeth clamped down on him. "Mother!"

"Definitely not." She giggled. He convulsed when she pressed her hand against his throbbing erection. "Oh my." She tsked. "Let's see what we can do about this." She shucked off his jeans and boxers, then skimmed her body up his, her hard nipples grazing his abdomen, making his hips rise of their own volition.

"Now, Kristen. Now," he growled.

"Soon." Kristen slid back down his body, her long red hair covering him like a silk blanket. He'd never seen anything so erotic in his life. A fantasy come to life. Kristen's naked body entwined with his, her slender arm thrown across his chest. Then her mouth began to do amazing things to him. Just as he thought he couldn't take another moment, she wrapped her hands around his erection and lathed him with her tongue. "Fuuuck."

Before he could come, he grasped her arms and hauled her up and onto her back. Reaching for his jeans, he fumbled with shaking hands for the condom he'd conveniently slipped into the pocket. His hands trembled so with lust he could barely get the thing on, but once he did, he entwined his fingers with hers, lifting them above her head. "I won't last long."

Thrusting her hips against his, she said, "I don't care. I just want you inside me. Now."

He plunged into her, making her gasp, but she wrapped her legs around him, taking him deeper. "Jesus, Kristen. I can't . . ." He drove into her once. Twice. And on the third stroke, he lost it, giving in to the demand for release. As his climax shook him, he took her mouth with his in a punishing kiss, not relinquishing his hold until the last of the tremors rolled away like the aftershocks of an earthquake.

Rolling off her, he pulled her half onto his still-heaving chest. "You okay?"

"Mmm." Her arm draped across him heavy and warm, her face pressed to his chest.

"I'm sorry. You unmanned me."

He felt her cheeks lift in what he presumed was a smile. "Good," she murmured. "That was the plan."

He tightened his arms around her. "I wish you could stay. I'd like to wake with you in my bed."

She groaned. "To be honest, I'm not looking forward to going back out into the cold. But duty calls."

Kissing the top of her head, he released her and rose to dispose of the condom. When he returned, she was sitting up, and had collected her clothes and was sorting through them. "I know my bra is here somewhere."

"Behind you."

"Oh. Thanks."

Her cheeks were flushed, her hair tousled, her eyes bright. She was gorgeous.

Still naked, he knelt beside her and, cupping her face, he pressed his lips to hers, soft and tender. Grasping his wrists, she sighed into his mouth, and his body sprang to life again.

Breaking the kiss, she glanced down then back up at him, a brow lifted. "Already?"

He gave her a rakish grin and shrugged. "I can't take the blame. It's all on you, babe."

Running her hands up and into his hair, she bit his

lower lip. "Well, since it's my fault, I should at least do something to, um, rectify the situation. It's the least I can do."

NOT THAT SHE didn't believe what Tyler had told her about her business finances, but she needed to hear it from another source. Growing up financially insecure, she had no basis for knowing how much was enough. No matter how much money her business was making, no matter how much she was putting into savings, it never seemed enough. She could run the numbers all she wanted to, but she still couldn't believe it.

The receptionist interrupted her thoughts. "Kristen? Marshall is ready for you."

She entered the all-too-familiar office with her laptop tucked under her arm, knowing Marshall would tell her the cold, hard truth.

"Morning, sugar. Come in. Come in."

Marshall's warm demeanor never failed to soothe her. "Thanks for seeing me on such short notice."

"It's no trouble. Had a client reschedule a meeting, so I had an opening. What can I do for you?"

"Could we just go over my monthly reports?"

"Sure. Is there a problem?" His brow furrowed in concern as he put his horn-rimmed glasses on.

"No. At least I don't think so. I was hoping you would tell me what you think."

Marshall joined her at his small conference table. "Let's see what you've got."

After showing him the last six months' numbers. He sat back in his seat, removed his glasses, and rubbed his eyes, his movements making her nervous. Chewing her lower lip, she waited for the verdict.

He replaced his glasses, looked her in the eyes, and said, "I knew you were a smart business woman, but even I underestimated just how smart. You've built yourself a successful business, Kristen. I'm proud of you. Damn proud."

His words settled deep into her bones. Kristen McKay had made Marshall MacKinnon proud. There were no more powerful words than that. Tears burned her eyes. "Thank you, Marshall. Coming from you, that means a lot."

He patted her hand. "Keep up the good work."

"I plan to, especially if the Town Council approves the film location application."

"They will. They may be hard-headed, but they aren't stupid."

"Tyler suggested paying more on the principal of my two loans. What do you think?"

Marshall studied her a moment before responding. "Tyler, huh?"

"Yes. We're, uh, working together on the investigation for the EDC."

"Well, considering how successful he's been, I think only a fool would disregard his suggestions when it comes to money."

Kristen nodded. "I'll start paying toward the principal next month." She closed her laptop and rose. "Thank you, Marshall, as always."

"My pleasure, sugar."

As Kristen turned to go, Marshall spoke again, "And, by the way, you could do a lot worse than that young man."

❄

Tyler checked the $CO_2$ gauge on the fermenting tank and absent-mindedly rubbed the tightness in his chest. He shouldn't have picked up that bag of barley yesterday by himself, but no one else was around and he wanted to get it out of the way. He must have pulled something.

Jotting the numbers into a spreadsheet on his iPad, a tremor of awareness ran up his spine, and he paused.

After his morning run today, he'd been coughing, but had chalked it up to the cold, dry air. Now, with the tightness in his chest, a memory nudged him. A memory from five years ago, when he'd thought he'd had a chest cold or pulled a muscle in his chest. Two seemingly innocuous symptoms that changed the course of his life.

He knew half the recurrences of Hodgkin lymphoma happen within two years of primary treatment, and up to ninety percent occur before five years. He was months away from his five-year mark.

Tamping down the paranoia, he reminded himself that he had just had his check-up in October and that everything had been fine. But still, as another cough fought its way up his airway, the concern nagged at him. Had he been tired lately? Sure. But that could be the result of late nights with Kristen. Did he lack his usual stamina during his run? Maybe. But again, see above.

Determined to set it aside for now, he moved on to the next tank and the next $CO_2$ gauge in his inspection.

"You okay?" Kristen asked him a couple of hours later, as she set a glass of water on the counter in front of him.

He leaned against the island in his kitchen and gave her a wan smile. "Not so much." He lifted his arm and coughed into the crook of his elbow. He'd only put in a half day at the brewery, leaving the rest of his to-do list in the capable hands of his staff, but he felt like he'd run a marathon.

Reaching out, she touched his forehead with her cool hand. "No fever." She studied him. "You should call your doctor."

"Yeah, I know. It's just . . ."

As if reading his mind, she continued. "Tyler, it's likely nothing, and why borrow trouble when you can just see your doctor and get answers?"

"You're right." He smiled to reassure her, and maybe himself. "It's probably nothing."

"I'll go with you." She laid her hand on his shoulder and it felt warm and comforting.

"You will?" The offer shocked him. After what she'd been through with her mother, he knew it couldn't be easy for her to sit through doctors' visits and lab and radiology tests with him.

"Of course."

That she would offer meant everything to him. "Can you stay a little while?" He nuzzled her neck, reveling in the shiver that rippled through her, then withdrew to look at her.

She rolled her eyes. "Men. Nothing keeps you from sex."

He tugged the hairband from her hair. "Neither snow nor rain nor heat nor gloom of night . . ."

"That applies to mail carriers," she scoffed.

He shrugged, "Same goes for men and sex." He brushed his thumb over her lower lip and watched as her pupils dilated and her breath caught. "What do you say?"

"Mmm. You keep that up and how can I say no?"

❄

"That's the plan." He buried his face in her hair, his breath warm on her neck. "I need you, Kristen." He shuddered against her.

Her throat tightened, and she lifted her hand to stroke his hair. "Shh. I'm here." Taking his hand, she drew him along behind her to his bedroom. "Sit."

He sank to the edge of the bed, and she removed his shirts, baring his smooth muscular chest. Grazing her nails across his skin, she knelt to remove his shoes and socks, setting them aside. Skimming her hands up his denim-clad legs, she reached for the button at the fly and popped it open, her eyes on his face, she slid the zipper open. "Lift up." He obeyed, and she shimmied his jeans and boxers off and tossed them aside. "Lie back."

Rising, she quickly shucked her own clothes beneath his heated gaze. Naked, she crawled up the length of his body.

He hissed in a breath at the delicious friction of heated skin against heated skin. "Kristen." He cupped her jaw, skimming his thumb over her cheekbone. There was something in his eyes, something that set her heart aflutter and made her stomach quiver.

Straddling him, she bent and took his mouth with hers, melding their lips in a kiss that held more than physical passion. Bracing herself on one arm, she guided him home with the other. Their eyes met and held as he entered her, slow and easy, and her breath caught at the raw emotion on his face.

"Don't move. I just want to feel you against me, around me." He stroked her from nape to ass and back again, his fingertips eliciting a frisson of pleasure. Finally, he began to move with long, slow, sure strokes, and she threw her head back at the sheer enormity of the feelings coursing through her. Joy. Tenderness. Contentment. All overlaid with the pure carnality of riding him, taking her pleasure from him, even as she gave pleasure in return.

She knew at that moment things were different. That their relationship had grown beyond just passion and into something . . . more.

Clasping his hands in hers, she raised them above his head, taking the lead as her hips picked up the pace. The orgasm hit her with the impact of a meteor, shattering everything in its path, tearing down barriers, leaving her exposed and vulnerable.

Tyler slammed into her once more, then with a strangled cry, followed her into the wreckage that had once been her fortress. "I love you."

Oh God. She squeezed her eyes shut. What had she done?

# CHAPTER TWENTY

Memories of her mother's battle with cancer haunted Kristen. She had hoped to never set foot in a hospital again, and yet here she was, with the possibility of losing another person to the shitty disease.

A person she cared about. Deeply.

And Seth? Could he lose the father he doesn't even know he has before he even gets to know him?

Tyler had confessed his love for her. A confession she was not yet ready to make. He'd been composed in the face of her failure to reciprocate the declaration. He'd simply gathered her in, kissed her forehead, and in his physical and emotional exhaustion, fallen asleep.

For her part, sleep was long in coming after she got home. She wrestled with her feelings until the wee hours of the morning. Did she love him? She didn't know. And if she loved him, shouldn't she tell him the truth?

*Damn right, you should tell him.*

But not now, she argued, rationalizing this was not the time to break such news to him. Not with the possibility of recurrence hanging over his head. All the reassurances she tried to give Tyler, and here she was jumping to a terrible conclusion. In need of a distraction, she pulled out her phone and texted Calypso to see how the morning rush had gone.

The radiology waiting room was full of people—young and old, sick and well—waiting their turn. Tyler had been called back about ten minutes earlier for a CT scan of his chest. Then they'd head over to the lab for a blood draw. Tomorrow, he'd see his doctor for the results. Almost twenty-four hours from now. And until then, they would both be on pins and needles.

She tried to keep a positive attitude, especially in front of Tyler, but she was worried.

She'd sat in waiting rooms like this when her mother was ill. She snorted. Well, not quite like this. Her mother had been treated at the indigent hospital in Atlanta, since her mom had had no insurance. This was like the Taj Mahal compared to where her mother had received treatment.

Her phone buzzed with an incoming text from Calypso: *All Good. No worries.*

Now what?

She picked up a glossy home décor magazine and flipped through it without actually seeing the photos or the text then put it down. Rising, she walked over to the coffee pot and poured herself a cup, splashed a bit of cream in, and stirred. *Blech.* Apparently, even state-of-the-art hospitals weren't immune from serving bad coffee.

Or maybe she'd become a coffee snob.

The hands of the utilitarian clock on the wall appeared to have hardly moved. The radiology assistant had said it would take about thirty minutes. How much longer? Not that they would know anything, but she wanted him with her, by her side, where she could see him. Touch him. Assure herself he would be all right. Everything would be all right.

*It would, wouldn't it?*

Only it hadn't been for her mother. She collapsed in the chair behind her, her legs shaky and weak with fear. She caught the sympathetic glance of the older woman across from her, a bag in her lap filled with colorful yarn, her knitting needles clicking rhythmically. "I found that knitting helps," she said, her movements sure and efficient. "Occupying my hands takes my mind off . . . the what-ifs," she added, a sad smile lifting the corners of her mouth. "Would you like to help? I have a hank of yarn that needs rolling."

Kristen couldn't wipe the eager look off the woman's face with a no, so she nodded. "Sure."

"I'm Harriet, by the way."

"Kristen."

"Nice to meet you, dear."

The woman set aside her knitting and pulled a beautiful blue yarn from the bag and unwound it. After setting up the process, she unwound the yarn from the hank and into a tidy ball, speaking all the while.

"Is he your husband?"

"Oh. No. Just . . ." She shrugged, unsure what to say. *You know, the father of my son, who he doesn't know is his.*

"But you love him. Anyone could see that." Her hand flew, the ball of yarn growing bigger with each revolution.

"Oh. I—we've only been dating," if that's what they were doing, "for a few weeks. Too soon to fall in love," she said off-handedly. *But apparently not too soon for Tyler.*

"I don't know about that. I met and married my Phil in the space of six weeks. When the sparks fly, you just know. There's no minimum time requirement." Harriet leaned over conspiratorially. "I won't say there weren't times when I just wish the man would find something useful to do," then she sat back, "but I wouldn't trade a day of our fifty-seven years together."

Fifty-seven! Until now Kristen couldn't imagine spending a year with someone, much less fifty-seven. Would she still feel then what she feels now? she wondered. Or does it change? Does it ebb and flow, grow stronger, or worse, grow tedious?

"When Phil got sick the first time, we thought our time together was coming to an end." She shook her head, obviously recalling a grim memory. "Almost died." Her face brightened, "But then he went into remission and for six years had been clear of the cancer. Now it's back, and in more places."

Kristen's heart ached for the couple. They'd had so many years together, but when you loved like that, were they ever enough, she wondered?

"I'm sorry." Her words felt empty, but she knew nothing else to say.

Harriet shook her head. "Don't be sorry, dear. We've had so many good years together. And though it might sound trite, a love like ours never dies."

Kristen cleared her throat and blinked away the tears.

Tyler returned to the waiting room to find Kristen in conversation with an older woman, blue yarn wrapped around her extended wrists. The older woman wound the yarn into a ball with quick, practiced movements. Before he could say anything, she looked up and, for a moment, he saw tears shining in her eyes.

What had they been talking about to make her look so . . . not sad, but wistful? But a smile lit her face now, causing the woman to turn in his direction. He couldn't regret telling her he loved her, even though she wasn't ready to reciprocate. She just needed a little time, and he'd give it to her.

"Ah, your young man." She reached out and slipped the yarn from Kristen's wrists. "Go. I can finish this later. I'll enlist Phil's help," she said with a wink at Kristen.

Kristen rose and Tyler strode over to her, wrapping an arm around her and pulling her to him. He basked in the warmth of her after the cold radiology room.

"Tyler, this is Harriet." Kristen extended her hand toward the woman. "And this is Tyler."

"Pleased to meet you, Tyler. You've got a good one there." Harriet jutted her chin in Kristen's direction. "Don't let her get away."

"Thank you and no, ma'am."

"You two, scat. My Phil will be out any minute now and he'll be craving Cracker Barrel." She sat and began packing a knitting bag filled with colorful yarn and knitting needles of various sizes.

Kristen knelt in front of the woman and touched her on the arm. "It will be all right. Everything will be all right."

Harriet nodded. "It will."

"You can relax, Tyler. What you've got is a good old-fashioned viral infection."

After a long, lonely sleepless night running through worst case scenarios, the breath left his lungs in a *whoosh* and he sat back in his chair. "Really?"

"Really. It's been going around. You're like my tenth patient this week with the same symptoms. No fever, just a dry, hacky cough and fatigue. The soreness in your chest is just your muscles protesting the exertion."

Kristen reached over and gave his hand a squeeze.

"Go home. Go to bed. Get some rest. It should play itself out in a day or two. If not, give me a call."

After checking out at reception, Tyler and Kristen walked hand in hand out to the parking garage. He'd been grateful for her presence and support. He knew what it cost her emotionally, given what she went through with her mother. And it was one of the reasons he believed she loved him. She wouldn't be here if she didn't.

When they reached his car, he escorted her to the passenger side, but before he could open the door for her, she reached up, cupping his face and kissed him. Soft and tender, telling him with her mouth how relieved she was.

Then he remembered and pulled back. "No. It's a viral infection. I don't want you to get sick."

"I've been around you all week. If I was going to catch it, I already would have." She studied his face, her hands still warm on his cheeks, and kissed him again, this time pressing her entire body to his, from soft breasts to firm thighs. And infection be damned.

He turned them around, pinning her between him and the car. The primal rush of survival and the need to reaffirm life surged through him. He inserted his thigh between hers as his hands found the hem of her sweater and burrowed under the warmth to feel the silk of her skin.

She drew in a breath then, fingers grasping his hair, she changed the angle of the kiss, increasing the heat and want of it. Sliding a hand around and along her ribs, he palmed her breast through her bra, eliciting a breathy moan from both of them.

The *beep-beep* of someone locking their car door echoed through the garage, startling them apart, both panting like they'd just run the Atlanta Marathon. He pressed his forehead to hers with a rueful laugh. "Guess I'm not all that sick."

"No," she said on a shaky laugh.

"Come home with me." It wasn't a question.

She said yes, as if it was, and the relief he'd felt since he'd received the doctor's news turned to unadulterated joy.

"A game of Sexy Nurse McKay sounds like fun," he said with a wink.

LATER THAT EVENING, Tyler laid in his bed, Kristen's luscious curves tucked up against him. A fire in the fireplace set the room aglow with flickering oranges and golds, casting intermittent shadows around the room. Outside a cold rain whispered against the roof. He stroked his fingers up and down the curve of her hip, the silky skin rippling beneath his touch.

Tyler had noticed a softening in Kristen recently, but especially today with Harriet. Oh, she could still let a zinger fly, but she had a new warmth and compassion about her. Or maybe it had always been there and she'd just kept it tucked under the armor she wore. He'd certainly witnessed it in her relationship with Seth. And now in her relationship with him.

"Thank you," he whispered.

She lifted her head to look at him. "For what?"

"For coming with me today."

She laid her head back down on his chest and sighed. "I wouldn't have been anywhere else."

"But I know how difficult it is for you to get away from the café."

"I've got Calypso. I've got to trust her. After all, that's what I pay her for. And Seth helped out after school."

That was new. The controlling Kristen would never have said that.

"I hope it wasn't too difficult after what you went through with your mother."

"I won't lie, it wasn't easy, but not hard enough to keep me from going."

Recalling his mother's conversation about Kristen's childhood, he said, "Tell me about your mother. I didn't really know her."

Shifting so that she was lying on her back, she stared up at the ceiling, but a sad smile lifted the corners of her mouth. "She wasn't exactly June Cleaver. She smoked and drank, and after my father's conviction, had a string of no-good boyfriends. But she was my mom." She shrugged as if that explained it all. Her eyes closed, and he thought that was the extent of her response.

"Some were abusive," she continued, "her boyfriends, I mean."

He tensed next to her. "Did they ever touch you?" he asked, with barely suppressed anger.

"Once. My mother was at the beauty parlor. He backed me up against the ancient stove, stuck his tongue in my mouth." She shuddered, and Tyler's hands curled into fists. "But a well-placed knee to the nuts took care of the bastard, and he never touched me again."

"He live around here?"

"No. None of them did. Most were long-haul truckers like my dad. Why?"

"Because I'd like to castrate the son of a bitch."

Kristen laughed at that. "I heard he died a few years later—accident on I-85 just outside Atlanta."

"Karma."

"Maybe."

"How old were you?"

"Fifteen."

"Did you tell your mom?"

"No. They broke up a few days later. I'd like to think I had something to do with that."

She laid silent a few beats, lost in thought. "Anyway, Mom and I scraped by on the living she made from her tiny two-chair salon, but there were times when we didn't have food or heat. When I was old enough to work legally, I took waitressing jobs to help make ends meet. The tips I earned helped. We were always living on the razor's edge, but my priority became keeping the utilities on."

"That's why you hate to be cold."

She glanced up at him in surprise. "Yeah."

THAT HE'D NOTICED and figured that out touched her more than she would have thought.

"When did your mom get sick?"

Relieved that Tyler skipped over the Seth backstory, she said, "Seven years ago. She fought it for five years, then it finally got the better of her."

He pulled her close. "I'm sorry."

"Yeah, me too. The one plus from my mom's illness—if there can be a plus to having terminal cancer—no more asshole boyfriends. In the remaining years of her life, we became close—closer than we'd ever been, which made her death even more difficult." She blinked back tears, surprised that her mother's death still had such an affect her.

"And the café?"

Sounded like a change of subject, for which she was grateful. "One of the many places I'd worked was Dominick's, where I learned the secrets of dough and baking. Their garlic rolls are made in-house. Did you know that?"

"I didn't," he said with smile.

"I found solace in working the dough and transferred that to skills I'd learned working in a bakery in Doraville. I was taking classes online and the bakery hours worked well with my schedule—early morning hours at the bakery from four to seven a.m.—then I had the rest of the day for classes and homework. I loved the work so much, I even considered changing from a business degree to culinary school—until I saw the cost of tuition."

"Okay. So, that's where you gained your masterful baking skills. When did you decide to start your own business?"

"I was never going to get ahead working for someone else. About the time my mom died, the bookstore in town went on the market. I knew that was my chance. It was now or never, I thought. My mom had a small life insurance policy, and I used it as the down payment on what would become the café and bookstore. And the rest is history."

Other than the crackle of the fire, the room lay silent, and she thought he'd fallen asleep.

"You're the bravest person I know." His arms tightened around her, and guilt threatened to suffocate her.

"No, I'm not." *I'm a coward.*

He rolled over, covering her, his hands smoothing the hair from her face, as he pinned her with his gaze. "You are to me."

"Tyler, I—"

"Shh." He pressed his lips to hers. "Let me love you now."

And being the coward that she was, she let him.

# CHAPTER TWENTY-ONE

"What do you have going on this weekend?" Zach asked, as he pulled up a barstool Thursday afternoon in the Taproom. Still in uniform, Tyler knew he hadn't come by for a drink.

"My dad's sixty-fifth birthday is Friday. The whole family will be in town, and Mom's making a special dinner."

"Sixty-five? Wow. That's a landmark birthday. Tell them I say 'hi,' and tell your dad I say 'Happy Birthday.'"

"Will do." He nodded. "Why d'you ask?"

"I'm baching it this weekend. Olivia's been asked to teach a master class for the Miami City Ballet, so I thought you might like to go into Atlanta, maybe catch the Falcons' game on Sunday."

"I could do Sunday."

"Great. I'll check with my buddy to see if he's using his tickets." Zach tapped the bar in a sign of *that's all I needed,* and stood up.

"So, I've invited Kristen over for it," Tyler blurted. "My dad's birthday, I mean."

Zach sat down again. "Wow. Family function. Sounds like you two are getting serious."

Were they? Tyler wondered. He shrugged. "Nah. It's not like she doesn't already know my mom, and . . . it's just a big family gathering."

Zach rubbed his chin. "Still . . . involving her in your family's celebration is a pretty significant step. Things must be going well."

*Things* were going well. But what exactly did that mean? Were they a *thing*, or did *things* refer to the improvement in their relationship?

"Yeah," he responded with a touch of hesitation. Then he nodded. "Yeah, they are."

"Well it's about damn time. You've lusted after her for as long as I can remember."

Tyler paused in thought as he propped his elbows on the bar. "It's not just lust. It's—I don't know—strong like?" Heat suffused his face at the confession.

"I see." Zach grinned. "Well, lust and strong like is better than outright animosity."

Scratching his chin, Tyler said, "The animosity was totally one-sided. I never had anything against Kristen."

"You find out why she, well, loathed your very existence?"

Tyler laughed, in spite of himself. "No. And at this point, I'm not sure I want to know. Whatever it was, she's clearly gotten over it. Why dig up old hurts, real or imagined?"

"Can't argue with you there."

"I NEED YOUR HELP." Kristen pressed the phone to her ear

with her shoulder as she scanned the pitiful contents of her closet. She was angsting way too much over this. It wasn't as if she and Tyler were getting married, just because he told her he loved her.

"What's up?" Olivia asked.

Kristen told her about the invite to Tyler's parents' house.

"Chill. You be you," Olivia said. "His parents are going to love you. Besides, his mom already knew you and everyone else in the high school."

Yeah, thought Kristen, that's what I'm afraid of. His mom knew more about her than many in town do. Deep-rooted feelings of inadequacy sprang to the surface.

Tyler wasn't the only Kincaide child to attend a prestigious college. His younger sister Megan attended Brown University, and his younger brother Joshua graduated from MIT. And she was just Kristen McKay—from the wrong side of the tracks.

"But what should I wear? Jeans? Slacks?" Did she even own a pair of slacks? "A dress?" Not that she had many of those either.

"Well, you don't want to look like you're trying too hard. Since it's his dad's birthday and it's only family, I doubt it's dressy. I think a nice pair of jeans and maybe a sweater."

Nice jeans. Right. Kristen lived in leggings, *worn* jeans, T-shirts, and sweaters.

"Or maybe some leggings and a tunic," Olivia continued.

Leggings and a tunic. She might be able to swing that. Along with the boots she'd worn to Atlanta with Olivia.

"Done. Should I bring something?"

"Why not bring some of those sinful dark chocolate pecan brownies you were selling last week?"

She could do that. "But what if they have cake?"

"Then they'll have cake *and* sinful dark chocolate pecan brownies."

"Mom, you remember my . . . friend, Kristen."

Kristen didn't miss the hesitation, and felt certain neither had his family. But she didn't know whether to be relieved not to be introduced as his girlfriend or hurt.

She often saw Tyler's mom in Smith's Grocery, but other than a nod of greeting, they never spoke. She wore her dark blond hair in a stylish cut with shoulder-length layers. Highlights blended away the gray and enhanced the golden lights in her amber eyes.

"Of course."

"Mrs. Kincaide." Kristen extended her hand but found herself wrapped in a warm embrace instead.

Out of the blue, tears stung her eyes. Not that her mom had been that demonstrative, but she did bestow the occasional hug, especially after she became terminally ill. Realizing far too late how much she'd failed her daughter.

"Please, call me Abby," Tyler's mother said, releasing her.

"And call me Neil." A tall, handsome older man stepped up next to Abby and wrapped his arms around her waist. She saw where Tyler got his hazel eyes. Tyler's father had a head full of salt-and-pepper hair, making those gorgeous eyes stand out. She cut a glance at Tyler, wondering if she was seeing him in another thirty years. Not that she'd be with him thirty years from now. Maybe not even thirty *days* from now. Especially once she worked up the courage to tell him the truth.

"Thank you," Kristen said, as Neil helped her take off her jacket. She turned to see him hang it in the closet behind her.

"These are for you." Kristen handed the twine-wrapped baker's box to Abby.

"Oh! You didn't have to, but thank you! If you made them, I'm sure they're delicious."

The sound of girlish giggles came from the next room.

"That will be my granddaughters Maddie and Shelley." Abby's face beamed with pride. "Come in and make yourself comfortable."

Kristen had been in Tyler's house. Once, seventeen years ago when they'd sneaked into his basement bedroom for the night Tyler apparently didn't remember. She hadn't noticed her surroundings then, she'd been too focused on the boy she'd been with.

The living area was nicely furnished with soft comfy sofas, matching end tables and coffee table, and a fireplace that served as the room's focal point, with a cheerful fire burning. On the striped area rug, two girls, both towheads, were bent over coloring books, the older of the two instructing the other on the correct colors for hair. Not to be deterred, the younger sister insisted that purple was a perfectly acceptable hair color. A free spirit in the making, Kristen thought.

"Megan, Joshua?" Abby called. "Your brother's here."

"Coming."

"Be right there."

One voice, Megan's, came from upstairs, while the other voice, Joshua's, came from the basement.

"Maddie, Shelley, can you stand up and meet Kristen?"

The girls glanced up, took one look at Tyler, and launched themselves at him.

"Unca Ty!" The little one squealed and threw her arms around his legs, gazing up into his face.

When he bent to pick her up, Kristen's heart rolled over in her chest, and her gut clenched with guilt.

"This is Maddie," Tyler presented her to Kristen, blowing a raspberry on the little girl's neck, sending her into a gale of belly laughs. So that's where he acquired his love of blowing raspberries, she thought with a smile.

"'Gin!" she ordered, and Tyler obliged.

"What about me?" The older girl stood, hands on hips, a pout on her little pink mouth.

"And this is Shelley." Without releasing Maddie, he scooped up the girl and set her on his other hip, then blew raspberries on her neck too. The girl scrunched up her shoulders and giggled. "That tickles," she said laughing.

"It's supposed to." Grinning from ear to ear, he glanced between the two girls, then gazed into Kristen's eyes. The love she saw there held her spellbound, and something powerful and not a little overwhelming passed between them, leaving her shaken and . . . longing.

The moment was interrupted by his sister, and she assumed his sister's husband, followed by Joshua and another woman.

"Hey, bro." His brother nodded at Tyler. "You remember Hailey?"

"Yeah. Okay, either you girls are getting big, or your uncle is getting weak."

"Weak?!"

Everyone turned to his mother at the strident refrain, followed by some eye rolls.

"Mom, he's fine," Megan said on a sigh.

A sibling message flowed between Tyler and his sister

as she took Maddie from him. Tyler let Shelley slide down his leg to her feet, as Megan gave him a one-armed hug.

Stepping back, her presumed husband stuck out his hand for a bro handshake. "What's up? You still brewing beer?"

"You know it."

"Everyone, this is Kristen." Tyler reached out and pulled her next to him, his arm around her waist. While he made the introductions, Kristen stood pressed against his warmth and tried to relax. Being an only child, Tyler's large, gregarious family overwhelmed her.

"Dinner's ready! Wash up and come eat," Abby called from the dining room.

You apparently didn't have to tell this crew twice. Everyone parted to wash their hands, some went to the kitchen, some to the guest bath, and some upstairs.

Kristen and Tyler squeezed into the laundry room and washed their hands over the laundry sink. He took her hands and soaped them along with his, the gesture both sweet and oddly sexy. As he lathered their joined hands, a warmth flooded Kristen's belly and pooled between her legs.

Who knew washing your hands could be so sexy?

She leaned close to his ear and whispered, "You are so getting lucky tonight."

WITH HIS WHOLE family at the dining room table, Tyler's father presided over his birthday dinner like a king over his court. And who could blame him? Looking around the table at his parents' legacy, he felt the now-familiar twinge of regret. Regret that he will never be able to do the same. Never celebrate a birthday surrounded by his own kids.

Now was not the time.

His mother entered the dining room and presented her delicious pot roast to his father like she was presenting a delicacy to a king, before setting it in the center of the table. She beamed with pride as she took her seat to his right.

"Don't be shy, Kristen. Dig in or you might not get any."

As food was passed around, the family muttered compliments and thanks until everyone had filled their plates. Talk turned to the trip to Niagara Falls his parents had planned for next spring to celebrate their forty-third wedding anniversary.

"We're returning to the scene of the crime," his father joked, letting Kristen in on the secret.

His mother laughed. "Don't listen to him." She waved her hand as if shooing a fly. "Niagara is where we honeymooned."

"We got married the same month I graduated from college," his dad explained around a mouthful of mashed potatoes.

"SUNY Buffalo," his mother said.

"You two met in college, then?" Kristen asked.

"Yes. He was a year ahead of me," his mother said. "We met at a mixer."

"I took one look at her and knew she was going to be mine," his father said.

"Cocky much?" Joshua asked with a grin.

"Neil got a job in Atlanta at a small—I guess you would call them 'boutique' now— accounting firm, so we moved here. I finished up my last year of school at Georgia State University, and we lived in a dreadful little apartment in Inman Park. But when we decided it was time to start a family, we wanted to live in a quiet community where the kids could have a backyard to play in and could walk to school."

"So you moved to Northridge?" Kristen asked.

"We did. And never looked back."

"Megan and Jeff met in college too," Abby pointed out.

"It's a great place to meet your future spouse."

"Megan and Jeff are also accountants in Chicago," Neil said with a bit of fatherly pride.

"College is also a great place to sow some wild oats too," Joshua put in.

"Joshua Stephen Kincaide!"

Everyone laughed at his mother's effrontery. Unabashed, Joshua just shrugged his shoulders, and Jeff offered him a fist-bump of support.

Megan rolled her eyes. "Men."

"Oh, come on. You can't tell me you didn't have a good time in college before you met me," Jeff goaded.

Megan gave a lazy lift of her shoulder. "Well, yeah. But I had a better time once I met you."

"Aw!" Hailey sighed.

"Remember the time we took a gondola tour on Halloween and it snowed?" Megan asked.

They descended into stories of college life, each telling stories in turn, and Tyler joined in, telling a few stories of his own.

"Lord, help me," his mother intoned. "You three couldn't have left me in blissful ignorance?"

Tyler had noticed Kristen's descent into silence, but he thought it was just his overwhelming family. Now, however, he noticed she pushed the food around on her plate, barely taking a bite.

"We all made it out alive," Joshua joked.

"No thanks to your behavior," their mother muttered.

"How about you, Kristen?" Megan asked. "You have any crazy college stories to share?"

Kristen looked up, her eyes wide, her mouth open, as if shocked to have been invited to join the conversation.

*Shit.* Tyler closed his eyes. Of course. She'd felt completely left out of the conversation having never gone to college. She never had the opportunity to go like he and his siblings had.

Tyler reached over and squeezed Kristen's leg, giving his sister a look.

Before he could smooth over the moment, his mother, bless her, spoke up.

"Who's ready for cake?"

"I'D LIKE to go home, please." Kristen wrapped her arms around herself, not against the cold of the truck's interior, but against the emptiness in her heart. After seeing Tyler's warm, loving family, she realized she denied not only Tyler, but all of them by keeping Seth's paternity a secret. She'd also denied Seth the opportunity to grow up with an extended family. Assuming they would have accepted him, but after tonight, she had no doubt they would have.

Maybe it would have been better for Seth if what she feared most had come to be—that she'd told Tyler all those years ago, and Tyler would have taken Seth from her to raise. He'd have been loved and cared for, and more importantly, he'd have grown up with more opportunities than he had now.

But that wasn't the only thing troubling her. Tonight reminded her she would never be good enough for Tyler.

She didn't fit in among his family. College-educated professionals with experiences and lives she couldn't begin to understand. A family who'd grown up in a perfectly nice middle-class home, had enough food to eat, heat to keep them warm, and who didn't wear hand-me-downs to school.

She scoffed internally. She *still* wore hand-me-downs most of the time.

Tyler's parents were solid middle class, college-educated as well, but their children had surpassed them. And likely their children's children would surpass them as well. She would never be anything but white trash. No matter how hard she worked or how successful she was. Here, in this town, her history would always be a part of her. Just like Jonah the Jerk had reminded her.

Tyler's warm hand landed on her thigh and he squeezed. "You okay? Did you have a nice time tonight?"

She simply nodded and said, "I have an early morning tomorrow."

On the short drive to her apartment, Tyler let her be. When he pulled to the curb, she opened the door before he could throw the truck into park. "Good night."

Even in the dim light of the dash lights, she could see the hurt and confusion on his face.

"Hey. What's wrong?" His right hand reached for her.

"I have to go." And without another word, she closed the door and ran the few steps to the stairs up to her apartment. Inside, she walked over to the window and looked down, but his truck was gone.

*Mew.* Bending down, she scooped up Cinnamon and pressed her face into her soft fur. The cat's purring calmed her, but did nothing to stop the tears that rolled down her cheeks.

He loved her. And she'd made a mess of everything.

❄

TYLER PACED through the dark rooms of his house feeling very alone.

He'd just spent several hours in the company of his big, growing family, but it was Kristen's absence tonight that made him acutely aware of his single lifestyle more than anything else.

What he had hoped would make Kristen feel welcome had turned out to make her feel alienated. Which couldn't have been more wrong. It had never been his family's, nor his, intent to make her feel anything but welcome, but as the evening progressed and talk at the dinner table moved to college and careers, he noticed her descent into silence. It was almost palpable. As if she were folding into herself.

Would she ever realize just how amazing she really is? How proud she should be of what she's accomplished? Would she ever overcome her apparent feelings of inadequacy?

But how could he talk? Seeing his beautiful nieces, his own inadequacies had surfaced, reminding him he will never hold a child of his own, thanks to the after-effects of the cancer treatment for his lymphoma. The *lifesaving* cancer treatment, he reminded himself.

He knew he should be thankful to be alive. And he was. But at times like this, the ache in his soul felt like a different kind of cancer, one that threatened to consume his gratitude, like lymphoma tried to consume his body.

And yet, spending time with Kristen—and Seth—made him feel whole again.

He loved her, loved them both. Maybe it was time to do something about that.

# CHAPTER TWENTY-TWO

THE NEXT DAY, the bell over the door tinkled, followed by a blast of cold air, announcing another customer. Kristen looked up from wiping coffee grounds off the work counter to see Tyler's mom glance around the café before approaching the coffee bar.

"Oh. Just the person I wanted to see," she said when she spotted Kristen.

And here it comes. She's going to tell her to leave her son alone. A dull ache formed in the pit of Kristen's stomach. Should she gracefully step aside, or should she defy his mother's request? The rebel in her wanted to stand her ground just for contrariness' sake. But in that moment she realized that wasn't the only reason.

She'd grown close to Tyler. Closer than she ever had to any man in her life. She didn't want to lose that. To lose him. But she'd lose him anyway, she reminded herself, as soon as she told him about Seth. So why should his mother's rejection hurt so much?

Because—you're not good enough. And if anyone knew that, it was Tyler's mom.

"I'd like to buy you a cup of coffee if you're not too busy."

"Shouldn't that be the other way around?" Kristen asked, trepidation making her nauseous.

Abby smiled, but shook her head. "No, I'm buying."

"All right. What can I get you?"

Abby perused the blackboard behind the counter and said, "I'll try that fancy triple mocha frappe. With whipped cream."

"Have a seat and I'll bring it over." Tamping down her fears, Kristen set about making Abby's coffee. After pouring herself a cup of hot, black courage, Kristen carried the drinks to the out-of-the-way table Abby selected.

Perfect for an uncomfortable conversation.

Abby took the drink as Kristen pulled out the chair across from her, her entire body humming with the anticipation of the confrontation.

"Ooh, this is delicious! I'm not much of a fancy-coffee girl myself, but I could get used to this."

*Lovely.* Just what Kristen needed. A new customer who thought she was good enough to make decadent coffees, but not good enough for her son.

She looked around before turning back to Kristen. "You've done a wonderful job with the café, the bookstore. You should be proud of yourself." Abby's voice didn't have the note of surprise Kristen expected. It didn't carry that tone of *who would have thought?* Softening me up for the cut-down, she wondered?

"Thank you. I work hard." The hand under the table gripped her thigh in agitation. She waited for the "but." Why didn't the woman just get on with it?

"I want to thank you for supporting Tyler through this scare. He was lucky to have you by his side."

*Um, what?* All Kristen could do was stare open-mouthed at the woman's comments.

"I'm sure after what you went through with your mother, it couldn't have been easy for you—bringing back memories better left in the past." Abby reached out and squeezed Kristen's hand.

Staring at their two hands clasped on the tabletop, still unsure she'd heard right, Kristen blinked back tears.

Sitting back in her chair, Abby withdrew her hand and Kristen immediately felt its absence.

Abby fiddled with the napkin dispenser, sighed, then took a sip of her coffee before setting the cup back on the table as if it were made of fine crystal rather than heavy white-glazed pottery.

"When he went through this after his initial diagnosis, he essentially went through it alone. Of course his father and I were there as much as possible, as were his brother and sister. And Zach. But he didn't have the one person whom he could rely on, day or night, every day of his battle."

She looked as if she wanted to say more but shook her head. "I'll just leave it at that."

Abby must be referring to Celeste.

She lifted her gaze to Kristen's and offered a tender smile. "So," she shrugged, and blinked back tears of her own, "I just wanted to thank you."

The only sound in the café was the murmur of voices from the other customers, punctuated by the click of someone typing on their laptop.

Kristen couldn't have been more stunned if someone had told her she'd won the lottery. The fight-or-flight adrenaline that had been pulsing through her since Abby walked through the door fled, leaving her both exhausted and relieved.

She sat back, cleared the tears pooling in her throat, and said, "Your coffee's on the house."

Abby laughed, then sobered. "He cares for you. And Seth."

The ache in her stomach was back, but for a different reason. Guilt. Shame.

"Tyler's told me so much about Seth. It's so great that Tyler is spending time with him. Maybe even forming a bond. Especially since Tyler can't have children now."

The ache detonated, spilling noxious fumes into her belly and chest. "What?" The word barely came out as a whisper, and the heat of the explosion left abruptly, leaving her cold as an arctic winter.

"Oh, dear. I shouldn't have spoken." Abby's face had gone pale. "I thought—I thought he would have told you." She took a deep breath and blew it out. "The cancer treatment that saved his life left him sterile. Unable to have children."

Bile rose in Kristen's throat, and she swallowed hard to suppress the need to vomit. Oh God. She squeezed her eyes shut, hoping to block out the truth. Oh God, oh God, oh God.

What had she done? Denied him all these years with his son when he'd never have another child of his own. He'd never forgive her. Never. Why should he?

"Kristen? Honey?" Abby touched her hand, and Kristen opened her eyes to see Abby staring back at her, concern in her amber depths.

"I hope this doesn't change your mind about how you feel about him."

She shook her head. The only communication she was

capable of. No, but what she has to tell him will change his mind about how he feels about her. More than she ever realized.

Tyler opened the front door to see Kristen standing on the doorstep in the frigid cold, her arms wrapped around herself for warmth. He grinned broadly at her. She really did hate being cold.

"Hey, you. I was just thinking about you, and here you are. Come in." He reached out his hand to her, thinking she would take it, but she didn't. She stepped into the light from the foyer, and he closed the door behind her. He took a closer look and saw that she'd been crying, and his heart sank. Was she here to break things off? Or . . .

"Seth? Is he okay?"

She paled. What the hell?

"I need to talk to you." Her hands twisted and gripped one another, as she waited for his acquiescence.

This didn't sound good. Flashes of Celeste's breakup crossed his mind. "Okay." He lifted his hand to indicate the living room and followed her in. Maybe his relapse scare had been too much for her. Or maybe the evening with his family had been. His stomach ached, the ham and cheese omelet he'd just eaten for dinner sitting there like a brick, all heaviness and sharp corners.

She'd perched herself on the edge of the sofa, as if ready to take flight at any moment. Her watery gaze met his and she looked as if she were about to tell him the dog died. Oh!

"Cinnamon?"

She shook her head and a tear spilled down her cheek.

"Kristen, you're scaring me."

She nodded, took a deep breath and blurted, "Seth is your son."

For one brilliant flash, joy swept over him. His. He had a son.

Then reality hit, and he crossed his arms over his chest. "What? How? He's sixteen years old! We never . . ."

"We did. Apparently you just don't remember."

He planted his feet and set his hands on his hips, and huffed out a mirthless laugh. "I think I would remember something like that, Kristen."

She squeezed her eyes shut. "The night before you left for college."

Then it hit him. He felt as if he'd been socked in the solar plexus, as his breath left in a *whoosh*. Grateful for the chair behind him, he dropped into it trying to make sense of what she was telling him. It was true, he remembered little about that night after he'd had those tequila shots. The next thing he knew, he woke up in his bed with a headache the likes of which he hadn't experienced since.

"It's why I hated you. I thought you had used me. That you thought the only thing I was good enough for was a one-time fuck."

He winced at her words. "But . . ." He popped to his feet. "Christ! That was seventeen years ago!" He stalked into the middle of the room, then spun back to face her. "You got pregnant?"

She nodded.

"And you never told me? You never," his voice faded as tears and anger clogged his throat. "You never thought to tell me I had a son?"

She jumped to her feet. "I tried, goddammit. I tried."

"Must not have tried very hard because Seth is sixteen

fucking years old! Sixteen years!" His voice boomed off the walls.

She stalked over to him, her face a mask of rage. "Don't you dare! I called you. I left you messages. You never called me back!" She poked him in the chest with her finger.

"No!" He turned his back on her. "Impossible."

"You don't believe you're the father? Because of course, Kristen 'McKay the Lay' could have fucked any number of men who could be the father, right? Would a paternity test make you believe it?"

He spun and grabbed her by the shoulders. "No. I believe you." He recalled his loser of a roommate, who often neglected to give him his phone messages. His mail. Hell, one time his mom sent a box of her special chocolate chip cookies, and because Tyler had been out of town, his room-mate had eaten them and never bothered to tell Tyler. Only when his mother had asked about them did Tyler find out.

"Shit!" He scrubbed a hand through his hair. But he'd been home over a year and she hadn't told him. She'd kept his son from him.

"Does Seth know?" he asked, his voice strained.

"No. No one knew."

"Knew?"

Kristen drew in a shuddering breath. "Olivia figured it out."

He scoffed, and threw his hands up in the air. "How long? How long has she known?"

"A couple of weeks."

"Zach?"

"I made her promise not to tell him," she whispered, wrapping her arms around her waist.

He paced the floor like a caged beast. The anger, the hurt, roiled inside him, threatening to engulf him.

"All these years, no one knew we slept together until I told Olivia two weeks ago. That's when she put two and two together."

His back still to her, he stopped, hands on hips, shaking his head. "I'm surprised you didn't tell the world. Pregnant with my child. It could have been your ticket out. I, my family, we would have taken care of you. The child."

Fury surged through her at his accusation, as if she were some gold digger only after money. "Or taken the child *from* me. I couldn't let that happen. I couldn't—" her voice broke, and the anger fled as quickly as it had come. "Besides, I was ashamed. Ashamed that you slept with me then walked away, making me feel like the slut I was reputed to be. I hated you. And then I learned I was pregnant and tried to tell you, but you never called me back. I hated you even more. You threw me aside like so much white trash." Her voice sounded small in the room.

"That's not true!"

"I know that now!"

Sixteen years! He had a son sixteen years old, and he never knew. And the last five years, dealing with the fallout from his chemotherapy. Learning recently he would never have children. And all along he had a son.

Anger burned deep. Anger at Kristen, at his dipshit roommate, at himself. But mostly at Kristen. A year! She'd had the last year to tell him, and she didn't. Instead, she'd sent Seth away. Then he thought about the times he'd come home to see his parents. All the Thanksgivings and Christmases. All those opportunities, and she'd kept the truth to herself. And what about the last two months? Had they meant nothing to her? How could she, goddammit?

She said she'd tried to tell him. But had she?

"I hope maybe someday you can forgive me."

A sob had escaped with her statement, but he hardened his heart, and without looking at her, he said, "It will be a cold day in Hell. And I know how much you hate the cold."

He braced his hands on the fireplace mantel, gripping the wood so hard it should've splintered under the force. A few silent moments passed, then he heard the click of the front door closing.

Unable to restrain his rage any longer, he grabbed the object nearest him and flung it across the room, where it hit the wall. The metal clang of the pewter beer stein echoed in the now silent room.

# CHAPTER TWENTY-THREE

Hot tears of guilt and shame ran down Kristen's face mingling with the hot punishing spray of the shower, as sobs wracked her body. She felt as if the world had rolled over on her. But she had no one to blame but herself. Her anger, her pride, her shame. The grudge she'd held. The forgiveness she never gave.

Finally, she'd found a man to love. To love her. And she'd wrecked it.

Despite her hurt, the only thing left was to make things better. To do her best to rebuild her relationships. Even if Tyler never forgave her, she had to tell Seth. She had to step back and give Tyler and Seth the opportunity to become father and son. Even if she wasn't in that family picture.

Stepping out of the shower, she pressed the towel to her face, trying to stem the flow of tears. It had to stop. She couldn't face Seth like this.

She pulled on her warmest pajamas, still cold despite the heat of the shower. In the living room, she slumped on the couch, recalling Tyler's expression, the utter surprise when she told him they'd slept together seventeen years ago.

That told her, even if nothing else did, that he truly didn't remember.

But then the look of anguish on his face when he'd learned he had a sixteen-year-old son he'd only just now come to know would be forever etched into her mind.

He would never forgive her. A mirthless laugh escaped at the irony. She never forgave him for something he didn't even remember doing. Now, the tables were turned. What goes around comes around and all that.

Her phone buzzed with an incoming text, surprised to see Tyler's name on the screen, she snatched up the phone.

---

Tyler: I'd like to see my son. Alone.
Kristen: When and where?
Tyler: Tomorrow. My house. 11:00.
Kristen: He'll be there.

---

SHE SET the phone on the coffee table and sighed. Well, that's progress. At least Tyler didn't intend to let his anger affect his relationship with Seth.

A ball of orange fur landed in her lap and Cinnamon began making biscuits on her thigh, her motor running at five hundred-twenty RPMs. This time the soft vibrations did little to ease Kristen's stress. She had another difficult task ahead of her to atone for her many sins.

Then *both* the men in her life, who meant more than anything to her, would hate her.

The irony wasn't lost on her. "I've been the one withholding forgiveness, and now I'm the one who needs it."

WHAT HE WOULDN'T GIVE for some alcohol right now, Tyler thought. Oblivion was preferable to the conflicting emotions colliding in his chest like limbs in a wind storm. He scrubbed his hands over his face then massaged his temples in an attempt to sooth the burgeoning headache.

A son. A son! Who is sixteen years old! My God! Even if he wasn't sterile, how could she think he could ever forgive her for keeping that from him? All these years wasted! All these years he could have watched his child grow up. All these years he could have been a father to him. It was too much.

Pacing the floor, he allowed the fury to roll through him like violent waves during a storm. One wave crashing into the other in a rapid, steady succession. Then it hit him again like a tsunami. He had a *son*. He collapsed onto the sofa, breathless and shaking. A beautiful, healthy, talented son. Just when he thought he would never have a child, here was this . . . gift. A gift made even richer by the fact that Seth was, and always would be, his only child.

He swiped at his face, wet with the tears he hadn't realized he was shedding.

As angry as he was with Kristen right now, he wanted to talk to her about Seth. To ask her questions, to get to know him as his son. What had he been like as a baby? What was his first word? When did he learn to walk? Did he learn to ride a bike? Throw a baseball? What brought him to the violin? He already knew he was wicked smart. Talented. Kind. He shook his head, and in spite of himself, he recognized that Kristen had done a brilliant job raising him. He couldn't ask for a better kid.

He wondered how Seth would take the news. Would he want Tyler as his father? Would Seth let Tyler become part of his life, even if Tyler and Kristen were no longer together? There was no question he and Kristen were over. How could he ever trust her again? Maybe someday, when the hurt faded, they could become cordial again, but not a couple. Never a couple.

And yet the thought pierced him through.

Lying back on the couch, he put his feet up. The adrenaline that had flooded his system ebbed, leaving him exhausted.

He recalled the night last week when he and Kristen had curled up on this very couch watching one of her favorite shows, *The Walking Dead*. They weren't fifteen minutes into the episode when their attention—and hands— began to drift elsewhere, just as their clothes had drifted to the floor. He'd told her again that he loved her, then showed her with his lips, tongue, hands, and body. When their hunger for one another was banked for the moment, he'd felt sated. Loved. Happy.

Dammit! He threw his arm over his face as if it would block the memories that bombarded him. How beautiful she'd looked over that fancy French dinner. How sexy she looked after their lovemaking, her hair a tumble of red waves, her green eyes half-closed in contented drowsiness. How she'd reach out and brushed a lock of Seth's hair away from his face, her touch gentle and loving.

Tyler rolled to his side and curled into a ball.

He had a son. But in gaining him, he'd lost the love of his life.

❄

THE SOUND of Seth's key in the lock woke Kristen, and Cinnamon jumped down from the couch with a *mew* to greet her human brother.

Kristen sat up and groaned at the ache in her back. Wiping the sleep from her eyes, she braced herself. This was the moment of truth. As difficult as it had been to tell Tyler, Seth would be more difficult. The last thing in the world she wanted was to hurt her son and potentially destroy their relationship.

"Mom? What are you doing sleeping on the couch?" Seth closed the door behind him and lowered his violin case to the floor by the door then bent to lift the cat in his arms. "Ooh. You're so warm," he muttered into her fur. "It's cold as hell out there tonight."

About as cold as Kristen's heart felt.

"How was rehearsal?"

"Fine. Easy." He shrugged.

She knew he wasn't being challenged by the high school orchestra teacher. Seth needed to get back to Juilliard. If he didn't run away after she talked to him. "You hungry?"

"Went to Dominick's for pizza with Hannah and Eduardo." He set Cinnamon down and unwound his scarf before hanging it on the hook by the door.

"Come. Sit. We need to talk."

He got a wary look in his eyes. "Mom, if this is about Juilliard—"

"It's not." She patted the cushion next to her. "But I need you to listen." He sat, and she took his cold hands in hers. "You know I love you, right?"

He drew back, "Mom, you're scaring me."

Because I'm scared to death, she thought. Scared of

losing both my men in the same night. She took a deep breath, flashed him a tentative smile, then decided to broach the subject with care, rather than blurt it out like she'd done with Tyler.

"Haven't you ever wondered who your father is? I mean, you've never said anything."

He shrugged. "Maybe in an existential way."

She shook her head. "What do you mean?"

"You know, I'd wonder if I got my musical talent from my father. Is he good at math and science like me?" He grinned, and her whole world lit up. "Because we both know I didn't get those from you."

She laughed, despite her fear. "No. That's a given." She lifted his hand and examined it. So like his father's—long, agile fingers and strong, square hands.

As she got to know Tyler, to spend more time with him, she saw him in his son. Seth had Kristen's green eyes, but he had a mix of his father's dark blond hair and his mother's red hair in his strawberry blond locks. But his expressions. They were all Tyler.

The first time she saw Tyler concentrate on the data he'd collected for their presentation, she saw Seth. Seth had his father's deep, throaty laugh, his smile, with its asymmetry, even his father's walk. And God knows he got Tyler's brains. His paternity would have been impossible to deny if anyone had known she and Tyler had had a one-night stand.

"Seth, I need to tell you who your father is."

"Okaaay," his voice wary as he eyed her.

Taking a deep breath, she let it out. "Your father is Tyler Kincaide."

Kristen watched as Seth processed this information,

nausea roiling in her stomach, as she braced for the anger. The resentment.

"Really?"

"Yes."

He processed this revelation a moment longer then nodded. "I can see that."

"That's it?"

"Well, no. I have questions."

"Okay." She hesitated, as if Seth were a ticking bomb and she didn't know how much time she had before it exploded.

"I'm sixteen. My birthday is April thirtieth, which means I was conceived in August the year you graduated from high school."

She blushed. "That's right."

"Were you and Tyler high school sweethearts?"

"Well, no. I did have a crush on him. But he . . . he had other plans."

"To go to college."

"That's right."

"Does he know?"

Her mouth had gone dry, and she licked her lips. "He does now. Just a few hours ago I told him, but he didn't know."

"And?"

"And he was angry." She reached out and touched Seth's arm. "At me, not at you," she reassured him.

"Why did you wait until now?"

She told him about Tyler and his sensitivity to alcohol, and how he didn't remember the night Seth was conceived, and how she'd tried to tell him, but he never got the message.

"I'm not proud of myself. I harbored a deep resentment

for Tyler all those years because I thought he, um, used me. I didn't know he had alcohol-induced amnesia. I didn't know his roommate never gave him my phone messages. I just assumed he wasn't interested in me or in knowing what I had to say."

"But I've been home since September. Why haven't you told him? It's clear you no longer hate him."

She blushed. "I tried, several times," she gnawed her lip, "but I'd either chicken out or we'd get interrupted. You're not angry?"

"I'm . . . hurt. I mean, I get that you thought he was a jerk and that he didn't care about you the first fifteen years of my life. But after he came back to Northridge . . . you could have told him. *Should* have told him. And me. So, yeah, I'm not going to lie. I'm hurt."

She nodded in understanding. Of course he was hurt. And it was all her fault.

"I hope I can make it up to you somehow."

"Does he hate you?"

She released a mirthless laugh. "Let's just say, I'm pretty sure he doesn't *like* me."

"Tyler? He, wants to see me?"

"Yes! He does. Again, he's not angry at you. It's all me."

"Then I can have a relationship with him—if he wants it? Even if you two . . . don't, you know, work out? I won't if it would be too difficult for you."

"Oh, baby! Now that the truth is out, I would never stand in the way of a relationship between you and Tyler. Even if I'm not in that picture."

"I like him." He took her hand and squeezed. "He's a cool guy."

"Good. I'm glad you do. I hope you will come to love him. As your father."

# CHAPTER TWENTY-FOUR

Tyler opened the door to Seth's knock and there stood his son. Of course, now the resemblance was clear.

He glanced behind the boy. Kristen leaned against her car, arms at her sides. He wasn't prepared for the gut punch when his eyes met hers. A sucker punch for sure. He should hate her with every depth of his being. But he couldn't.

His gaze flicked back to Seth. His son. She'd given him a son.

And then kept it from him for sixteen years.

Without another look her way, he asked Seth in and closed the door. On her. On their possible future.

A sudden awkwardness took hold. He'd always felt easy around Seth. Now, as his father, he felt . . . nervous, as if they'd only just met.

"So, want something to drink?"

"No, thank you." Seth surveyed the house, clearly feeling the same awkwardness.

Should he hug him? Shake his hand? What does one do when one meets their almost-grown son?

"Let's sit down."

Seth preceded him into the living room and dropped into the same place his mother had sat last night. His gaze skipped over objects in the room, looking everywhere but at Tyler.

Okay, he was the adult in this situation. It was time he took charge. "Seth." His son looked him straight in the eye for the first time since arriving. "First, I want you to know, I didn't know . . . anything about you."

"I know. Mom told me everything."

"And how do you feel about it?" Tyler winced inwardly. He sounded like a therapist.

"I'm cool with it."

Anger flared, but he tamped it down. "Cool with it? Cool with me being your father? Cool with your mother keeping your paternity a secret? What?"

Seth sat up as if preparing for a speech. "Look, Mom told me what happened. That you don't remember. That your roommate was an asshole. All of it. I get where she was coming from. I get why she didn't tell you. Or me."

Tyler's heart sank. Not that he wanted Seth to turn against his mother, but he expected the kid to be upset over the sixteen-year omission.

"I also get where you're coming from now. I get your anger and your hurt. But I won't have you talk bad about my mom. If you have more to say, then say it to her, not to me. I won't be a go-between."

Tyler nodded, impressed. He'd known the moment he met Seth, he was an old soul, brimming with a wisdom and thoughtfulness far beyond his years.

"The last thing I want to do is put you in the middle. Kristen and I are adults. We need to work this out. Somehow. But I need to know . . . will you have me in your life? Will you let me be your father?" Tears clogged the back of his throat. "Because I want that. More than anything."

Seth's eyes filled, and he choked out, "I'd like that."

Tyler couldn't wait another moment to hold his son. To feel him in his arms. He rose, and of the same mind, Seth joined him in a hug that said everything.

Stepping back, Seth asked, "Should I call you Dad?"

"You can call me whatever you're comfortable calling me."

Seth nodded. "Okay . . . Dad."

"Mom!" Tyler called as he let himself into his childhood home. The sounds of water running came from the kitchen, so he followed the sound. "Mom."

"Jesus!" she gasped, a hand to her throat. "Tyler! Don't sneak up on me like that!" She smacked him with the dishtowel in her other hand.

"Sorry."

"I wasn't expecting you. Is everything okay?"

"I just need to talk to you and Dad."

"Your dad's in Charlotte visiting your uncle Charlie."

"That's too bad, but this can't wait," he muttered to himself.

His mom studied him a moment, her brow knitted in concern. "You're not—"

"No, Mom. I'm not sick."

She breathed a sigh of relief, then her face changed from concern to joy, and she laid a hand on his arm. "You're engaged!"

"What? No. No, that's not it." *Great.* Not only was he

not engaged, he and Kristen were over. "Can we go into the living room?"

With a look of confusion, his mom folded the dishtowel and draped it over the kitchen sink then followed him into the living room.

He sat in his father's chair, while his mom sat on the edge of the couch, as if ready to jump to her feet at a moment's notice. Propping his elbows on his knees, he dropped his hands between his thighs, trying to figure out how to tell her. "Do you know Seth McKay?"

"Kristen's son? Yes, of course. Polite young man. Why? Is he okay?"

Despite the situation, he couldn't help the grin that broke out on his face. "He's fine. He's more than fine." He inhaled, then slowly let out his breath. "He's my son."

"I'm sorry? Did you just say Seth McKay is your son?"

He clapped his hands together and lifted his gaze to hers. "Yes."

"But I don't understand." His mom stared into space as if trying to remember where she placed the car keys. She shot to her feet, hands on her hips, and glared down at him. "And you never told me!"

Reaching for her, he took her wrist and pulled her down to the sofa again. "I didn't know."

She sank to the edge once more. "Okay, start from the beginning because I'm completely confused."

Tyler told his mom as much as he remembered of the night before he left for college, then filled in the gaps with what Kristen told him. When he finished, his mom stood and moved across the room in front of the fireplace, her hand to her mouth. "Your child was conceived in our basement?" She pointed at the floor of the living room.

He winced. Not a detail he'd want to share with his mom. "Um, yeah. Apparently."

"The note," she muttered.

"What note?"

She wrung her hands. "That morning, I came into your room to check on you—it was so late and you didn't usually sleep that long—and I found a note on the nightstand."

He sat up. "Who was it from? What did it say?"

"There was no signature. It just said something like 'I had a great time. Call me tomorrow.' I had no idea it was from Kristen, or that you had, um, entertained her in your room." A blush covered her cheeks, and she glanced away.

Heat flooded his face, and he cleared his throat. "What did you do with the note?"

"I put it in the nightstand drawer so it wouldn't get lost."

He shook his head. "Well, I guess I didn't need whatever was stored in that drawer when I left for college because I never saw it."

"I'm sorry, sweetheart."

"It's okay, Mom. Without a signature, I wouldn't have known who it was from anyway." He hunched his shoulders, ashamed of his behavior that night. But if he'd known there had been a note he would have at least known he'd slept with someone and maybe he could have tried to figure out who.

His mom paced a bit then stopped and shook her head. "I have a grandson." Her eyes shone with unshed tears, and a soft smile lit her face. Then her mouth thinned into an all-too-familiar line of displeasure.

He recognized that expression from his childhood misadventures that ended with this mother's censure. "A sixteen-year-old grandson. Right under my nose," she murmured, as she folded her arms across her chest in a pose of parental disapproval. "Wait till I see Kristen McKay! I have a few words for her."

Tyler stood and approached his mother. "Mom, please, let it be for now."

"But you and Kristen—"

He cut her off. "No. It's over. It ended when she told me she'd been hiding Seth's paternity from me."

He expected to see his mother nod in agreement and understanding. Instead, she gaped at him. "But, you could have everything you want." She threw up her hands. "Everything you thought you would never have. A wife. A child. A family. It's there for the taking!"

"She kept my son from me for sixteen years. How do I get beyond that?"

"Are you going to cut off your nose to spite your face?" At his look of astonishment, she continued. "Look, I'm not happy to learn that for sixteen years my grandson has been growing up right in front of me and I never knew. But you're throwing away happiness with both hands," her voice rose with each word. "She told you the truth, and it couldn't have been easy for her. And now, my grandson," her face lit up at those words, "is yours to claim. To love. Don't give that up."

"I don't plan to. I'm going to spend as much of every day with him as possible before he returns to New York. Getting to know him. Letting him get to know me. I don't need a relationship with Kristen to do that."

His mother sighed. "You're right, you don't. And I feel confident now that she's told you, she would never try to keep you from Seth, but she gave you a gift. She gave you a son."

She took him by the arms the way she used to when she wanted to get her point across. "She could have had an abortion. She could have given him up for adoption. But she didn't." She shook him. "She raised that boy. Sacrificed for him. Loved him. And from what I can tell, did a damn fine job raising him. That says more about Kristen McKay than anything."

He set his jaw, but she continued despite it. "You could have lived the rest of your life not knowing you had a child. But Kristen told you. She had to know telling you now would only damage your relationship with her. But she told you anyway. Despite the secret she's kept all these years, she came clean, and damn the consequences to her. That's pretty selfless." Finally, she laid a mother's hand on his cheek. "And, you love her. I know you do."

His heart squeezed. "Correction, *loved* her. How can I ever trust her again? How?"

"It's called forgiveness, son."

"Wowzer. You look like something Cinnamon coughed up."

"Gee, thanks." Kristen settled herself in the front seat of Olivia's van, fastening her seatbelt.

"What are friends for?" Olivia grinned at her. "Late night with Tyler?" She waggled her brows then clearly realized her mistake. "Uh-oh." She threw the car into park and turned to face her friend.

Tears welled in Kristen's eyes and she blinked furiously to restrain them. Dammit, she'd cried more in the last two days than she had her whole life. Well, with the exception of when her mother died. Olivia reached across the console and squeezed her hand. "What happened?"

"I told Tyler. And Seth."

"Ah. And I take it didn't go well."

Kristen huffed out a laugh. "That's the understatement of the century." She wiped a tear from her cheek and related the course of events to Olivia, finishing with, "I'm not proud of myself. I've robbed Seth of his father and Tyler of his son all these years. He will never forgive me, and I can't blame him. Go ahead. Tell me 'I told you so.'"

"Okay, wait. I'm not going to do that. You did try to tell him, initially. And, in your mind, Tyler used you and then discarded you. What woman wouldn't be pissed off about that?"

"And since he's been back?"

"Well, you've got me there. But whenever you were in the same room with him, you got your back up like a cat's. I guess I can't blame you, given how you thought he'd treated you."

"But was that really a good reason to keep it from him now?"

"Probably not." Olivia chewed her lip as she stared through the windshield and the swaying branches of a tree. "So, what made you tell him? Because you love him?"

Kristen felt the heat rise in her face. "Yes, and no. I mean, I had been trying to work up the courage to tell him, even tried on a couple of occasions, knowing when I did he'd walk away from me and never look back." She heaved a sigh then gazed out the window. "I should have told him as soon as he returned to Northridge. At least then I had less to lose," she muttered, almost to herself.

"So, what gave you the courage after all this time?"

"Something his mother told me." She twisted her hands in her lap. "Something I can't share without his permission."

Olivia studied her face, considering. "Okay."

"And Seth? He knows?"

"I told him the same night I told Tyler."

"How'd he take it?"

"That kid." She shook her head and smiled, despite her heartbreak. "He just takes everything in stride."

"Like Tyler."

Kristen huffed out a laugh devoid of humor. "Yeah. Well, Tyler's not taking this in stride, let me tell you."

"And Seth and Tyler?"

"I dropped Seth off at Tyler's this morning."

"So, I take it Tyler wants to be a father to Seth."

"Yes." And why wouldn't he, since Seth is, and will be, his only progeny.

"That's good at least. Not that I would ever expect Tyler not to. And you're good with that?"

"I am. Truly, I am. It's just . . . Seth has gained a father, but I've lost Tyler in the process." Her vision blurred this time, as the tears filled her eyes to overflowing then ran down her cheeks. "And I have no one to blame but myself."

Olivia unfastened her seatbelt and leaned across the console to give Kristen a hug. She'd never been much of a hugger, but the knowledge that Olivia cared for her overwhelmed her.

"Honey, we don't have to go to Atlanta today. You've got a lot on your plate."

"No, I want to go. I need to give Seth some room to process everything, and honestly? I'm happy to get away from Northridge for the day. I know it won't be long before this hits the town gossip mill." She will do her best to protect Seth from the harmful things people will say until he leaves again for New York, but it won't be easy.

Olivia sat back into her seat, tapping her lip with her finger in thought. "Well, there must be a way for Tyler to forgive you. We just need to give it some thought."

It might be cold outside, but it wasn't a cold day in Hell yet.

Tyler pulled up in Zach's driveway and shut off the ignition. A table saw screamed from the backyard, so he followed the sound around to the back of the house, leaves swirling at his feet in a brisk wind.

Spotting him, Zach shut off the saw and removed his safety goggles. "What's up?"

"What are you working on?" Tyler hedged.

"Building some shelves for the room I'm converting into Olivia's home office."

Tyler ran his hand over the oak. "Nice."

"Found it in an old sawmill they were about to tear down. It's about time for a cold beer," Zach pointed at Tyler. "You?" Sweat poured down Zach's face, despite the cold.

"Sure." Tyler ran a hand down his face.

"Sounds like you could use one."

"You have no idea." Tyler followed Zach into the house, glancing around. "Olivia at home?"

"No." Zach opened the fridge and grabbed two of Tyler's Firehouse Dogs and handed him one. "She just left to pick up Kristen for a trip into Atlanta. 'Wedding things,'" he said, using finger quotes.

Tyler popped the top on his beer but didn't take a drink. Now that he had it, he'd lost his desire for it.

"Seth is my son." He winced, not planning to blurt out the news.

Zach had the bottle halfway to his mouth then froze, cutting a stunned glance at Tyler, and tilting his head. "I'm sorry?"

Tyler heaved a sigh, set his bottle on the counter behind him, and leaned against it for support. "You heard right."

Tyler could see from Zach's expression the he was doing mathematical calculations in his head. "He was conceived before you left for Princeton?"

"Yes."

Zach gave Tyler a shove. "You never told me you slept with Kristen."

"Because I didn't know I did."

Confusion bloomed on Zach's face before the explanation hit him. "Oh."

"Yeah. The night of my going-away party."

"Well, that explains it." Zach lifted the beer to his mouth again then stopped. "Wait. You just found out?"

"Yes."

"Well, shit." Zach took a long pull on his beer, swallowed, then set it down.

"Exactly." Tyler told Zach the whole sordid *Lifetime*-movie-worthy story. When he finally finished, he added, "There's something else."

Zach's head jerked up, his eyes filled with concern.

"No. Not that." Zach's shoulders visibly relaxed. "I'm sterile."

"You're—what?" Confusion creased his brow. "Then . . . how?" Then it dawned on him. "The cancer treatment."

"Bingo."

"So Seth." He leaned against the other counter.

"So Seth."

"But why tell you now after all these years?"

"I think my mother may have let my, er, condition, slip and Kristen felt guilty."

"A gift then," Zach muttered, and Tyler shivered at the echo of his mother's words. "What do you plan to do?"

"Claim my son."

"So he knows then."

"Yes. Had our first father-son pow-wow this morning."

"Shit. And?"

"He's . . ." Tyler shrugged, "good."

"And Kristen?"

"I don't know. I haven't spoken to her since she told me last night. I don't know if I can forgive her for keeping this from me. For robbing me of all this time with Seth."

"But you admitted that," he held up a finger, "one, you didn't even remember sleeping with Kristen, and," he lifted another finger, "two, that your dipshit roommate never gave you her messages. Neither of those things is her fault. She tried."

"And since I've been back?"

Zach nodded. "Right. I get it." He crossed his arms over his chest. "But given her false beliefs, can you blame her? She likely thought you couldn't care less about her or her child." Realization dawned on his face. "This explains why she hated you."

Tyler winced, but anger also surged through him. "You're taking her side on this?"

"I'm not taking anyone's side. This whole situation is fucked up. All I'm saying is what do you have to gain from holding a grudge against her? Nothing. And you have everything to lose. Including Seth."

Tyler's head shot up.

"If you alienate his mother, he may not feel inclined to have a relationship with you." He paused. "And then there's Kristen. You love her. You told me that several weeks ago. Are you willing to forsake that love out of resentment or pride?" Zach laughed. "Seems to me that's what got the both of you in this mess in the first place. Her misguided resentment toward you kept her from telling you the truth. Now she has. Are you going to let your resentment get in the way of the best thing that's ever happened to you? What's that quote? 'Resentment is like drinking poison and waiting for the other person to die.'"

Tyler's anger deflated like a child's balloon.

He recalled the instances where Kristen had said she needed to tell him something. The instances that were interrupted. Had she been trying to tell him about Seth? Maybe telling him now wasn't just because she felt guilty after learning about his sterility. He rubbed a hand over his forehead where a headache had begun to form. "Honestly, I don't know. It's a lot to ask."

"It is. But here's the key question: will holding onto your resentment make you happy?"

# CHAPTER TWENTY-FIVE

The situation with Tyler made Kristen realize she had some unfinished business with her father, so the next visitor's day, she left the café in Calypso's capable hands and drove to Buford.

Seated at what had become their customary table, they exchanged an awkwardly polite conversation, until she finally leaned her elbows on the table and said, "I need to know. I need to know . . . why."

Her father's mouth compressed into a thin line, and she thought he'd refuse to tell her. Then he nodded, appearing to gather his thoughts. After a moment, he said, "I loved your momma."

Kristen scoffed. She might need to clear the air with her father, but that didn't mean she had to swallow his fairytales.

"We had our struggles, and even if I hadn't gone to jail, I knew it would never last. We were oil and water. And . . . I loved—love you."

Anger and resentment surged through her like electricity through a power cord. "Don't." The words caught in her throat. *Love me? Love me?* If abandoning her without another word was his way of showing love, she'd just as well do without it. Tremors shook her as she tried to control her rage. Her pain. "We barely got by in that shithole of a trailer after you left. Days without electricity. Without heat. Sometimes without food. Momma did her best, but it was never enough. I worked from the minute I was allowed to under state law—sometimes two jobs—all while trying to keep up in school."

"You didn't love us. You only thought about yourself when you decided to commit a crime. What? Did you need the money to buy beer and cigarettes? So excuse me if I don't melt into a puddle of sympathy for your situation." She thought she could do this, but she'd been wrong. If he wasn't going to come clean and tell her the truth, it was useless. She slapped her hands on the table and rose. "We're done here."

"Dammit, girl. I robbed that gas station to pay the rent," he blurted as she walked away, drawing the unwelcome attention of others in the room, including the prison guard.

She froze, then turned to him. "Bullshit."

"It's true. You said you needed to know why. I'm trying to tell you, if you'd just listen. Your mother had had a bad month at the beauty parlor. She could barely cover the rent on the place. Then I lost my job with the trucking company. We were going to be evicted. I couldn't let that happen, not with you just a little girl, and it cold and snowing."

"Don't you dare put this on me." She pointed a finger at him for emphasis. "Your arrest humiliated me—and Momma. Some people stopped coming to the salon, making a bad situation worse."

"I'm not blaming you, sugar. You were just a little girl." He looked up at her, his eyes yellow and glassy.

A little girl who needed her daddy *and* her momma, she thought.

"My first mistake was throwing in with crazy Calvin Phipps."

"No, your first mistake was thinking you could rob a gas station and get away with it." She folded her arms across her chest and maintained her distance.

He snorted. "Yeah, you're probably right. But, I swear to you, I never meant for anyone to get hurt. Cal and I were going to split the proceeds. I was going to cover the rent until I could get another job. Easy peasy."

He stared into the distance, not seeing the other prisoners and their visitors but that long-ago night. "It all went to shit when the gas store clerk pulled a gun out from behind the counter and Cal shot him dead."

And though the men had worn ski masks, the store security cameras caught the snake tattoo that wrapped around her father's arm, ending with the head of the snake on his right hand.

"I'd never seen anyone killed before. Let's just say it left a lasting impression. Worst decision of my life. And I've made some pretty bad decisions." He gave her a wan smile. "I hurt you, your momma, and the family of that poor store clerk. I have to live with that every day of my life—what's left of it anyway."

"Okay. But none of this explains why you waited until you were dying to contact me."

"Please, sit down. Sit down, Kristen." He reached out a hand to her, then set it on the table when she didn't take it. She sank back into the chair feeling as old as her father. "I thought you were better off. The more you distanced yourself from me, the better. And I didn't want you or your momma thinking you had to come all this way to visit me, to send money—"

She snorted and crossed her arms over her chest. "News alert! We didn't have money to send."

"No. You didn't."

They sat in silence a few beats. Her gaze roamed the room and she wondered how the other visitors found it in themselves to forgive their incarcerated family member or loved one. She shifted her focus back on her dad's face. "You left me. You made a choice that had a greater-than-not chance you wouldn't return. You could have been shot that night. Or arrested. Oh wait. You were!"

"I know. All I can say is I'm sorry. I should have found another way."

She looked away again but felt her father's eyes on her.

"Your momma used to send me your school pictures. You in your cheerleading uniform. Your high school graduation photo. I still have them, taped up on my wall. I was so proud of you. Still am. You've grown into a beautiful woman. And Seth," he shook his head with a smile, "you're a great mom. I'm sorry I missed all those years watching you grow up, watching Seth grow up. I can't go back and change my actions, but I can make the best of what I have left. If you'll let me."

Despite herself, her eyes filled with tears. Tears for her loss, Seth's loss, and her father's loss. Tears for a life wasted. We were only given one life. Did she want to look back one day and regret not forgiving her father before it was too late? Did she want to deny him the opportunity to make amends?

Tyler may never forgive her, but there was something she could do here and now.

Her hand slid across the table toward her father, and

she turned her palm up in invitation. A sob escaped her father as he laid his hand on hers and clasped it.

A tear trickled down her cheek, and she drew a shaky breath. "I forgive you."

A weight she hadn't realized she'd been carrying lifted from her heart.

Kristen entered the conference room with some trepidation. She hadn't laid eyes on Tyler since she'd dropped Seth off at his house last week, and she had no idea what kind of reception she would get from him. Would he treat her with outright animosity? Or would he be cordial for the sake of their presentation?

At least they'd agreed that Tyler would present the findings and recommendations to the committee, so she didn't have to tag team with him under the present circumstances. Her contribution had been her self-acquired skills to create a professional, polished, and sometimes humorous Power-Point presentation. On one slide, she'd included a photo of an extra in full-on zombie gear strolling down Senoia's Main Street.

A quick perusal of the room, and she breathed a sigh of relief when she saw Tyler was occupied with setting up his laptop and didn't see her.

She took a seat toward the back corner of the table, hoping to remain inconspicuous. Even so, her gaze drifted to where Tyler stood, leaning over his computer typing. He looked good. No. Better than good in his open collar dress shirt, the cuffs rolled up past his forearms, and a pair of tan slacks. He'd had a haircut, the shock of hair that usually fell across his forehead a little shorter and more controlled.

As if feeling her eyes on him, he glanced up and their eyes locked. His a deep blueish green today, intense and focused. Forcing herself not to look away, she gave him a slight nod, as if to say, *you've got this.*

His mouth lifted at the corner—just a momentary gesture—then his attention returned to his computer.

She took a deep cleansing breath. *Well. That wasn't so bad.*

Sliding her copy of the meeting agenda closer, she saw a few items listed before the presentation on the film location application.

"Hey." Tabitha pulled up the chair next to hers.

"Hi." Kristen offered a polite smile.

A few other members filed into the room, taking up seats around the table, exchanging friendly greetings, and engaging in small talk. Too nervous to join in, Kristen pretended to be concentrating on some notes in her notebook.

Carter took his place at the head of the table and called the meeting to order. Clearing his throat, he said, "We have a few business items I thought we'd get out of the way before we turn the floor over to Tyler and Kristen for their report on the film location application. So, first up, the Main Street holiday celebration next month."

Kristen fidgeted in her seat for the remainder of the meeting until Carter finally turned it over to Tyler.

Gripping her knees with her hands, she blew out a nervous breath. As important as this was to her business and the town of Northridge, if she had a choice between the EDC recommending approval of the application to the Town Council and Tyler's forgiveness, she'd pick Tyler's forgiveness, hands down.

Tyler was a consummate pro. He took the members

methodically through the data they'd collected, the comments and feedback they'd received from citizens of Senoia, the proposal for the additional application fees and necessary forms, the security requirements, and the support of the Northridge Police Department.

But the *pièce de résistance* was the final slide. Tyler had used his mad number-crunching skills to extrapolate the data they had gathered into dollars in the form of positive economic impact to Northridge and its businesses specifically, as well as its citizens as a whole. After taking a few questions from the committee members, he yielded the floor to the chair.

"Excellent presentation. Excellent. You'd think you'd done this sort of thing before," Carter said with good humor. "Any other discussion, or do we have a motion?"

Tony lifted his hand. "Based on that data, I move we recommend approval of the film location application to the Town Council and add Northridge to the list of camera-ready cities in Georgia."

"You've convinced me. I second," Tabitha said.

"All in favor, raise your hand." Carter's gaze swept the room, mentally tallying the hands raised in favor, including hers and Tyler's. Unanimous.

"The motion passes. The EDC will recommend to the Town Council that the film location application be approved and that Northridge become a film-ready city."

"Any other business for the good of the order?" Hearing nothing, Carter said, "Meeting adjourned."

The coward in her wanted to gather her things and beat a hasty retreat. But she couldn't do that. She at least owed Tyler her congratulations. So, sucking up her courage, she walked to the front of the room where Tyler gathered his laptop and papers.

"Great job," she said, feeling a little like a breathless groupie mooning over her idol.

"Thanks." He didn't lift his head as he stored his computer in its case. "But it wasn't all me." He looked up then, his eyes shining with victory. "You had a hand in this as well."

She shrugged. "Not really."

An awkward silence fell as committee members exited the room.

"Well, I'll, uh, see you around." She turned to go, but his voice stopped her.

"Kristen, I'd like to help with Seth's expenses. We can decide on a number for his monthly maintenance, but I'd also like to help with his school and living expenses in New York when he goes back."

"You don't have to—"

"I know I don't." His voice hardened. "And it's not really an option. If you won't take the money, I'll open an account for Seth and he can access it."

She tamped down her temper. She wasn't angry that Tyler wanted to help, but rather his assumption that she wouldn't allow him to. "Fine. But he already has an account, and I'd rather you put it there. Seth's old enough to control his own finances, but you can keep tabs on his spending, if you'd like. I'll leave that between you two."

Tyler nodded, "I'll get the information from Seth." Then he picked up his computer, took his jacket off the back of the chair, and walked out.

So much for a peace treaty.

A FEW DAYS LATER, shortly before closing time, the bell

over the café door chimed in the otherwise quiet café. From her location in the back of the store where she'd been stacking a few copies of the latest bestselling historical novel, Kristen caught a glimpse of worn jeans, brown work boots, and a flannel shirt, and her heart flip-flopped in her chest.

Dammit. Would she ever get over him?

Abandoning her task, she moved to the front where Tyler was searching the café for her.

"Hi."

He jumped then turned to her. "Hi." He shoved his hands in his pockets and offered a tentative smile. She'd take it. Better than the iciness she'd experienced at the end of the EDC meeting. "The Town Council voted to approve the film location plan. I'm to contact the film liaison in Gwinnett County so she can get the ball rolling."

"That's great! Really." But Kristen's enthusiasm over the news wasn't what it would have been just a few short weeks ago. Then she'd have given just about anything for that news. Now it didn't hold the luster it once held. Nothing did. Except for Seth.

She and Tyler stood only a few feet apart, but it seemed an entire ocean.

He looked at his feet, then back up at her, and tears clogged her throat. "Kristen, there's something I have to say."

The final blow? Hadn't enough been said? She wrapped her arms around herself as if she could hold her heart together in the face of Tyler's excoriation.

"You should be so proud of yourself, and of Seth. You have done the most amazing job raising him." He shook his head. "I can't think of a better mom, outside my own, of course," he said, a hint of a smile lighting his face.

The tears clogging her throat now filled her eyes. "Thank you," she whispered. "That means a lot."

He nodded, then after a moment's hesitation, stepped closer. "Thank you for my son." His eyes filled, and her chest tightened.

His tears were her undoing. Even if he never forgave her, the knowledge that she gave him the one thing he thought he could never have would be enough for her. It had to be.

"My beautiful, talented, kind, smart, gifted son." He took her by the shoulders and pulled her against him. Wrapping his arms around her, he sobbed on her shoulder as she held him.

She found herself comforting him, offering soft words and tender caresses, even as she sobbed with him. Crying for the pain she caused him, the years lost between father and son. The loss of his love for her. But also for joy. Seth couldn't ask for a better father. Now, maybe they could put the past behind them, and Tyler and Seth could forge an even stronger bond. Even if that bond didn't include her.

After a moment or two, he retreated, his face wet with his tears, but he didn't let her go. "I didn't think I could ever forgive you. But I was wrong."

Her heart hammered in her chest. *What?*

"You have given me such a gift. I'd be a fool to throw that away. I love you, Kristen McKay. And if you can forgive me for my behavior this last week, I'd like for us to try again."

"Forgive *you*? But—what about *me*? I kept Seth from you all these years—"

He kissed her then, his mouth warm and soft on hers, and her heart nearly burst.

Withdrawing just an inch from her mouth, he pressed a folded piece of paper into her hand.

Confused, she opened it to find the note she had left him seventeen years ago.

---

I had a great time tonight. Call me tomorrow.

---

She looked up at him, heart pounding, and he pressed his forehead to hers. "Forgiven."

# EPILOGUE

KRISTEN STUDIED the new certified copy of Seth's birth certificate, the previously blank space for the father's name now complete:


TYLER MICHAEL KINCAIDE


SHE SLIPPED it into her bag, as Tyler and their son exchanged a man-hug that made her heart squeeze.

Never in her life did she think she could ever be this happy. The day of Seth's birth had been life-changing, but seeing them together as father and son at last filled a void in her heart that had lingered for sixteen years.

"Let's celebrate!" Tyler said, as he leaned forward to kiss her. Wrapping an arm around her waist, and throwing the other arm around Seth's shoulders, he led them out of the Atlanta Vital Statistics Building and out into the cold crisp, January day.

Seth would return to New York tomorrow and take up

his weekly classes at Juilliard, but she and Tyler already had a visit planned for Seth's spring break in March. The only big city Kristen had ever been to was Atlanta, so Tyler promised her the full tourist experience from a Central Park carriage ride to visiting the Statue of Liberty, with Seth by their side.

A few minutes later, they were seated at a table in a College Park restaurant, Kristen and Tyler on one side of the booth, Seth on the other. Kristen squeezed his thigh, drawing his attention. "I love you," and she knew her eyes were shining with her happiness.

"I love you too." Taking her hand, he clutched it in his, a broad grin lighting his face.

"Do you have a sparkling apple cider or grape juice?" he asked the server when he took their drink orders.

"Yes. We have two options." The server pointed to the drink list on the menu.

"Perfect. We'll take a bottle of the Martinelli's and three glasses."

The server left to get their drinks, and they all perused the menu.

After placing their orders, Tyler did the honors and poured the non-alcoholic bubbly into their glasses. "A toast." He lifted his glass, and she and Seth followed suit. "To family!"

After guzzling the sparkling apple cider, Tyler set his glass on the table and rubbed his hands together in anticipation. "What do you think, Seth? Should we make it official?"

With a glance at her, Seth nodded, a broad grin on his face.

Confused, Kristen set her own glass on the table. "Official? We just did."

"I've already asked Seth's permission, so . . ." Tyler rose

from his seat at the table, reached into his jacket pocket, and dropped to one knee.

Other patrons in the restaurant paused mid-conversation and a hush fell over their seating area. Kristen's head swam, and her heart beat so hard she expected it to leap out of her chest.

Tyler presented a blue velvet box to her and lifted the lid. A gasp escaped at the sight of the ring inside. Brilliant green flashed from the emerald-cut stone, set off with two diamond trillions in a gleaming platinum setting.

"Kristen Melissa McKay, best friend, love of my life, mother of my child . . . will you make our little family official and marry me?"

Kristen lifted a shaky hand to her mouth and sat, speechless, her eyes filling and blurring her vision.

"Say yes, Mom!" Seth prompted.

"Yes!" She laugh-cried. "Yes!"

Tyler slipped the cool metal onto her left ring finger, and the diners applauded, cheered, and lifted their beverages in toast.

Through her tears of joy, Kristen saw Tyler rise from his knee and could have sworn his cheeks were glistening with his own tears.

She leaped from her seat, flung her arms around his neck, and pressed her lips to his.

Seth muttered jokingly, "Get a room."

She extended her hand to him and he joined her and Tyler in a big family hug.

Amazing what forgiveness brings, she thought. Her life couldn't get any better than this.

# ABOUT THE AUTHOR

Rebecca Heflin is a bestselling, award-winning author who has dreamed of writing romantic fiction since she was fifteen and her older sister sneaked a copy of Kathleen Woodiwiss' Shanna to her and told her to read it.

Never quite sure what she wanted to be when she grew up, Rebecca didn't attend college until age 30, and earned her bachelor's in literature, before going on to complete her law degree.

Ever the late bloomer, Rebecca finally turned her attention to fulfilling her dream of writing, and published her first novel at age 48. When not passionately pursuing her dream, Rebecca is busy with her day-job at a major state university.

She and her husband are also co-founders of a non-profit organization, which raises money to help cancer patients and their families.

Rebecca's pen name is an abbreviated version of her great-great grandmother's name: Sarah Anne Rebecca Heflin Apple Smith. Whew! And you wonder why she shortened it.

Rebecca writes women's fiction and contemporary romance, and she is a member of Romance Writers of America (RWA), Florida Romance Writers, RWA Contemporary Romance, and Florida Writers Association. Rebecca and her mountain-climbing husband live at sea level in sunny Florida.

Sign up for Rebecca's monthly newsletter, Rebecca's Readers, for all the latest news on upcoming releases, appearances, and contests.

facebook.com/RebeccaHeflinBooks

twitter.com/RebeccaHeflin

pinterest.com/rheflinbooks

goodreads.com/goodreadscomrebecca_heflin

bookbub.com/profile/rebecca-heflin

# REVIEWS

Did you enjoy this book? Please let other potential readers know.

Reviews are the most powerful tool in an author's toll box when it comes to gaining new readers–more powerful even than the most expensive ads. Honest reviews help bring them to the attention of other readers.

If you enjoyed this book, I would be grateful if you could take a few minutes to leave an honest review on the retailer's website. Even a short review can help.

Thank you!

ALSO BY REBECCA HEFLIN

*THE PROMISE OF CHANGE*

*RESCUING LACEY*

**DREAMS COME TRUE SERIES**

*DREAMS OF PERFECTION, BOOK 1*

*SHIP OF DREAMS, BOOK 2*

*DREAMS OF HER OWN, BOOK 3*

***STERLING UNIVERSITY SERIES***

*ROMANCING DR. LOVE, BOOK 1*

*WINNING DR. WENTWORTH, BOOK 2*

*EDUCATING DR. MAYFIELD, BOOK 3*

***SEASONS OF NORTHRIDGE SERIES***

*A SEASON TO DANCE, BOOK 1*